*I'm Here: Alaska Stories*

*I'm Here: Alaska Stories*

stories

DAVID NIKKI CROUSE

Book Design by Mark E. Cull

Library of Congress Cataloging-in-Publication Data

Names: Crouse, David, author.
Title: I'm here: Alaska stories / David Nikki Crouse.
Other titles: I'm here (Compilation) | I am here
Description: First edition. | Pasadena: Boreal Books, [2023]
Identifiers: LCCN 2023019523 (print) | LCCN 2023019524 (ebook) | ISBN
    9781597099349 (paperback) | ISBN 9781597099356 (ebook)
Subjects: LCSH: Alaska—Fiction. | LCGFT: Short stories.
Classification: LCC PS3603.R685 I45 2023 (print) | LCC PS3603.R685
    (ebook) | DDC 813/.6—dc23/eng/20230426
LC record available at https://lccn.loc.gov/2023019523
LC ebook record available at https://lccn.loc.gov/2023019524

The National Endowment for the Arts, the Los Angeles County Arts Commission,
the Ahmanson Foundation, the Dwight Stuart Youth Fund, the Max Factor Family
Foundation, the Pasadena Tournament of Roses Foundation, the Pasadena Arts &
Culture Commission and the City of Pasadena Cultural Affairs Division, the City of
Los Angeles Department of Cultural Affairs, the Audrey & Sydney Irmas Charitable
Foundation, the Kinder Morgan Foundation, the Meta & George Rosenberg Founda-
tion, the Albert and Elaine Borchard Foundation, the Adams Family Foundation, the
Riordan Foundation, Amazon Literary Partnership, the Sam Francis Foundation, and
the Mara W. Breech Foundation partially support Red Hen Press.

  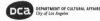 

First Edition
Published by Boreal Books
An imprint of Red Hen Press
www.borealbooks.org
www.redhen.org

# Acknowledgments

The stories in this collection have previously appeared in the following magazines: "The Black Bear Month" in *Agni*; "The Alaska Girl" in the *Beloit Fiction Journal*; "Make Me Whole" in the *Bennington Review*; "Marriage or Wolves" in the *Florida Review*; "Shapeshifters" in the *Greensboro Review*; "Fare Forward Voyagers" in *Grub Street*; "Nomads" in the *Literarian*; "The Gift of Flight" in *Meridian*; "The Wolves Again" in *Natural Bridge*; "I'm Here" in *Prairie Schooner*; "A Wrong in the World" in the *Sycamore Review*; and "The Alphabet in Reverse" in *Western Humanities Review*.

Any book is not just the product of individual effort, but also the work and support of many people. These stories would not exist without the love and care of the following: my wife, Bonnie Whiting, who inspires me with her devotion to art and life; my children, Dylan, Noah, and Beckett, who have given me more joy than I could have ever imagined; my parents, Alfred and Marie Crouse; my sisters, Jane and Karen, and my brother, Michael; and dear friends Stephanie Clare, Laurie Marhoefer, and Hattie. Thank you to Greg Moutafis and Jon Dembling for unwavering friendship lasting decades and long discussions about art stretching from our teenage years until now.

Thank you to Nicole Stellon O'Donnell for support both spiritual and pragmatic, and to Peggy Shumaker, who has supported my work since I was a numbskull student in one of her graduate workshops. Thank you to Madara Mason for the beautiful cover image. Thank you to the staff at Red Hen and, in particular, to Rebeccah Sanhueza, for all the hard work in stewarding this book to publication. Thank you to my colleagues at UW and to my students. Thank you also to those I might not have mentioned, but who have helped me somewhere along the way. Lastly, thank you to Frank Soos, life-changing teacher and good friend, and sweet R.T. I miss you both more than I can say.

# Contents

*For Bonnie, with much love*

# Nomads

I was born with the umbilical cord curled tightly around my neck, my face as blue as a bruise, and as the midwife tried to extricate me from my predicament my mother leaned forward and grazed her fingers lightly over my full head of black hair.

"She's beautiful," she said.

This is the story my father told me as we sat across from each other at the worn kitchen table in his small cabin in Fairbanks, Alaska. There were many reasons to tell it. My father and I had not seen each other in more than a year, and in the bedroom one of his dogs was going into labor on a nest of blankets pulled from the bed and tossed to the floor. We could hear her panting and whining and it did not sound much different than what I imagined a person might sound like going through the same thing. "It'll take a while," my father said. "Finish your bread. Then we'll see how she's doing."

I had never tasted warm bread before, at least not that I remembered, and I liked the heat on my tongue. He tore pieces from the loaf in chunks and slathered it with butter before handing it to me. "So that's what she said, huh?" I asked.

"Surprised?"

"A little," I said.

The other dogs scratched against the door, trying to get in to their mother, and occasionally my father yelled at them, but in a fake-angry way, smiling as he raised his voice and slapped the table. He seemed infected with their energy, their joy at what was happening in the bedroom, and some of their anxiety too. I could tell because of the way he ate—ripping pieces of the bread in half and then eating first one half whole, then the other—although maybe he ate everything that way. It was hard to know. It had been a long time, after all.

"It was the first time and last time your mother ever complimented you on your appearance," he joked as he stood up, wiping crumbs on his jeans.

I stood up too and followed him, trying to copy the assured swing of his legs. The simple way he crossed a room was a wonder to me. He had covered the bedroom windows with blankets and the room was dark and cool. It felt good to escape from the sunshine, which streamed into the house even though it was ten at night. My father knelt down and I knelt down behind him, a polite distance apart. "You were amazing," he added, after the first of the slick little puppies was in his hands. "And strong too." The second followed, wet into the world, and then the third. I was trying very hard to be quiet, to listen and watch and remember it all, as if this might be something I would be called upon to use in the future. I had seen so much already in my short time here.

His white T-shirt was covered with blood and sweat as he held the mother's jaws with one hand, pulling her head up and away so I could see the squirming mass of arms and legs and faces. One had been born dead, a still shape at the center of all the writhing movement. "We don't want the mother to eat that one," my father said, as he twisted her snout upward. Her eyes were rolling back, lost in some kind of reverie. "She doesn't know who I am right now," he explained. "She just knows I'm not one of them."

This was why we had rushed from Anchorage to Fairbanks two days before—*any day now*, he had said before we were even out of the airport, *any day now*—and it cast that whole crazy trip in a new light, made it seem small and less important, although I knew that was crazy. Important things had happened on that trip, things that made me see my father differently, and I knew I needed to remember them, but the way he held the mother dog, with gentle force, and spoke to me, it was easy to forget. Not forget, actually. It was more like letting one thing mask another, a problem with foreground and background. I wanted to touch the newborns but I held back. The puppies didn't really seem like dogs at all. Eyes shut, bodies thin and slick, they looked like amphibians, and the dead one did not look any different than the healthy ones except he wasn't moving. My father held it gently—as if it were still alive—and began rubbing its belly with two fingers. "Watch this," he said.

I could see the dog's bones under its loose skin, the points where the legs met the shoulders and hips. My father began to rub harder, pushing down his hand against its chest, and for a moment I wanted to pull it away from him—to save it—but I knew the time to save it had passed. It had probably been dead in the womb.

Its mouth opened and it coughed up something milky yellow. It was twitching in his hands. "Sometimes you just have to remind them to breathe," he said.

"Okay," I said.

He placed the dog back with the others and I lost it in the mess of bodies, until I couldn't figure out which one had almost died.

"A damned fighter," he said. And then his voice changed, grew softer. It had all the delicate control of a good actor approaching the lip of the stage for a final speech. "I'm sorry about all that talk earlier. You were a captive audience, I guess, in the truck. And there's not many people I can speak to about that stuff. I know it probably doesn't mean that much to you at all. But I'm telling you about your heritage too. I'm trying to pass along something. Too late, probably. I know that. But then again, it's never too late, right?"

It was summer then, his first year in Fairbanks, Alaska, and something had opened up in his heart. He told me many stories I had not heard before, not from him, not from my sister, and especially not from my mother who, after all, was not exactly cast in a good light in most of them.

✻

"It's the cancer talking," my sister said the next day, when I told her what my father had said about my birth. Her voice sounded tinny and faraway, which of course she was, back east with her husband and young baby. As I told the story to her I slanted it even further toward danger and death. The cord had been tighter, my breath harder, and the doctors told my parents that I might not make it, that I might simply tip back toward the darkness from which I had just emerged.

Something about this possibility thrilled me. I imagined my frightened mother and father wondering what might happen to me as my small body was connected to tubes and wires, the patient words of a kind nurse, my befuddled sister, slumped in a chair in the waiting room. She would have been ten years old then, smart and cynical. "It's what he said," I told her.

"Bullshit," she said.

She had begun to use words like that recently. She dressed crisply, in ironed black skirts and expensive high heels, with a tight knot of hair at the back of her head, and I think she liked the contradiction that kind of language created. She was more like my father than she would ever admit. "It's what he told me," I repeated, voice low but insistent.

It was mid-June and we had not spoken in the days since I had arrived in Alaska. But guilt had gotten the best of me and so I had decided to make the effort, which involved more than just dialing her number. My father did not own a phone—he said that if anybody wanted to see him they knew where to find him—so I rode his old two-speed bike on the dirt road into town. It was white with a red flame painted up the side and although my father must have bought the bike recently, I could picture him as a child my age, painting that flame and thinking it was cool. To change speeds I pedaled in reverse until I heard a click as the gear caught. I did this as often as possible, moving from forward into reverse like I was shifting speeds on a car. I dropped it into the dirt alongside the diner. "Hey, Nancy," one of the waitresses said as I came through the door and made my way to the counter. My father had told her about me, his daughter from New England, and she seemed to think it was amusing that a fourteen-year-old girl had come all that way on her own, to visit a man like my dad. But as long as I ordered a piece of pie they didn't seem to mind me using their phone.

My sister and I, we had arranged a secret signal. I would call her collect and give them the fake name I thought was beautiful. "Would you accept a collect call from Grace MacDowell?" the operator asked. My sister knew to refuse. "I don't know anybody by that name," she said, and then she called me right back. The phone rang, the waitress slid a piece of blueberry pie to me, and I began to tell her what had happened.

"It took us twelve hours," I said, about the drive from Anchorage into Fairbanks. "We got into town around midnight and the sun was still in the sky." I told her about the one dog, its silent heart and miracle comeback, and I waited for that word again, bullshit, as if I would have some reason to lie about something like that. But she didn't say anything. She just listened, and that made me want to tell her the next story, the one from the road. But I held it back. I wanted to show her a side of my father she had forgotten about, so all I said was that we had stopped to help some people on the side of the road. That's what had taken us so long. There had been a bad accident.

I didn't tell her about the land strewn with busted metal and rubber, and road curved and broken from what my father called frost heaves. I didn't tell her about the bearded man sitting all alone on the grassy slope, his face tilted up to catch the sun, his pale, distended belly. He was like someone who had wandered out of a fairy tale. That's how I saw him in my mind's eye, a secret that gave me power.

"What kind of accident?"

"Just an accident."

She said, "Do you want to come home early, Nancy? It's okay if you do, you know."

"No, really," I said. "I'm okay. And Dad's okay too. The dogs are doing great."

An elderly man came up next to me and pushed a few dollars across the counter, quarters and dimes. His face was sunburned and pinched and he looked angry, but when he saw me watching him, he smiled and moved on. I cut my pie with the side of my fork and moved it around my plate. "Well," she said. "You know best. I do trust you, okay?"

"I understand," I said.

"No, you really don't," she said, and she laughed. "I'm the one who re-members everything. You were just a little thing."

Which pushed me back into telling her my story. I wanted to show her that yes, maybe I didn't understand, but she didn't either, and our ignorance was something that could help us. I told her about the noise the dog made as the machinery of its lungs began to work.

"Are you really okay?" she asked me.

"I'm on the edge of something," I said.

When I arrived back at my father's cabin I leaned the bike against the back of the outhouse and walked to the side door. The blender was run-ning inside—I could hear it through the open window, whirling up another one of his health shakes. He stopped it as I came walking through the door. "Evening," he said, and then he started it up again. I walked into the other room and clicked our little portable television. The blender drowned out the sound, but I was more concerned with the pictures.

My father said the TV was a gift from a friend, but I knew even then that he had probably pulled it from somebody's trash. The back of it was splashed with white paint and the longer it was left on, the shakier the picture would become, until the image was flipping rapidly. So I watched it with my fingers on the vertical hold knob, adjusting the images as the show went along, trying to stay one step ahead of the defect. My father revved the blender like a car engine, grinding down apples and eggs and fish oil into a thick formless mass. "Want some?" he asked me, when he was finished and standing there in his gym shorts, holding the heavy metallic shake cup in his hand. It was a teasing little joke, because I was at the age that even a slightly burned piece of toast would make me curl a lip in disgust and push back my plate. "Can you feel it?" he said, taking a deep breath of the dry air. "All your synapses are coming alive again. The city isn't good for a young girl."

*Clarity* was a word he had used on the road, to describe the feeling he had from living close to the bone. The snack food in the small cabinet next to the washbasin, the local newspapers in the outhouse, and especially the TV, I knew these were all concessions, something he might see as tiny hypocrisies. "The dogs have taken over my room," he explained. "Looks like you're stuck with me."

I nodded but kept my eyes fixed on the TV.

"What are you doing?" he asked, although obviously he knew what I was doing.

"Nothing, really," I told him. "Just watching my show."

"Our little window on the world," he said, with a hint of irony and disgust. He tipped back his shake and drank a big gulp, made a show of wiping his mouth with the back of his arm.

I don't remember the name of the show, but I remember the faces of the actors, the cheap little stagy sets and costumes, and vivid little fragments of the storylines. One of the shows depicted insects the size of a human hand—dozens of them—crawling on a windshield, although I don't remember the rest of the plot or anything else but the shapes moving across the glass, the car going dark inside. "You could be writing letters," he said. "It's a lost art, you know. Think about what you did today. Write it down. I'll mail it for you tomorrow." He was talking about my sister, but he did not write to her either, at least not that I knew, and the only pencil I had seen in the place was a thick carpenter's pencil. "How about a journal?" he asked me. "You should be writing all this down, Nancy. Seriously. Time is finite." What he meant was that our time was finite, but the idea of time itself having an end made my heart beat a little faster. It was like an idea dredged up from the TV and put in my father's mouth to speak.

"I know," I said.

"I'll buy you a notebook," he said. "What's your favorite color again?"
"Blue," I said. "Electric blue."

"Right," he said. "I knew that." He seemed satisfied with this, and he re-treated to his bedroom, where he did chin-ups on a bar he had suspended in his doorway. I could hear him count from one to twenty, then stop and start up again. He seemed strong and confident and happy. I could imagine myself dying, in my infancy, or even from old age at some remote point in my future, the idea of *him* dying was the most impossible thing I could imagine. He was at number twenty-seven, and soon he'd be at thirty and I'd hear him grunt and drop heavy to the floorboards.

I think my father wanted to be preserved, even if just by his daughter's simple sentences, written in messy handwriting in this notebook he offered to buy me. The responsibility of setting down all the finely tuned things I had experienced made my head spin. The way the sun bathed the debris, my father's slow, even walk after he had climbed from his truck to the stream of wreckage running along the gulley, and not just that, but the clicking of plates as I washed the dinner dishes in silence after that first meal at his home, how could I get any of this right? I had made a mess of it on the phone, after all, and even in my own head.

※

"I think we gave up too easily," he said, "we" meaning, I think, all the dead Pequot. For a moment when he said this, it seemed like he had been alive then as the settlers moved into Connecticut, converting some natives to Christianity, killing others. His regrets flowed back that far and deep. We had not been in his truck for more than twenty minutes when he had start-ed in on this, his new subject. My sister had warned me, but it was still a surprise—the sheer feeling in his words as he spoke, his eyes scanning the road. The truck swayed and rose like a ship navigating a difficult wake, and sometimes he moved into the oncoming lane to avoid especially bad road damage. When a car passed us going the other way, he opened his hand in a wave. They always waved back. "The meek inheriting the earth, that's a lie," he said. "A line they feed you. We were as meek as they come."

Ever since the diagnosis, my sister said, he had become interested in what he called his heritage. He said he was half Pequot Indian, although he had never mentioned this while we had been living back in New Hampshire, and he did not look like any Indian I had seen in the movies. His hair was short and brown, graying at the temples, and his face was like mine—round and flat, although on him the features had come out handsome. "Did you know that our ancestors, they never waged war? They were as peaceful as deer, and when the white man came, they greeted him with open arms. That's why there are so few of us left. We didn't run and hide, and we didn't attack. We just assumed they were like us. We walked out of the woods and shook their hands."

I imagined my father walking out the woods and shaking hands with these new visitors. He looked like a white man to me, a white man with a ruddy complexion maybe, but a white man, and he had been raised in a tenement building in south Boston. But I liked that he was angry and fighting, and he drove with casual assurance. The road, he explained, was one straight shot all the way into Fairbanks, a busted-up little line running north to a busted-up frontier town. And he was smiling, driving one-handed, as he explained it all to me.

"Dad," I said. "What's this?"

"Fires," he said. "We've had them all month. We'll pass through."

A white fog hung around the road and blocked our view of the birch trees that lined both sides. It grew harder to see ahead too. It was like the world was dropping away from us bit by bit. But I didn't feel afraid. He was still smiling, and he said he was sorry, because he had done all the talking and he wanted to hear more from me. How was high school? The first year would be the hardest, he said, but then I'd make good friends, and it would be smooth sailing from there. I said, "Is this dangerous?" meaning the fires. I pictured them moving quickly across the land, destroying everything, just like the settlers my father had been talking about. "They're farther away than you might think," he said. "Miles and miles."

"Sure," I said, because that seemed like it could be true. I wanted to tell him that school was harder than I had anticipated. Not the work, that was easy, but all the alliances and double-talk. I had gotten in a good deal of trouble just a couple of weeks before for punching a girl who had made fun of my clothes, and I had already decided that I would do it again if she tried it twice.

After a while my father said, "I love your sister and she loves me. We just don't understand each other very well." I wasn't sure what to say to that so

I said nothing, and neither did he. The road moved under us in waves of jagged land and coughed up asphalt.

It took almost an hour for the world to come back to us, bit by bit, tree by tree, until the sun was strong in our faces and the road stretched out in front of us to the horizon. "There we go," he said, when we had been clear for a good twenty minutes. We were both quiet, but he seemed to be thinking about something. The windshield was spattered with overgrown mosquitoes and sometimes he ran the wipers, smearing them all over the place. "There's only five hundred of us left," he finally said, meaning the Pequot nation, the string of people who had come before him. Most of them, he said, were back in Connecticut. Some of them did not even know who they were and what had happened to them. "It's a crime," he said.

"What is?" I said, thinking he meant the settlers moving across the country.

"Not knowing who you are," he explained. "It's a crime against yourself."

I asked him what he meant again, but he didn't respond except to say he had a surprise for me when we hit Fairbanks. He asked me if I liked animals. "Sure," I said, and then, "Depends what kind."

"The pregnant kind," he said, and then, "I've been taking care of a few sled dogs. Greyhounds, really, well, greyhound and husky mixes. Amazing looking animals. Bodies like daggers."

"Is that what you've been doing?" I asked, and I didn't mean it to sound rude.

"A little bartending," he said. "The people here are good people. Everybody here is from somewhere else, so that makes me feel less lonely."

"Do you like it more than Raleigh?" I asked, which is where he lived last, the previous summer, doing seasonal work for his brother's landscaping company.

He made a face like he had just tasted something awful. "That town is history," he said. "It was probably a good place once, but not anymore. It's all chewed up and spit out."

What had my sister said? That my father was the kind of man who had to run to the edge of the world to find himself. It was certainly not the kind of thing he could do sitting in chair, surrounded by his family, and he had discovered through experience that South Carolina, New Mexico, Colorado, Nevada, none of these places were far enough. When she told me this I had scowled and said nothing, watching the planes out the wide airport windows, because things were different now since the diagnosis. This was a man with a black spot on his brain, and the old jokes didn't work anymore.

⁂

I had meant it when I told my sister I was on the edge of something. There was so much to tell, and I did not know how to start, and if I did not know how to start then how was I going to know how to end? So I told her the simplest of stories, and not even that. I told her just part of the story. I did not tell her that, just three hours outside of Anchorage, we stopped at a roadhouse with a sign that read *Beer Inside* and another one, a metal one, reading *Coke Refreshes*. That one was shot up with bullet holes from so long ago that the holes and dents had turned brown with rust. My father ran up the steps to the entrance two at a time, held the door open for me like a gentleman. The inside was as dark as a cave and smelled of damp, but the woman behind the counter smiled to see my father. "I thought you might drop by again soon," she said, and then she smiled at me. "Is this your new girlfriend? Should I be jealous?"

"My daughter," he said. "Nancy. Isn't that a nice name? She's a long way from home."

"Not really," I said, because I did not really think of New England as my home. I never had, although maybe I didn't realize it until that moment. But this was a conversation for just the two of them. I tried to recede into the background as they talked. My father said, "I bet you didn't think I had a daughter. But I have two."

"What other secrets are you keeping from me?" she asked, and she was still smiling, handing out little paper menus.

"I think you know everything now," he said.

She glanced at me and said, "Do you think I should trust him? He's a charmer, but I'm not sure I should trust him."

"You should trust him," I said, surprised at the conviction in my voice.

"She's had a rough life," he told me when she had gone back to the bar, and I looked over my shoulder at her cleaning a glass with a white rag. She looked happy to me, or at least content, and I wondered what it would be like to trade places with her. "I'll tell you sometime about Tlingit women," he said, and I guessed there was some connection between her hard life and this new fact, although I didn't know what that could be. She had opened a newspaper and had spread it open on the bar. Someone was talking to her from the kitchen and she was talking back, but I couldn't make out the words.

When our food came she pulled the extra chair back from the table and sat down. "Don't blame me if you don't like it," she said. "Blame the cook." We ate slowly, and the food was good. She talked about her family, five brothers and four sisters who were scattered all around the state, and her cousins, and her grandmother, who was sick in a Seattle hospital. My father seemed to have heard some of this before, but he asked questions, and complimented the food, and then he threw his napkin on the plate and said, "I want to stay longer, but we have to hit the road. We have some obligations back in Fairbanks. We're going to tear up the road today." He looked at me and grinned and winked.

"Sometimes I think he loves those dogs more than he loves people," she said, and there was an edge in her voice even though she was still smiling. He was standing, reaching for his wallet. He said something about loving all of God's creatures, including people, but he was the only one laughing.

"Two girls," she said. "I can hardly believe it. You really are full of surprises."

"I try not to be," he said. "I try to be an open book."

She was looking at him, but talking to me. "Nancy," she said. "Your father thinks we're the same, me and him. But look at him. Does it look like we're the same?"

I considered the question, but I didn't answer. Nobody really seemed the same as anybody else, really, and I wanted to tell them this, but we were already at the door, squinting our eyes against the sunshine. Once we were outside everything changed again then and they hugged each other briefly. She said that it was the most beautiful day she'd seen lately and that we were really lucky people. There were lucky people and unlucky people and we were definitely on the lucky side of the ledger, she said. She felt lucky just being around us. They were both joking and relaxed again, and when we were pulling out of the parking lot my father said, "I hope you liked her. She's a nice person."

"Do you really think that?" I asked after a while.

"Of course," he said. "She's great."

"I mean, that you try not to be full of surprises."

"Sure," he said, and I could tell he didn't want to talk anymore. But I asked, "Does she know you're sick?"

"I don't think of it that way," he said. "That's a defeatist word."

"Okay," I said.

"It's not as big a deal as your sister thinks," he added, and his voice had a real edge to it. It reminded me of the way he could talk to my mother, those times he came to visit, and I didn't want to be talked to like that—I didn't want to be like my mother—so I quieted down and let the scenery slide past. He smiled and began to talk about the next town about two hours up ahead, a little place he had only visited once, when he had first arrived. "You can stand on one end and throw a rock across the thing," he said.

"More fire," I said, after a while.

He put his hand out the window, palm up, like he was checking for rain. "This isn't fire, Nancy."

He was right. It was dust and dirt, billowing around us in a cloud. He slowed down to a crawl. "What is it?" I asked.

"I'm not sure."

We drove at almost a walking pace, my father's window still open, and I could feel the dust tickle the back of my throat. "There's something in the road," I said, when I saw what I thought was a small, black animal, crouched right in front of us. It was a piece of tire, a long strip of threads and rubber, and that was followed by a few more pieces, and then a hubcap, a litter of broken wood and bright red plastic. My father leaned forward close to the windshield, and then he pulled over and stopped the car altogether.

"Car accident," he said, although there was no sign of the whole car. I opened my door and peered outside. Either the dust was clearing or I was getting used to it. The embankment was covered with small birch trees, and some of them were ripped up and broken, like a tornado had just passed through. "Where are you going?" he asked.

"I'm just looking," I said.

"We need to head home," he said. I wasn't sure if he was talking to me or to himself. Then he added, "There's a gas station about twenty minutes ahead. We can make a call there." That seemed to be for me, but my feet were touching the ground now. My hand was still on the door handle. Maybe I was driven by curiosity or maybe concern—probably a weird mix of both—but as my father said, "Wait," I released the door handle and stepped into the dust cloud. The truck was about fifteen feet up the embankment, turned on its back like a dead beetle. I felt the odd urge to sneak around the edge of the spectacle, watching for signs of life. If I was discovered, it seemed, I would be in serious trouble. I could hear my father hollering out my name.

This was the part of the story I had not wanted to share with my sister. The boy sat on the grass, his hands on his knees, his face turned up to the sky. By boy I mean he couldn't have been more than twenty, although maybe he was older, and he simply seems young in my mind's eye. He wore a peach fuzz beard, long hippie hair, ripped jeans, and sandals, and it was the mix of his little costume and his circumstances that made me feel sorry for him. I walked over to him and said, "Are you all right?"

He seemed to accept me as a new addition to the chaos. "No bones broken," he said. My father came up behind me and put his hand on my shoulder. The boy seemed to finally notice us completely, and he turned his head and gave us a quizzical look. "It wasn't my fault," he said.

"Do you need a ride?" I asked him.

"You should get back to the truck," my father told me, and he stepped forward to the boy, still five or six feet off, like there was something poisonous about him. He said, "Which way were you headed? South?"

"Anchorage," the boy said. "Homer. All over."

"Right."

"And it wasn't my fault at all."

"Back to the truck, please," my father said again, but I stayed where I was, watching them talk. It had the feel of an interrogation—the quick questions, the simple answers. It's true that he didn't seem hurt at all, although he did look starved and dirty. There seemed to be a little defiance in this, in his relaxed pose, his casual answers. After all, couldn't he have just stood up if what he said was true?

"He might be hurt," I said, and suddenly we were talking about him like he wasn't even there.

"He's fine."

"I don't think he is."

"What do you want to do?" my father asked, and the boy said he wasn't sure, that he felt fine though, and that none of it was his fault. "Are you the only one?" my father asked him.

"I'm fine," he said.

"Stay here," my father said, but I didn't listen to that command either. We walked together to the truck and he bent down and looked inside the cab. The windshield had been blown out and playing cards, cassette tapes, and scraps of food covered the ground. He reached inside, straining, found the keys in the ignition, and gave them a turn, then stepped back. It was an old truck and it seemed to have been involved in many smaller accidents before this big one. The driver's-side door was bright yellow, and the words *Young and Poor and Happy* were spray-painted down one side, in increasingly smaller letters. Flowers too, painted with brightly colored paints, blues and greens and pinks. I could imagine a party where all this happened, the crazed hopefulness of it. "Christ," my father said. "What a mess."

"Over there," I said.

"What?"

I indicated the baby's car seat further up the hill. It sat there as if it had been placed there carefully, by the boy, by someone else, and for a moment it seemed as if it was not part of the accident at all. I began to walk toward it, my father just behind me, and when I reached it I bent down and saw the baby's face, staring out at me from its safe place. "Christ," my father said from behind me. "Jesus Christ."

"It's okay," I said.

I unstrapped the buckles and only when I lifted its tight weight into my arms did it begin to cry. I patted its back and shifted it to my shoulder and then carried it down the hill to the boy. "Everything's going to be okay," I said, when he looked up at me. It was like he was seeing me for the first time.

"Take her," I said, and I held her out.

That's when his shoulders began to shake, and he reached up and took her and pulled her in close. "She's very important to me," he said. He began to ramble, something about a divorce, a girl in Montana, parents in Arizona, a brother in Florida, and how he had decided to become a wanderer, escaping all of those stupid places, all those people who told him he was a failure. Nothing was working out as he planned, he said. All his troubles came spilling out, but the baby was quiet and content now. They seemed to fit together perfectly, her small bulk against his skinny chest.

"You're both going to be okay," I said, although I did not believe it. Saying it made it feel as if it might be true.

"I wanted this drive to be fun," my dad said, when we were back on the road.

"Dad," I said.

He laughed. "It's been interesting, at least." We pulled down the long, dirt road that led to the box of a gas station. He left the car engine running while he climbed out and headed inside. I could see him through the plate-glass window explaining it all to the guy behind the counter. He put the phone to his ear and turned and noticed me and he smiled and waved. "Man," he said, when he climbed back into the truck. "No good deed goes unpunished." But he refused to talk about the phone call. "Only good things," he said.

"Okay," I said, and then he reached out and gripped my hand hard.

I thought of the baby looking up at me and realized that I did not know if it was a boy or a girl. Its hair was thick and black, its eyes floating as if seeing the world through a haze.

"I want every second to count," my father said, and then, gripping even harder, so that his nails pinched my palm, "I'm sorry. I really am. I'm not sure what I was thinking." I wanted to ask him, what for? Because I wasn't the one to whom he should apologize, right? There was the boy thirty miles back, after all, holding his kid.

"Helpless," he said.

"What?"

"People like that," my father said, as he released my hand. It was as if he knew what I had been thinking and was angry with me for thinking it. "The moment I saw him, I could tell what kind of person he was. He reeked of it. His family was right." He put both hands on the wheel and we listened to the engine idle. He seemed to be considering the right words. "He's just doomed, Nancy," he finally said. "If not now, then sometime later. And I'm not even going to talk about the little one." He pushed the truck into drive and backed us out. "Still a couple of hundred miles to go," he explained.

I did not tell my sister that postscript, but when I called her a week later, from that same diner phone, I told her some of it. Maybe I was scrambling around blindly, trying to find an ending. "We should have insisted," I told her, and she asked me, insisted on what? "The boy. He should have come with us," I told her, because we had left him there, sitting on the hill. I'm sure he was still sitting there when the police arrived, bemused by his own predicament, stroking the baby's thick hair. What did he do when he saw them walking up the hill toward him? Did he still pretend that everything was okay? He had not seemed upset by our leaving.

My sister said, "There was nothing you could do."

❧

My father's dying was an impossible thing to imagine, but that's what he did. Not six months after my visit to see him a woman called from a hospice in California and explained that he had passed away quietly and peacefully. She wanted me to know that he spoke often of me and my sister, and that he was proud of us. He could see what we were becoming. Alaska hadn't worked out for him, she explained, but she didn't tell me the details. He had never shared them, except to say that the winter was too long and dark. Somehow, he had saved some money and she wanted to send it to me. "Who are you?" I asked. "A nurse?"

"No, nothing like that," she said. "Just a friend. I helped take care of him though."

"You can keep the money," I said. "I don't need it." Although I did. My mom wasn't working again, so the checks from her had stopped, and my sister had decided to go back to school part-time.

"I don't think he would have wanted that," she said.

"Okay, send it," I said, and then, "What did he think we were becoming?" That question seemed to surprise her. She said she didn't know what to say. "Because I'm not sure," I added. I was finding danger without my father's help, and finding amazing pleasure in it. I was discovering a certain kind of lean, sullen boy, and I liked to skip school with one or two of them, hang out at home while my sister was away, smoking and kissing and talking dirty. I laughed and tried to make it into a joke—I figured I should give this woman an easy way out, a clearly marked exit to our conversation. But I closed it up as soon as I opened it. "I went to Alaska to visit him, you know," I told her. "He had a good life there."

"I'm sure," she said. "I think your father could make a good life anywhere."

"Not here," I said.

She was quiet again, polite to a fault, because she didn't just say goodbye. I would have been fine with that. She was waiting for my address, I suppose, so she could send me the money, or maybe she had more to tell me, instructions from my dad. She said it wasn't just the money. There were things to send too, things he had wanted to give to me in person. I did not bother asking what these things were. I had noticed the plastic beads and eagle jewelry around his cabin, the leather-banded watch he seldom wore, imprinted with animal symbols. I tried to explain about the light, the sheer intensity of it, enough to make you crazy. I remembered—but didn't speak about—the way that light had fallen all over that wreckage, and the expression on my father's face as he came away from the overturned truck. It was a blank, just a set of features and nothing more, and I had allowed myself to hate that impassive face, just for a second, as a sort of experiment.

My second and last week in Fairbanks my father hung signs on telephone poles with arrows pointing in the direction of his cabin. Or rather, I did. We drove around and he'd stop and I'd jump from the truck, hammering the sign into place. Then I'd scramble back to the car and we'd be off. "Good job," he'd say. This was how I got to know the town better, and him too, because he talked and talked. He told me more about the Pequot, how they fled inland as the settlers came and then kept moving around, from state to state. "I guess they weren't really states then, though," he said. "It was all Indian land, and it was beautiful. More beautiful even than all of this." And it *was* beautiful. We rolled on the broken dirt roads through stretches of untouched land, emerged to clusters of little cabins nestled in the valley. Sometimes a moose stood in the road and my father would brake slowly and carefully and we'd watch it lope off into the trees from a safe distance. He did not talk about his illness, but he did say once, "Sometimes I wish they'd stay longer for us to look at, you know?" and he seemed sad. It was a moose and its calf he was talking about and they were almost out of sight.

At his cabin we were quiet. Occasionally a car drove slowly up our long dirt road and someone walked along the side of the place and knocked on the door, probably surprised that anyone was living out here. It was my job to speak to them, to show off the puppies one by one. "This one is kind of shy," I'd say, or, "She's a real handful."

The dog mother stayed close to the puppies—she knew what was going on—but the males were even more energetic than usual, testing the limits of the cabin and then the land beyond. Sometimes I chased them like I was one of them—filling in for their missing pack member. Or at least that's how I wanted to see it, I suppose, because when I was playing with them, I became someone half my age, someone who had grown up out here, under this wide sky, breathing this pure air. The magic of my father's broken two-room cabin had done this to me, made me feel as if innocence could recede, then return as simply as a tide.

We gave away four of the five dogs, two to a kid not much older than me, two more to a woman and her young children, who stood waiting by her car where she had commanded them to stay, like the kids were her pets as well. She eyed the place suspiciously, as if I might be selling all kinds of things out here, and asked me if my mother was around. I told her no, she wasn't, and showed her into the bedroom where the puppies were waiting for her. Behind the house I could hear my father chopping wood. I could tell from the sharpness of the sound how clean the cut was, if he split the log on the first swing or if he had to lift it up again, held aloft by the axe, and bring it down a second time.

# *Shapeshifters*

The doctor was writing a long-delayed letter when she heard the commotion from the rear of the cabin, the sound of people trying hard to be quiet but failing badly, and she thought simply, *Another distraction.* She could feel the cold sweeping across the floor and over her feet, even through the door, closed with the double click of the jam and the heavy iron latch. With more than a bit of disgust, she decided to finish her half-completed thought across the middle of the page: an observation about the weather and her own tendency to mirror it, as if she were merely an extension of the difficult season.

How bored she had grown of treating every alcoholic shake, every fist-fight's aftermath. Sick of confession without any desire for absolution. She had come from the Salvation Army in Skagway and journeyed north to the Yukon Territory. Everybody in this place had an interesting story to tell and many reasons for not telling it. And yet roll up their sleeves to inspect an open sore, and they'd spill it all with pride, the drunken quarrels, poor business deals, the petty and not-so petty crimes. In the absence of priests any learned person would do, and a doctor might serve better, especially one with a frail voice and sensitive hands, a person who kept to herself in the priestly way. Sometimes men showed her long-ago injuries—missing fingers, bones healed badly. A man with burns on his face told her he was the only one of a dozen to survive and he was grateful except on certain days when he missed the camaraderie of his friends.

She did not care if they paid up front but she insisted they call her "sir" and not mock her habit of dress. If they had no money then food would be fine, and if no food there was wood to be split in the back. *I am somber in these winter days.* That was her thought, a pedestrian one if ever one existed, but she completed it across the page in neat script and anointed it with a period. What she had wanted to write was, *For a place with such fullness—caribou blotting out a hillside, the sea of white birch—there is an empty space here, one that begs to be read even though it is blank, as if it contains the solution to a mystery.* Or, *I am sorry for our separation, dearest, but what can be done? Trust me when I say that nothing can be done.* Standing up from the table meant losing all of that. She knew it would return but not in that exact form and not necessarily for days after. But possibly it was best for Theresa to be spared all that, best for both of them.

She barked out to the noise at the back of the cabin, "Hold on now. No need to tear down the place." She buttoned her shirt and thought of a new line for the letter. *So many have found fault with me and it is best to live alone so that the only enemy will be myself.*

Voices then, musical, and she recognized the speech of the two Nantuck brothers from up on the mountain. She had treated them on several occasions, once for a bad sty and once for a beating from their father, Arie Nantuck, a drunkard who liked to boast that he had been a cowboy in northern Missouri and met both Annie Oakley and Buffalo Bill. "Here he comes," someone whispered from beyond the door.

The sound of the masculine pronoun pleased her.

When she opened the door, she first noticed the youngest, a boy of no more than five who looked past her with such intensity that she wanted to ask him what he saw. There were five children, holding hands as if standing in a storm in the dark of night, a chain ordered from smallest to largest. She wanted to tell them that they were safe, nobody would be getting lost here. Each face was painted with flour paste, and she wondered if they had been playing at some kind of masquerade up there on the mountain, a play or performance. Each small nose tipped with ash, but their expressions solemn. "There's been some trouble, sir," the oldest said. He could not have been more than twelve and he wore some kind of cap on his head, ornamental in design and as bright red as anything she'd seen in weeks.

"It's our mother," the girl said.

The youngest made a sound of agreement.

The doctor remembered the mother, a Tlingit woman with that youngest boy's same stare and deep rubeola scars along her forehead. She had spoken to her once but couldn't remember the nature of the exchange. She imagined her now as the victim of some brutality, a body in a dark room. She asked the children, "Has someone been hurt? Has one of you been hurt?"

"Please, sir," the oldest said.

The children looked to each other. Evidently, they had nothing else to say. They'd come down the mountain through snow and ice, but this last step, passing along these words, seemed the most difficult thing. She said, "Very well. We can go. But take this," and she passed around salmon bark to each of them. They all looked to the oldest, who nodded, and then they began to eat.

As she found her boots drying on their sides by the potbelly stove she thought of one more line and cradled it in her mind. *If you were here we could share this melancholy together, and you'd find that it's actually quite pleasant, and a better cure than marriage.*

✹

She chose five of the dogs and dragged them one at a time to the sled. They had not run in more than a week and they were overflowing with desire. She reached for Charlotte, the lead dog, who went calm when the doctor's hand touched her head.

"Not that one," the oldest boy said.

"She's the best of them," the doctor said. Without looking at the boy, she continued fastening each dog to the sled, speaking each name as a litany. The dogs she had not chosen were barking in desperate excitement and the ones she had chosen were jumping and pacing and breathing ice.

"I'm not insulting her," he said. "I just don't think you should take her with us."

But she ignored his words, and he said nothing else about the matter. They progressed out through the legion of snow-heavy trees. This was familiar terrain, land that she loved, and as her heart filled with her own goodwill she was aware of a quick turning away, at least for a moment, from her thoughts of Theresa. But of course, in this awareness Theresa returned to her again, as quickly as she had left.

The youngest boy was still eating his salmon, his sister holding him steady. It was four miles to the ridge and she wondered then if she should have inspected the children for frostbite. Fifty toes and fifty fingers and she could not convince herself that all of them had gone unscathed. The upper curve of the ear, what she considered one of the most beautiful parts of the human body, was also one of its most sensitive and that too needed scrutiny. But they were moving now and it would have to wait.

They reached the edge of the trees and emerged into the open field where last spring, when first arriving here, she had settled down into the damp wildflowers and sprawled to look at the sky. The field had become a flat plane of ice with trees about half a mile in the distance and then a slow rise to the first plateau. The winter made the land seem burned and open, but of course it was all temporary.

"See," she shouted above the sound of the runners. "There's never been a better lead." But the boy would not respond.

Theresa could not be persuaded either, but that would not stop the doctor from recording the nature of her thoughts and sending them to San Francisco. *We are beyond friendship. We are beyond the rules of law and possibly nature and you can choose to live an easy life with that dull man, that is your right, but it's mine to remind you.*

But remind her of what? That once in a rented room they had lain together and the sunshine around the edges of the drapes had formed an attractive pattern across the carpet and for that short time everything had made sense.

Up ahead the dogs were not doing well and it was only the second mile. It was Charlotte; she was the problem. She lifted one of her front paws and half skipped on the trail.

They stopped and the doctor knelt to find the foot uninjured, but when they started again the dog immediately fell into her strange dance. Could the foot be broken? The dogs circled around and the children did too. The doctor nursed the foot with her thumb and it seemed fine, but she couldn't be sure. They'd have to bring the dog to the basket, but they were already six there, which meant the doctor would have to trot the rest of the way, just behind, holding the reigns. She picked the dog up and carried it across the snow, her boots crunching through the hard surface, and said to the oldest boy, "You're going to have to hold her steady," which he did, gently, a hand on her collar and his legs parted to cradle her length. The oldest girl stroked Charlotte's scruff. "So you were right," the doctor said. "How were you right?"

The boy said, "I just had a thought. That's all."

She checked the feet of the other dogs and reconfigured them, and when she returned to the sled the boy had taken the hat from his head and placed it on the dog, who accepted the indignity with a dog's grace. Charlotte seemed so at peace that for a moment the doctor considered hitching her up again, but that would have been cruel to the dog and cruel to the woman waiting for them. She had to keep reminding herself the mother might be in pain, most likely from a drunken beating, and what little light the day had given them would soon withdraw.

They lurched into motion again across the white expanse and she felt the thrumming of her breath in her head as she ran alongside the sled. The four dogs worked harder and she was proud of them and proud of herself for having strong legs and a strong heart. She was only thirty-three and she was proud of most of the things in her head, her knowledge of the body she occupied. There was no place for a person like her in San Francisco, but in Skagway she had thought she could recast herself. The Salvation Army had needed doctors badly, after all, but eventually they too had spat her out because she did not believe in God and she did not believe in romance in the way God constructed it. And what was especially not right about it was that it was easier for two men to do it in secret, or at least that's the way it seemed to her from the outside. In the mission there had been some of that, glances between men she knew meant more.

Lying Theresa. First one thing and then another. Theresa who tucked her hair behind her ear whenever she laughed. Theresa who did not belong in this cold place, except that maybe she did. The memory of her had become a slippery fish. Lord, she was fed up with trying to hold the pretty wriggling thing. She wanted to drop it along the way except that would be like throwing away nourishment, wouldn't it?

⚜

Just as they reached the next stretch of trees the new lead dog began to skip and then hop. The others grew confused and irritated by its hesitation. She was winded anyway and they stopped again. The world had gone dark except for the slightest yellow haze covering everything, including her hands as she untied the rig. Her fingers ached but she forced them to move.

"There's that one too," the boy said.

The same paw even. She moved it up and down like a lever. "I'm not sure what to do," she said. She spoke to the dog as much as the children, but none seemed to understand. The dogs had become part of the game too, even Charlotte, and it made her feel like the one standing outside the circle. Perhaps she had always felt that way.

"I'ma hold her," the girl said, and she picked the dog up gingerly and carried it up close to her chest. A difficult bundle, but it was the runt of the litter and manageable even for someone her age. It wanted to be held and went limp in her arms like a tired child.

"These dogs aren't no dogs," the boy said. He motioned to the five-year-old with a slight nod of his chin. "My brother is a fox. And these dogs aren't what they seem to be."

They were playing with her. Their mother might be dying and they were continuing whatever game of pretend they had started on the mountain. Except the world seemed to be playing along. How else to explain the strange alignment of coincidence? Even her past suddenly arranged on that axis: God playing at existence, Theresa pretending so well she convinced herself for a little while.

The doctor said, "I don't believe in God. The one I was raised to believe in. So don't be insulted when I say I don't believe you either. Spirits. Whatever you want to call them." She waved her hand as if shooing it all away.

"The names for things don't matter much," the boy said.

"We need to go," she said, turning back to survey the sled. In the girl's lap, the injured dog raised its front paw in a dainty motion that reminded the doctor of her mother holding a teacup and looking out the window, describing the day as *luminous* or *golden* or *full of great promise*.

Her family had given two brothers to the war, and as she pushed through her books she began to wear the clothes they had left behind: heavy coats, button shirts, loose-fitting pants. She had never been one to move quietly through a house but now she cultivated a strong footstep and a louder voice. She liked to look her father square in the eye and say something like, "You're wrong on that count."

The men with the worst of the facial injuries sometimes wore masks to cover the deformities. They reminded her of a costume one might wear to a masquerade. The insufficiency of this was comedic. Possibly her first step in wanting to be a man was feeling sorry for them, although she sometimes remembered names she had given herself as a child, masculine names like Grant or Howard, the names of presidents. She winced when her mother called her by her given name. Finally she cut her hair short and told her father that he might as well lose the last of his children. Her mother she felt horribly for, but what was there to say?

Perhaps once she completed the letter to Theresa she would write another and send it back east to her family, but the one to Theresa had taken weeks of difficult labor already and was not close to being finished. Pages had been torn up and others scratched out. Much of it passed through her mind like a muddy creek. And it was getting more complicated the further she moved up the mountain. How could she tell Theresa any of this?

"Sir," the boy said. "Is this the right way?"

"Of course," she said. "Look. There. There's your home."

She pointed toward what they called the mountain. It was more of a hill but with the foreboding attitude of a mountain, all craggy and misshapen. A few lived there. The lesson in that? There was always some more remote place to hide oneself. She let her voice crack out through the permafrost-stunted trees and the dogs dug in harder, three good dogs, but still only three, and she leapt from the sled again to give them some relief. She could turn and see her own place across the valley now, modest, with a plume of smoke still rising from the chimney. The letter on the desk. The fire would be dead by the time she returned, the letter a foreign thing. Possibly she'd have to start over. Was there still a chance for them and how could kind words bring such a thing about? Entertaining the possibility made her want to spit against the rocks.

Harder work now through snow thrown up in odd shapes, rocks, trees shattered and uprooted. She pushed and the dogs pulled. Now the sled was moving downward and she held to the runner, breathing hard. Yet another lead dog began to limp. It settled down into the snow as if to sleep and didn't even look in the direction of her voice. She pushed to the front and yelled at the dogs and grabbed one by its harness and sought to drag the lot of them by sheer force of will. It might have been easier for her to continue on alone but that meant leaving the sled and dogs and the children. She had a feeling the children could take care of themselves, even the youngest, but the dogs were dear to her, especially Charlotte.

She asked the oldest boy, "If it's not a dog then why do you stroke it like a dog? Why are you holding it like a dog?"

"I'm not," he said. "I'm stroking it like you should stroke a crying person. And I'm holding it like you should hold a child."

"What ails her?" she asked.

"You saw yourself," the boy said.

"Your mother, I mean," she said.

"I think she would want to explain in person," the boy said, and she realized then, looking from the boy to the dog on his lap, that, yes, the black mark on his nose was supposed to be a dog's nose. His face was as white as a husky. And the tips of his fingers were dotted with black, possibly coal, to make them look like the pads of a dog. For a moment he seemed ready to say something else but he pushed his fists against his coat and turned away to review the others.

※

The camp consisted of two buildings on opposite ends of a snow-blasted field, the smaller obviously in disuse, its roof splintered as if something had fallen through it. The filthiest chickens she had ever seen moved around the building and each one seemed to radiate a false pride that repelled her as they marched in circles, chests pushed out. She traced a line across the trees to find their coop at the edge of the forest. It was cracked open, apparently recently, for otherwise the chickens would be frozen tight as stones, dead, and not prideful at all.

She held the smallest child and the smallest dog, the child on her shoulders with his hands on her head, the dog in her arms. Each other child held a dog by the collar. The sled remained a good mile back, and she'd have to get it in the morning because her legs were weak. "Is this your home?" she asked the boy on her shoulders.

"You don't believe in God," he said, "but you will believe in us."

"Even if I didn't, your weight on my back would convince me," she said, "and I said I didn't believe your brother. Of course, I believe in you. The fact of you."

But some small doubt remained.

She went to the larger of the buildings. It wasn't inviting but was at least whole and warm. When she came around the corner she saw the door open. All the heat had been sucked out. Snow had even blown into the rooms. "Is this your home?" she asked again, with more irritation.

"No," the boy on her back said, although for a moment, in her tiredness, it seemed as if it was the dog who answered her. "Not no more," he said. "Where is my mother? My legs are gone on me. It's just my upper part I feel." She saw the body on its stomach at the far end of the cabin, its legs covered in a snow drift and one hand holding a skillet. She could not see the face but it was surely Arie Nantuck, who was probably as stone-solid as the chickens would be soon. He had shared their mindless confidence too. He wore expensive deerskin boots with embellished trim. One poked out of the snow. She turned from him with the boy above her and said, "Nothing to see."

"I already seen it," the boy said. "Now and yesterday too."

The others had come up around the house holding the dogs and they all stood there waiting for her to do something.

"I can't bring him back," she said.

She didn't know what made her say that, but immediately she felt like a fool. The oldest laughed in a way that made her embarrassment double. The one on her shoulders had begun to stroke her cheek with his mittened hand, and she wondered if that was what he had been staring at all along, all the way back there at the cabin: the sight of his father face down on the floor. She reached up and disentangled the boy and then went to look at the body. He was frozen hard to the floorboards and she couldn't even extricate the pan from his grip. She said, "There's no helping your father. We should think about helping ourselves now."

"It's momma who needs the help," one of the girls said.

"If what I believe is true then your mother is going to jail," the doctor said. "Beatings or no, you can't just shoot a person." Because she noticed now that it was the blood from the chest that had frozen the body to the floor. The man's shirt and jacket were expensive too, most likely purchased in Anchorage in a fit of extravagance.

She felt no disgust, just caution. At the mission she had worked on the hardest cases: broken bones emerging from the skin, a rib cage crushed by a rockslide, feet blackened by cold and needing the mercy of clean amputation. She kept her hair short and spoke in short, curt sentences. The other men seemed more than happy to let her care for those shattered people but not so pleased when she cursed or threw instruments. She tried to speak to the oldest boy in a voice flattened by her own measured will. "You need to start telling me everything you've kept from me now. Who did this to your father?"

"Sir," he said, and this time she detected just a bit of mockery in the word. "Our mother did it, but she had reasons."

"I'm not doubting that," she said. "I know your father's reputation."

The youngest boy had sat down in the snow.

"Stand up!" she barked. "Get some wood together and light a fire," she told the lot of them. "We're spending the night here."

"Do as he tells you," a new voice said. "Don't be rude."

She turned. The mother stood in the threshold with a rifle, but she held it all wrong, butt down, as if she might lift and fire from the wrong end. Her chin was painted black and a ring of beads and thorns circled her head, but she wore a military parka unbuttoned at the chest, below that a white undershirt.

She remembered her more clearly now. They had spoken once in town, very briefly, about Governor George Alexander Parks, who had visited a few weeks before on his tour of the Yukon Territory and made a speech to a crowd of a few hundred. The woman said he was a great man and he would do great things for the Tlingit people. When he spoke to a crowd he had a way of making it seem like he was speaking to you and you alone, that he had a cure for your specific problem. She had said she had almost shaken his hand, but he glanced away and found someone else in the throng. She had almost shaken the governor's hand and now here she was: she had killed her husband with a shot through his chest.

The doctor glanced around at the little ones and she looked to be counting them, making sure each one was present and accounted for before looking up past them to the threshold, the body beyond that. "You're a good man," the woman said, "to come all this way and bring them all safe back to me. I've been shot too. I shot myself."

"I see," the doctor said, and she wondered if she should just reach out and take the gun. The dogs, she realized, with a rush of blood to her head, were off killing the chickens. Let them have them, she decided.

The oldest boy and the oldest girl were picking up kindling. The woman took the sticks and said, "That's good. That's enough. Now me and this good gentleman need to talk. Why don't you go off to the back room and finish your play. We'll light the fire. Don't worry at all. Everything is going to be fine. Remember to speak loud so the trees can hear you."

The letter had been too small a vessel already, and now, how could it contain all of this? They sat across from each other with the fire going in the stove and the floor had turned wet and the doctor knew she should touch the body, turn it over and see, but that other body, the woman across from her, held her like a counterweight, the two a perfect balance. The voices came from the next room, sometimes words and sometimes pretend barking, howling, the sounds of hunting and fighting.

"You shot yourself in the neck," she said.

"I was aiming for the head," the woman said.

No gesture needed to be made toward the man on the floor. "Should I look at the wound?" the doctor asked.

"It's nothing," the woman said. "My hands were shaking bad. I hardly scratched myself." She seemed ready to sleep. Her head occasionally nodded forward and back as if in agreement to a question that had not been asked. And yet her confidence—the siren quality to her story—called the doctor deeper. She considered those other stories, the otter spirits appearing at the edge of the forest and asking for help, calling you inside, telling you, *Come with me.*

"Are you a Kushtaka?" the doctor said.

Of all the questions she could have asked, to ask that one. Her own words perplexed her.

The woman was silent for a moment. "I wouldn't expect you to understand," she said. "It's not him kicking me around. That I handled pretty well. He was gone a lot of the time anyway and my father had done the same. You just have to brace yourself for it. But those boots and that shirt. That money could have been spent on fishing gear, a new roof, anything, but what he did spend it on? That fancy costume. You understand?"

In the other room where the children played, salmon hung from ropes crisscrossed at the ceiling. The doctor watched the children from where she sat. The oldest held the youngest up on his shoulders, just as she had done, and they walked like a single beast with four arms. The others curled back, retreated, surged forward again.

The woman said, "Let me tell you, mister. We had a way of talking. He'd knock me down and then he'd say, I'm sorry, I'm sorry I did that. Why did you make me do such a nasty thing in front of our children?"

Theresa with hair so long it touched her tailbone and if you said, *You are beautiful,* she glared at you as if you called her ugly. Theresa feeding her oranges she could still almost taste. The decadence of such a thing. The decadence of her pain too. The luxury disgusted her.

"Enough," the doctor said. "Stop."

And she stopped, although her head started up with its ever so slight yes, yes, yes motion again.

"You asked if I was a Kushtaka," she finally said. "Not when I killed him. Then I was just a woman. But now, yes, now I believe I am." She looked herself over, her chest, the slope of her big body, her squat thighs and feet. "I think you are one too, mister. And if you are one then you must be here to trick me."

"I'm not here to trick you," the doctor said. "I'm here to help."

Except that was just what a Kushtaka would say as it whispered to you from behind your locked door, speaking in the friendliest of voices. She had heard about them from the oldest of the old-timers: spirits who appeared with a smile and an offer of assistance. *Come with me,* they'd tell you, *I want to show you something.* Sometimes they wore the skin of people you knew, people you trusted, until you found yourself in the middle of nowhere and then the skin would peel back, the mouth open into jaws.

"I don't know. There's something about you," the woman said.

"There is nothing about me," the doctor said. She wasn't sure what she meant but it seemed the exact right thing to say. The woman still held her rifle and the doctor inched forward, put her hand around the barrel, and guided it out of her grasp. In the other room one of the children said, "We need somebody to be raven. Who wants to be raven?"

A chorus of voices emanated from the next room: *me, me, me.* "What now?" the woman said. "One Kushtaka to another?"

"Women's prison for you," the doctor said. "An orphanage for your children. For me, I don't know. Life as normal."

"Don't you want them?" the woman asked. "Each one is perfect. You opened your door to them."

The doctor made a noise of disbelief, a throaty grunt that was as close to a laugh as she could come with a dead man on the floor.

The woman leaned in. "When did you become a man?"

She would not answer that. She thought of herself heading out into the woods and returning, crossing back into the world of people. In the other room the children were barking again, all but the youngest, who made a high-pitched keening wail. He was the bird, soaring above their jealous heads. His lamplit shadow stretched across the wall, two arms extended and moving as wings and he stretched upward and the shadow bent where the wall met the ceiling and then continued on its way. On the ground the others made noises of amazement, but the doctor couldn't see what they saw, what they pretended to see.

"Where's my gun?" the woman asked.

"I have it now," the doctor said. "I'm sorry." She held it up for scrutiny, the length of it in both hands, but she did not give it up.

The great bird danced across the far wall and then back again as a clock keeps time, moving in a circle but also always forward. The children were chasing it now, or following it in a slow parade, lifting their legs and shaking their fists. Something important was happening, but she didn't know what or why except that it was full of great solemnity and it seemed to be only beginning.

Eventually she finished the letter in her own way, by reducing it to a single page, throwing out the rest the way she might splash dishwater out behind the cabin.

The men came to her still, occasionally, with gashes across their foreheads, tales of betrayal and bad deals bursting out before they had even taken a seat and continuing in one long story told by many in a chain that linked them and weighed them down. They sat wide-legged and described the stupidity of the dead and boasted about their own survival, their own gumption and shrewdness and yes, their luck. They had to travel further now because she lived on the mountain, but they didn't seem to mind. The challenge of it buoyed their stories, made them true.

The doctor did not tell them about the Kushtaka, the shapeshifter who took your soul but sometimes, very occasionally, performed some kindness for you too, a small token, the saving of a life or the gift of a pretty stone at your feet while you slept. Possibly to keep you guessing, to hurt you more the next time, or maybe because it had taken a fickle liking to you. She did not believe it, of course, she was an educated person, but in the end, anything was possible, at least here in a place still unclaimed by reason. She watched the world with an eye to putting it down on the page. And letters came back to her, from the women's prison in Anchorage, asking about the children, the homestead—all the normal questions that might be asked between a husband and wife if one were on a long journey, the other at home.

The dogs barked whenever the wounded came calling and sometimes the children joined in and made the most magnificent noise.

# A Wrong in the World

We had driven across British Columbia and through Resurrection Bay and all that time my mother kept reminding me that we weren't running, we weren't escaping, we were *going* someplace, and when we got there all the hardship would be worth it. This was 1977 and half of the gas stations along the Alaska Highway were closed and the rest were charging crazy prices. She had begun paying with balled dollar bills and change and once just before the border—I remember this distinctly—she filled the tank, gunned the engine, and laughed as she peeled out onto the main road. "Stealing is wrong, Daniel," she told me. "There are a lot of things that are wrong. Your father might say that this whole adventure is wrong. But sometimes you have to do those wrong things anyway. The best you can do is make it up somewhere else along the line."

I looked up in the rearview at the gas station growing smaller and smaller. A human figure emerged, hands on its hips, and watched us go.

Her brother worked in Seward on the boats and I think she was hoping he'd have some money for us once she reached him. After all, she had helped him out many times when he was down and out. "Remember that time when he came with us for a few weeks in the winter? We didn't tell you this then, of course, but he was getting out of his own bad situation. Remember your father pouring wine down the drain before he got there?"

"I don't," I said, which was the truth.

"Well," she said. "He did."

We camped so close to the road that sometimes the headlights of passing cars woke me up in the middle of the night. I was twelve then and she joked that in a couple of years I'd be ready to work right alongside my uncle. "It's not dangerous work if you know what you're doing," she said. "Better than selling cars. People should take risks, don't you think, Daniel?"

"I think so," I said. "I think you're probably right."

I was imagining my father at the dealership waiting for people to come on the lot so he could jog out of the building and tell them all about the new Chryslers and Chevrolets. I wondered if he was at work right at that moment. Time had gotten all mixed up and it shocked me to realize I didn't even know what day it was or what time it might be back there in Colorado Springs where my father possibly sat at his desk watching out through the glass wall of the building at the expanse of shiny cars and potential customers.

We had left Colorado Springs heading due west in the middle of the night and I think my mother was thinking about California, the place where she had grown up. After three days we changed direction and began our move upward into the Dakotas and then Montana and then the Canadian border. Somehow, she convinced the border guard to let me through without my birth certificate. "We're attached," she said to him, and she clasped my hand and held up the grip for the guard to see through the window.

"Your uncle came here when he was nineteen," she said. "Can you imagine that? Nineteen and he hitchhiked all this way. Your grandfather was a bit of a tyrant. We both rebelled in our own ways."

At the tops of the mountains you could see sheep standing in clusters of five or six. Nothing more than specks against the snow but if you looked long enough you could see them moving, changing configuration. That's how you knew they were alive: the way the points formed different shapes. Anything could be alive and you had to really look closely or you might miss it. I had never seen so much beauty. It overwhelmed me. "Over there," I told my mother whenever I saw something interesting, and she'd turn her head and give the sight a quick acknowledgement.

She had brought binoculars, but it was hard to focus them from the moving car. I wore them around my neck, though, in case we should stop, and sometimes even in the tent at night. I counted up the sheep so I could have a story to tell. Something like, "I saw forty-six sheep," and I'd know it was exactly correct because I had been meticulous. That's what I was trying to do in everything: in the way I ate our peanut butter and jelly sandwiches in the morning, slowly, tasting each bite, and the way I spoke to her when she talked about my father and why she had done this thing.

"I always wanted to live an interesting life," she said. "I don't think that's too much to ask, is it?"

⚕

Just over the border into the Yukon we camped again and my mother spoke to me in the dark about my father. "You should have seen him in his glory days," she said. "This was before you were a baby, before I trapped him, you might say. Before everything trapped him. Should you blame a whole country for your failures or just yourself?" I felt her hand reach out to touch the skin of my arm just below my elbow. "You're going to have to worry about this too," she said. "In a way that's my fault. For not falling in love with someone different. My parents thought I did it to get them angry, just like Adam heading off to Alaska, but it was true love, or honest feeling at least."

"Do you hear that?" I asked, because something was out there.

I could hear her move upright, the shuffle of her sleeping bag. "Bear," she said, but that wasn't it. I could hear a voice, two voices, growing louder. "It's someone talking," she said, and then the voices called out to us. "Don't talk," she whispered to me, "and they'll just go away."

The first voice called out and said something about almost hitting our car and the second, a deeper tone, but still a lot like the first, wondered if we were okay. A couple of flashlights strobed down the nylon of the tent and I could see my mother's face briefly in the glow. She held a gun in both hands and I couldn't help but think of a child holding a teddy bear the same way. I had never seen the gun before and I would never see it again but the fact of it—stubby and black, small as a toy—impressed itself on me and for the first time on that long trip I knew things were not going to work out. It was just a question of what accidents might befall us and when. The voices called out again, asking if there was anybody there, if we needed any help, and finally she whispered to me, "Tell them to leave. Yell it." She had pulled the pistol into her chest, flat, as if she were protecting it from theft.

"Go away," I yelled, trying to put on my gruffest voice. "Get out of here." That didn't seem good enough so I barked out another, "Go. Go now."

I could hear the two men talking to each other. The flashlights dropped lower and then vanished altogether, skittering off in the opposite direction, maybe back toward the way they had come or over to the station wagon. One of them said, "Are you alone in there?"

I didn't say anything else. In the dark my mother's pistol had ceased to exist and in a way she had too. I needed to do something and the hardest thing to do was to sit still, quiet, and let them talk. The longer I waited the longer I felt I could wait, and after a while I could hear them moving back to the road. An engine started and they drove away, slowly, and when they were gone I sat there listening for any sign that my mother was still with me. After a long time, she said, "Let's sleep."

In the morning, driving in the early sunlight, it was as if it had never happened, or at least something very different had happened than what I had remembered. Nosy, she called them, and she told me not to worry, the gun didn't even have any bullets. "A knickknack from our time living in Brooklyn," she said. "People used to shoot up in the hallway of the first floor of our building. A different kind of danger. Hey, look at that. Are you going to count those or what?"

A half dozen specks dotted the snow on the mountain off to the west, clinging to the side in a way that seemed impossible. I wondered how they could do such a thing. "Already saw them," I said.

"You're getting good at this," she said.

We had forgotten to make sandwiches that morning but I was eating a candy bar and rested both of my bare feet on the dash. My mother had washed her hair by pouring a jug of water over it and now it was tied back in a tight bun and she looked much like she did back in Colorado Springs. I imagined her on stage speaking out above the heads of the audience, reciting something profound from memory, and it was easy to believe that a person who could do such a thing could get us to Seward and get us back again.

But that had been a long time ago. Now she was a massage therapist and a healer and she liked to talk about the previous lives of the people she loved. Mine had been a king, way back there somewhere, and she had been a queen, but on different continents in different times. This, she said, was the first time we had ever met, but we had a lot in common. My father, who had also been an actor—that's how they met in Los Angeles—liked to say that he had been a horse carriage salesman in his previous life, and before that he had sold chariots. "And before that the wheel," he said. "But that was a long, long time ago." That one even made my mother laugh and he liked to bring it up whenever she was talking about all the lives that trailed behind us back to the beginning of time.

"You have to be on guard," she was saying as we drove. "You have to be *prepared*. Is that how the scout motto goes?" She pointed out again at another mountain peak, but there was nothing there. "I'm not just talking about protecting yourself against strangers. I'm talking about everybody. You can't just glide around with your heart on your sleeve. I've learned that the hard way, let me tell you." She stopped the car and way, way up ahead on the road I could see a bear, a small one, moving out into the center of the road. We let the engine idle until it crossed down the embankment and into the trees. "He's got the right idea, doesn't he?" she said. "Can you believe it? Did you ever think this would be happening to you?"

⁂

Just past the Alaska border the mountains receded and the land turned to scrub brush and dirt and stunted trees sometimes exposed at the roots, all tilting in the same direction as if blown by a great storm. It all reminded me of bad weather and disasters, something half-destroyed and then forgotten.

My mother pulled over and said, "You know what, kid? We're either going to have to sleep or you're going to have to drive. What do you say?" So I drove, slowly, while my mother cracked the window and let her fingers dangle out, moving them as if waving to someone just past my line of vision. She reminded me of myself when I was eight or nine, playing with the rush of air, feeling the pleasure of it and not really thinking about much else. "You're doing really well," she told me. "Just don't ride the brake so much. How long has it been since we've seen another car?"

"Hours," I said. "The Chevy with the broken grill. Remember that?"

"Right," she said.

That's how we arrived in Seward, with me driving, maybe thirty miles an hour, until buildings began to appear among the damaged landscape and my mother told me we should switch again. "Good job," she said. "Really good job. You're the kind of person a woman can trust, do you know that? Don't ever lose that. It's a precious commodity." She scooted across the seat and I walked around the front of the car. My palms were sweating and I wiped them on my jeans. They came away dirty. I had worn the same pair all week and they were dark with campfire smoke.

"I know what you're thinking," she said. "You're thinking that this is crazy. But I trusted you and you have to trust me. Everything I'm doing is because I love you. I know you hate hearing that word but there it is." She made a sound like our cat puking a hairball and she laughed. "Right there in the car with us. So trust me. When you're an adult you'll look back at this and say, 'Man, she did right by me.'"

Seward came into view: a long road wet with that morning's rain crowded by low buildings. Out in the bay another crowd of boats and beyond them a wall of mountains, smaller and gray in the foreground, towering snow-covered ones looming behind them. I realized that what my mother had been telling me—that the sight would take my breath away—had been sincere, and that she was amazed too. She slowed the car down and we watched the horizon and the ships and the play of the light on the water. It was blue and green at the same time, sometimes one, sometimes the other, and sometimes both, and the white of the mountains was like no white I had ever seen. My mother must have glanced at my face because she said, "I told you so."

I remembered my uncle as a big man with a thick beard who had slept late during his time at our house, sometimes rising at noon and grunting as he moved around upstairs. He told funny little stories about growing up with my mother, stories that always showed her in the best possible light, as smart and courageous and funny and more than a little rebellious, and I believed that she was still all these things in the right proportions.

My father had looked at my uncle like he was a thing he was trying to figure out, a puzzle spilled all over the kitchen table, but they had joked good-naturedly and when he left at the end of the two weeks, my father said, "Independent thinkers. That's what this country needs. I'd probably last a day up there, don't you think? Maybe two?" And he produced a bottle of wine from somewhere—my mother laughed to see it—and poured two glasses. "A toast," he said. "To adventure," and they twined their arms together like the necks of swans I had seen in a picture book once, tipped the cups to the other's lips.

⋇

In 1977 Seward was a place you could go if you wanted to erase your name from society's ledger. My mother said that the people who lived there, my uncle included, did not want to be found, but he was in there somewhere, on one of those boats clustered into a miniature city. It would take patience and that was okay.

This is what he saw when he woke up every morning: the water and sky and the frame of mountains on three sides, the ocean on the other. We seemed to be falling into all of it. I could practically feel the tug of gravity as we followed the road down a long slope into the center of town. Trucks traveled the other way, moving slow over ruts in the road, turning and twisting around the worst potholes. Occasionally another driver opened a hand in a wave. We passed a sign for the Wells Fargo bank, another for a restaurant that said simply *Good Food*. I was still trying to remember the number and name of the day. We drove the wet main street at a walking pace and my mother said, "We'll need to handle this gently. Your uncle Adam is going to be a bit surprised."

I said, "I thought you two had talked this out. What about the phone call?"

"That was to your father," she said, "and I ended up not making that one either."

"Okay," I said.

"I didn't want to let him know," she continued, as she moved around a little crater of mud. "He would have talked me out of it. He's always liked your father, you know, even though it might not seem like it. Or at least he thinks your father is good for me. I guess that's not the same thing, but close enough. So yeah. There's going to be a reaction." She laughed a little. "Be sure to get a good look at his face. Another reason we should have brought a camera, right?"

"Right," I said.

We slowed for a group of men crossing the road. They wore bright all-weather gear even in the sunshine and took their time getting to the other side. One of them drank from a beer bottle and he tipped it up high to get the dregs, then kept moving with his arm draped to his side, holding the bottle by the neck in a gesture that was almost gentle.

The mountains seemed further away the closer we got to the center of town. I could see the mud flecked trucks, the dogs wandering free with lowered heads, sidewalks made of wood. I could see my mother's face smiling as she nodded, affirming this or that with a motion of her head. Possibly she had been able to imagine us making it all the way. What could she do now but let the joy wash over her and ignore what might come next?

I was fourteen then and I suppose young for my age. I'm more than triple that now and my work takes me many places, although I can't say many of them are especially interesting. Still, I know that impulse to move, the clarity of a suitcase full of clothes and car odometer putting on miles. It's like a lot of things—its power not any less so because it's illusionary.

I've often thought about my mother's words. She believed that time would judge her kindly, or maybe that was just her hope against the odds, a leap of faith similar to getting into the station wagon with a pup tent, a road atlas, and her only child.

※

Later when I returned from Alaska my father did not speak about my mother for a long time except to say that she would be back soon, he was sure of it, and that we should both have faith—both in the kindness of others and in her own love for us. But then he began to tell me things I had never heard before, filling that open space her absence had created. "I met your mother when she was acting in Othello out in San Francisco," he said. "She wasn't Desdemona, but she was the best performer in that play. You could tell just from the way she carried herself, before she even spoke a line." He had just come home from work and he still wore his white shirt and tie, although the tie was loose around his neck and his sleeves were rolled up his forearms. We stood on the back porch watching our small square of yard. He narrowed his eyes as if he saw something weird out there in the dark by the fence and bushes, a thing he didn't like. "Maybe it was a mistake to fall in love with someone on a stage. I don't know. I wasn't thinking much about the future. I certainly wasn't thinking about someone like you being in my life." He turned to me and touched my shoulder and smiled and then he looked down because he had always been shy with me.

"Who was she then?" I asked.

"Emilia," he said. "A minor character. Well, not so minor, but it's not important."

"And who were you then?" I said.

"What?" he asked.

"In the play," he said. "Who were you?"

He laughed. "That was a long time ago," he said. "I was the lead, but I crashed my way through it. All bluster and muscle. I think I screamed every line. What else could I do? An audience full of rich white people."

I could tell he was remembering it vividly, and even though he was looking out there at the edge of our property, what he was seeing now probably had something to do with that young man, the only Black man on stage, pacing as he yelled his lines. He looked embarrassed by the whole thing. He said, "These were the days of segregated lunch counters, so it was an important part. But you wouldn't know about that. You've grown up in a different world."

"Right," I said, although I'd been insulted at school plenty of times. I watched the place my father was watching and I swore I saw something move. A dog probably, but still, it made me happy to think that maybe something wild traveled through the neighborhood on all fours, digging beneath fences and searching for food.

"I wasn't old enough then to be playing a role like that," my father continued and it seemed like he was speaking to himself now as much as to me. "And now I'm a little bit too old. There was a very small window I missed."

He didn't seem old at all, although his shortly cropped hair was flecked with gray. I said, "I'm glad we live here," because at that moment it felt true and because I knew he was thinking about what might have been.

It had been more than a month since my trip to Alaska but our little suburb still seemed tight as a cage. Still, I was happy to be speaking with my father, happy to be back in school. The story was that I had been very sick but I was better now. "I should probably take that stupid thing down," he said, meaning the swing set. "You haven't used it in years, have you? And I just left it there. Let's take it down this weekend." He put his big hand to his chin and rubbed. "You've been through a lot, haven't you?"

"I really haven't been through anything," I said.

"You don't have to protect her," he said. "Let's talk honestly."

"I am," I said. "I'm talking honestly."

"Okay, then," he told me, and there seemed to be nothing left to say. He nodded, as if agreeing with himself that yes, the swing set needed to come down. Maybe he'd find out about that animal too, if it was an animal. Other things needed to happen. The lawn needed to be mowed. The garage needed painting. I could tell he was probably making a list in his head. He wanted a good life for all of us, me especially, and this was one way to do it.

"What else were you in?" I asked him.

"Nothing much. Too good-looking for character parts and not good-looking enough to be a leading man. That was my problem. And I didn't care that much when it came down to it. It was just a thing to do. A hobby."

He grimaced and took his tie off completely, let it hang down at his side. I thought of the man with his bottle crossing the road, all of those men exhausted after work, but I also thought that he was very good-looking, the most good-looking man I'd ever seen, and that in a way all of this was a performance. He seemed to be striking a pose, the pose of a tired family man finished with his day. I could tell he was thinking about sleep, but I had something else to say. I said, "You know, she didn't really want much. I learned a lot of things about her when we were traveling and that's one of the main ones."

He grimaced again and blinked his eyes, rubbed the bridge of his nose. "Maybe," he said. "Maybe that's true. But what's that little thing then? Tell me that." And then he smiled again and it was as if those words had never come from his mouth. "You're a good kid, Daniel. A really good kid. God knows you don't deserve this." He laughed and added, "Maybe in the next life we'll work it all out, eh? I wonder if she's going to be a queen again. There aren't as many of those as there used to be, but I wouldn't put it past her."

"Me neither," I said. "I bet she's working on it."

"I bet so too," he said.

"You know," I said. "She mentioned something in Seward. Can you tell me if it's true?"

"I'll do my best," he said.

"She said you performed in London once," I said. "In *The Black and White Minstrel Show*."

That grimace again. "It's a hard life when you can't trust your mother," he said.

"Right," I said, and that was that. I think that's when I made my decision, somewhere at the base of my brain, although it would be two years until I followed through on what my mother had begun. What she had said in Seward had actually been, "Your father was afraid of becoming a colossal failure so instead he decided to become a minor one."

She had still been pretty, I decided, and still young, young enough and smart and strong enough to get what she wanted. Anything could have happened in her life.

❦

We were waiting for her brother to return from the sea. We had thrown his name around town and although nobody knew him they said there were boats coming in that night and we should stick around, so we walked up and down the pier and she began to tell me about the past in small pieces. The word tyrants came up again, bigots, small-minded backstabbers. Her brother had solved all that by cutting the knot.

"Mom," I said. "I'm cold."

"Me too," she said. "And it's April. Who could have figured?"

Out on the water I could see small patches of ice moving, I decided, like the boats moved: in small clusters configured by a logic I didn't understand. The wind blew my mother's hair around her head and although she was smiling she looked frightened and alone. I was there, right with her, but I'm not sure I counted in the way she wished. My presence seemed to make her lonelier the longer we waited and she touched her fingers one at a time, rubbing them for warmth. I said, "Remember the caribou? That was my favorite part."

"Yes," she said. "We had to stop the car. A whole parade of them across the road."

"Like a train," I said, because it had taken them that long to pass and because they had walked in single file, almost as neat as a set of boxcars.

"London," she said. "Can you even imagine?" but I didn't respond. Then she looked out to sea and said, "They're coming. I can see them."

I held up the binoculars. A line of white hulls and a mess of rigging, at least a dozen boats, probably more, and they moved together like birds did, arranged in tight design. I moved my eye across them, acknowledging each one and then the next, and sometimes I could see smaller details.

He would be surprised and angry. They'd probably go away and have a talk and leave me to watch the ocean with his heavy coat around my shoulders.

But he didn't arrive. The boats came into the docks and the men came up the ramps but he wasn't one of them. Someone had caught a particularly large halibut and they hung it from a hook and gathered around. "That's bigger than you," my mother said to me and I could tell she was trying very hard to keep her good attitude. "I'm sure this is the place," she added. "I have the letters. I remember him telling me. You remember, right, Daniel?"

She took me by the shoulders and crouched slightly and stared right into my face. She repeated the question but I wouldn't answer. I think part of me wanted to see her this way, dumbfounded and frustrated, the beauty drained from her face and replaced with anxiety. Her lips were chapped and bleeding at the corner of her mouth and her hair whipped upward and around like a mad thing. "Daniel," she said. "Talk to me. Don't tell me that you weren't dying there too."

"I don't know what you're talking about," I said.

She released me and I stumbled back a bit, caught myself before falling. "Oh, great," she said. "This is it, isn't it?" And she clapped her hands together and laughed. "We've come all this way. Please don't quit on me now."

Just then someone walked up to us and we both turned and for a second I thought it was my uncle, but then I noticed the beard was dotted with gray and there was something distant in his eyes. He didn't know us and he didn't care to know us, but he did want a cigarette and when my mother told him we didn't have any he looked insulted. "I saw you earlier," he said. "With those things," and he pointed at my binoculars and I felt like a fool.

><

We tented out on the beach and even made a small fire of driftwood. The next morning, I woke before my mother and headed up the coast, picking up especially interesting stones and then sending them out to the breakers. I was debating whether I should head back to my mother or head out on my own to find my uncle, to find someone, to maybe just find a pay phone and call my father collect. We had been gone two weeks, but it seemed much longer and a childish part of my brain thought he might not recognize my voice if I called—that I had somehow grown beyond his recognition. It was a stupid thought, but I allowed myself to luxuriate in it, to find strange pleasure in it, and then I kept going until I could no longer see any sign of my mother's tent. I imagined that I had come here alone, that I would stay here and that my mother was back with my father in Colorado Springs and they were both happy. I knew I was happy right then, but I didn't really know why except that the little stones felt good in my hands when I picked them up.

I knew where to find him. He had mentioned the name of his boat, *The Bobbysocks*. He had mentioned it to my mother too, but she must have forgotten. I walked around the docks, up and down, until I found a small fishing boat with that name and sat down on the dock and watched it. People came and went up the dock, but none of them were my uncle. I could watch the sunrise and then the boats leaving, the smell of diesel. I tried to imagine myself as a native kid, someone who belonged there, but everybody I saw gave me a once over. I waited for more than an hour and then I stood and looked at the name again and decided that yes, I was right, this was the name of his boat. It had featured in a number of his stories and I thought of my father laughing at them and then waiting for another one. "That's nuts, man," he'd say, or, "What the hell are you talking about?"

Finally, my uncle appeared, but he was not surprised to see me and not surprised to see me alone either. "There you are," he said, and he took me in for a hug. He was with a couple of other men and they receded politely into the background. "Are you okay?" he asked. "I've been talking to your dad and we thought you might make an appearance." He looked me over from head to toe, as if checking for wounds, but he did it in such a good-natured way that I couldn't figure out if he was joking or not. "We've been worried sick but you're going to be okay now. What do you need? Do you need some food? I bet you're hungry as hell."

"I am," I said, and even that felt like a betrayal.

The four of us moved together in the same way I had seen the men crossing the street. We found a restaurant, the one my mother and I had seen entering into town, and slid into the booth. "This is my nephew," he told the waitress. "He's had quite an adventure, so treat him kindly."

"The opposite of the way you treat us," one of his friends said, and everybody laughed, including the waitress, including me. I found out that the halibut from the day before weighed three hundred and seventy pounds, the biggest my uncle had ever seen, and although he had nothing to do with the boat that caught it everybody in town shared in the pride of the thing. I remember my uncle shaking his head in mock disbelief. It gave them something to talk about for the rest of the year at least and sometimes you needed something like that to get through the winter. "Two miracles in one day," he said. "That's enough to talk about until March."

❧

When my mother found us on the dock she began screaming before she even reached us. Then she was running up the dock, sprinting, a ridiculous sight amid all that cold serenity. She grabbed me and pulled me behind her and pushed up into her brother's face and for a moment I thought she might strike him. I've been looking all over, she kept yelling, and my uncle's friends had to pull her back away from him. I remember them smiling as they did it, as if this kind of thing happened all the time here—or it didn't happen enough.

"Let's talk about this, Sherry," my uncle said. "There's a lot we need to sort out."

It seemed like the typical kind of lover's quarrel I had never seen happen between my father and mother: the hysterical woman, the placating man. One of his friends held her around the waist. She shook her body and he let go.

"Get in the station wagon," she ordered me, but I stayed put. She spun around and said it again, louder, "Find the station wagon and stay there," but I wasn't going anywhere. A few other men gathered around further up the dock listening to her.

"Sherry," my uncle said. "Everybody's fine. The boy's fine and you're fine. I've been talking to Don. He's sick with worry, but he's not angry."

"I'm not going to lose him," she said.

He said, "We should talk about this in private."

"I knew it," she said. "You were pissed off at me when I married him and now you're pissed off that I'm leaving him."

"In private," he said.

"You're my *brother*," she said, and something caught at the back of her throat. She seemed about to gag.

I realized then that even though I was full she had not eaten anything all day. She had probably been pacing up and down the beach waiting for me to return. The mountains and ocean must have seemed impossibly big to her then as one hour turned to two and then three. But we were together now and my uncle was at least part right. I was fine. And I believed that my father was not angry. I had never seen him angry in my life. At some point he had given up on that feeling, replaced it with something greyer and yielding. I thought of what my mother had said, that he had performed in a play I had never heard about before, and decided that if it meant nothing to him anymore then it was probably best if it meant nothing to me either. My mother was still yelling, but she wasn't saying anything new, and my uncle stood with his palms open, head slightly turned, as if he was prepared to take this all day. Finally, she turned and began to walk back up the dock and said as she passed me, "Let's go."

I began to walk with her, but slowly, so that she had to slow down too to match my pace. The dock shook beneath her heavy steps.

"My brother," she said. "My own brother."

"Mom," I said. "Stop. Where are we going to go?" and I grabbed her by her wrist. She pulled back her hand and we struggled for a moment. I could hear my uncle coming up behind us.

"My brother," she said, "and my *son*."

Then she headed up the dock. My uncle came up behind me. "Let her go," he said. "She just needs to cool down."

But when I went to look for the station wagon later it was gone and so was the tent. It was dark by then and my uncle kept insisting she'd be back. We sat on his boat and he took out two small glasses and a bottle of whiskey and said, "I don't think Don would mind if I gave you a little bit of this while we wait. And it's up to you to tell him." He poured me an inch or so and I took it and it burned the back of my throat. I could hear people on the shore yelling and laughing and I thought that my mother might be one of them but that seemed an idiotic thought and I tried hard to ignore it. Better to not think about it at all and hope that she returned the next morning, her expression more composed, and although she wouldn't be ready to apologize—I had never heard her say I'm sorry—she'd at least be ready to sit down and share breakfast with us. By then she'd be starving.

"I want to tell you something about your mother," my uncle said, and I noticed that he was glowering at some point in the middle distance. He looked to me like a man looking into a mirror and he didn't exactly like what he saw. At least I hoped that he wasn't looking at me. "This is a good one," he said, and did his best to grin. "Your mother, Sherry, she was two years older than me, see? She is two years older than me. She always will be." He grinned a little harder and I tried to smile too. "I always looked up to her, and when she met your dad, well, I had to get my mind around that, not for the reasons you're thinking, but just because I knew it was going to make it harder on her. But I guess I ended up looking up to him too. And when you came along, I thought, God damn, these are people who are going to have it all. I mean, they were going to have *everything*."

This didn't seem like a story at all. It didn't have a beginning or an end. It was just the state of things, once, a long time ago, and I wanted him to stop. I wanted to hear my mother's voice calling out down the dock, which is to say, that I wanted time to spin backward. Across the bay I could see lights strobing along the water from one of the larger boats and I wondered what they were doing out there. I could hear what I thought might be fish breaking the surface, but it could have been something else, it could have been anything really. Two miracles, my uncle had said. But both of them were just luck. One good. One bad. I grinned and wondered how well he could see me. "When I come home from school I walk in and there she is," I said. "Sitting in a chair."

That was important to tell him: her body reclined, her chin lifted to the door, fingers scratching at the armrest. She seemed to awaken from a stupor as I entered.

๖ৈ

They flew me home the next day, first on a single engine into Anchorage, then south to Detroit, and finally to Colorado Springs. I called my father collect from the Anchorage airport and when he answered the phone he was breathing hard. "I thought something might have gone wrong," he said.

"No," I said. "Nothing like that. I'm right here."

"Enjoy this if you can," he said, "and if not then just sleep through it. I wish I could have come out and gotten you, but this seemed the easiest way."

"Have you heard from Mom?" I said.

"Not yet," he said, "but who knows? She might be on her way back here right now. We'll both be here when you get home."

"Sure," I said.

"It's hard to hear you," he said.

Through the glass I could see them loading the bags onto my plane, the one I would be boarding soon, and I spotted the army green duffle my uncle had given me to pack a few of his oversized sweatshirts. My clothes were in the station wagon along with everything else except some change in my pocket and my binoculars and a few of the stones I had decided to keep. I thought of my mother during the first few days of the trip when I wasn't quite sure where we were going or why. We slept next to one another in the tent and sometimes she'd click on the flashlight and say, "Do you hear that?" And I'd say, "What?" and she'd say, "Do you hear the quiet? It's incredible. You can hear yourself think." She'd reach out from her sleeping bag and touch me, touch my cheek or my hair, and then withdraw, and the light would go out and I would do the difficult work of wondering what might happen next.

ﹸﹶ

For weeks after my trip to Alaska the phone would ring in the middle of the night and I'd hear my father speaking in a low voice from the kitchen. We lived in a small house and if I rose from my bed and stood by the door I could hear the words as clearly as if they were spoken into my ear. "It's not your fault," he'd say, and I'd know it was my uncle again, had known it the second the first ring of the phone jolted me awake.

I'd hear my father scrape a chair across the floor to get settled in for a good, long talk and the next morning he'd be blurry-eyed and distracted. They had found the station wagon a few hours from the Arctic Circle not far from a town called Coldfoot. The car had been parked just off the Dalton Highway, the tent set up a hundred yards off in the tundra. She'd found a pretty place to stay the night. That's how I pictured it, with nobody around and only the noise of ravens and maybe one of the quick-running streams I had seen on our trip together, streams so fast they churned up mud and stones on their way to wherever they were going.

My father told me the news in the early morning and before he had even begun I knew what he was going to say. "Where do you think she was trying to go?" he asked me, and I said that I didn't know, she hadn't told me anything.

I never spoke to my uncle again. What did he feel? This was 1977 and none of this was anything to talk about—except late at night when you've had a little too much to drink and you do the math on the difference in time zones and then decide, what the hell. You do that again and again expecting the man on the other end to ignore you, but he never does. I could hear it all. My father said, "What else is up there once you pass that line? Is it a place you'd want to live? What could a person like her do there?"

That went on for weeks after they found my mother's body and then, finally, it stopped, and I missed it. I would wake anyway, but there would be no sound, no voice. That was a little bit worse, I guess.

They found her in the tent. That's what my father said. I imagine her body resting there for days. A gun accident. He insisted on this when he first told me the news and he insisted on it the next week when I asked him again. He insisted on it to my uncle during those long talks. He insisted on it years later when I called him from the road, drunk myself, and full of snarling hostility. The first time it had seemed true. After all, so many strange things had happened recently. He seemed almost hopeful as he told me the news, as if some greater disaster had been averted.

My mother said a lot of things. She sometimes said people were made of light, and I thought of that as we sat at the kitchen table in the dark of the early morning. The refrigerator ticked behind him, some defect deep inside it that had been there since I could remember. The last light had gone out in my father. Or maybe not. I was still there, after all, and sometimes when I walked to the dealership to meet him after school he'd bring me into him with a slap on the back and a laugh. He would say this much to the other men in suits and ties: that I had been on some adventures you wouldn't believe. I had been across the country and I had seen a fish, and then he'd turn to me and say, "What kind of fish was that anyway? How much did it weigh?" An incredible actor, my mother had said. He had performed in London at the age of twenty-three. In the evenings he searched through my mother's pots and pans, flipped through her cookbooks.

The next time I made my escape I did it alone and this time it stuck. Years later, as my mother's voice traveled through me and I slurred out those insults over the phone, my father took them in with a perfect blend of generosity and indifference. "You know what?" he said after a while. "I've done amazing things with my life. Every day I wake up and go to work and I sell cars. Me. I'm the best salesman there and everybody knows it. The best in Colorado Springs. I sit there at my desk and the white people come in and they look surprised when they see me—they look petrified—and then I sell them a car." His voice broke and he said, "Have you ever done anything like that?"

At the time I was hitchhiking to the West Coast. This was 1981 and the sight of strange man, a man like me, on the side of the road elicited all sorts of reactions, but I was making slow progress. Soon I'd be in San Diego and I planned on taking off my shoes and running hard into the surf as if to win a race.

"Every day I get up," my father said. "Every day."

# The Alphabet in Reverse

Peter remembers it all with perverse clarity: the hard knock on the back door, his mother rising from the couch, the happy violence on the TV. His mother said, "If that's your little friend from down the street I'm going to kill him," and she headed to the back of the house, to the source of the irritation. He trailed her and the dogs trailed him, filling up the narrow hallway. He could hear the knocking ahead, the hollow door rattling in its frame. Whoever it was had interrupted a good part of the show—the part where the guns come out—and he was annoyed as his mother must have been at the prospect of his friend's smiling face bobbing in the doorway, all that unwanted sun shining into their lives. Except that it was raining—he hadn't noticed all morning—and it was his father at the door. He was hold-ing the new baby sort of sideways in the crook of his arm the way you might hold a package, but the child seemed happy enough. His mother had strong opinions about this baby, and his father, and their current situation. "He's using it as an excuse," had been her exact words, "but it's no excuse at all and the law agrees with me."

The baby's face was wide and flat. Although its eyes were open it did not appear to be seeing anything in particular. His father shifted the weight of its body slightly and said, "Sorry for the unannounced visit but I didn't know where else to go." And he smiled like a salesman who had been clever enough to come to the back door, a salesman who went up and down the street trying to sell people babies. *Let me in and I'll show you what it can do.* Of course, his father was not a salesman at all. He worked building houses, or picking up after the people who built houses, wandering the construction site sweeping up stray nails and scrap wood. His truck was still running in the driveway, the passenger's-side door open and the headlights on in the rain. The baby's hair was wet and dark as the fur of a Labrador retriever and Peter wanted to touch it and feel that softness.

The dogs tried to push their way out of the space between his mother's leg and the door but she kicked them and they scrambled backward. She said, "Where the hell did you come from?"

"From White Horse," he said. "Now are you going to make me a cup of coffee?"

"That's not my responsibility anymore," she said. "If it ever was. Doesn't what's-her-name make good coffee?"

"Yeah, well," he said. "About that."

But she interrupted him. "And where is your car seat? How did you get that poor kid here, bounce it on your lap the whole way?"

"I'm a safe driver," he said. "You know that. Now let me in. I want to see my sons. And this is a good thing that's happening. Let me tell you what's going on."

Peter's brother was upstairs pretending to read. *Finish his novel*, he'd say, and then head up to masturbate dreamily with his sleeping bag over his head. His mother would bang on the door. She knew what was going on.

That's what Peter remembers most about his mother. She was a woman who knew what was going on. She liked to say that about herself. In fact, he remembers her saying it as she held the door half-open. "I know what's going on." And even though he does not remember her as especially kind it would have been impossible for her to turn him away, a man who had just driven hours to his ex-wife's door, holding a baby in the rain. She had to let him in. Her son was watching her. So she opened the door and he moved inside, sniffling, looking around at the place, the pictures on the walls, the arrangement of shoes just inside placed in a long row, sneakers, boots, slippers. He had managed to remove his own boots while still holding the baby, lifting a foot and pulling at the laces, shifting his weight. He seemed as comic as the stuff on the TV, just as heroic too, and just as impossible.

"There's a difference between obligation and kindness," his father said. "And all I'm asking for is some kindness. Now how about that coffee?"

Peter and his mother ride the monorail across the city. Below them trees and people. A cluster of families surrounding a man on a horse, the man holding balloons, leaning down to hand them to children. Why is he doing this and why does Peter care? Because for some reason he's jealous of the man, of the children scrambling around him too, and even of the parents who look on as contented bystanders. It's a nice scene and if he could he'd spit on it that would make him feel pretty okay again, but the monorail is enclosed, of course, and he's never done anything like that before, even as a kid. The guy handing out balloons steadies the horse to perfect stillness, its head lowered to receive some strokes from little hands. What would it be like to fall into all that, to become the center of everybody's panicked attention? His mother sits rigid with her pocketbook on her lap. She gives the impression of being immune to it all—muggers, disaster, Peter's chiding corrections. She seems to have surrounded herself with an invisible bubble. If the impossible did happen she'd simply remain sitting there, staring straight ahead, everything dying below her.

The monorail reminds him of rocket ships and space travel, but it's rickety as a state fair roller coaster. He can feel the vibration in his thighs. Any second it seems like it might collapse. He reaches out to hold her hand—this is a very important trip for her—but he knows he's the one searching for comfort. Her hand is a cold, dry thing. He grips it tight anyway. Even now, on this trip to the memory clinic, her nails are polished and perfect, her hair freshly done.

Two weeks ago, when he called her in Fairbanks, she told him that she'd been getting lost in grocery stores. "I go up one aisle to get the milk and the milk's not there," she said. "Then I turn around and head to produce and I wind up in the bakery."

Of course, it was much worse than that. "She's been shitting herself," his father said, when he called from Montana. "You need to talk to her."

Yes, she'd been shitting herself and yet here she is with her precise makeup, her reassuring glance in his direction when they touch.

He's sure it's all going to just come apart around them. It feels like they are hurtling forward surrounded by an eggshell. Everybody else reads newspapers, trapped in their headphones.

If his father had not called him, he might not have known at all.

At first the call had displayed the usual symptoms: it arrived after midnight, his father's voice a little slurred, although maybe Peter imagined that. First, they talked about his brother, his own children, his wife. And then the call passed into an even stranger world when his father said, "When did you last speak with your mother?"

"I don't know," he said. "It's been a while."

The kids were coming out of their rooms. Carol too. All of them squinting through the hallway light. The phone had woken them up, but this was not that abnormal. It happened every couple of months and then Peter would move quietly all through the next day, work on his projects in the garage or go for a long drive. He motioned for them all to go back to bed and they inched into their rooms to their tropical fish nightlights and princess bedspreads. "Yeah, well," his father said. "She's in trouble and she's not exactly the kind of person to ask for help, right? Unless you know something about her that I don't."

He wasn't aware that his parents even spoke anymore, not for years and years.

His father said, "Peter, are you listening to me? This is important," and he felt like a kid who's been caught dozing off in class. But he reminded himself that he was the responsible one, the man who loved his wife and children. He's not a boy anymore, for Christ's sake, so why did he feel like one? He already knew what he'd do when he returned to bed: grab Carol, pull his head between her breasts. Then she'd stroke his hair until he was able to sleep.

He'd known his mother has been in trouble for weeks. The writing on the postcards had grown bizarre, the one last week a complaint about the price of gasoline, the one before that blank except for a few words, a list of household chores. Clean the floor. Wash clothes. Fold. But he had taken the postcards and put them on the fridge with the others, writing side down. Pictures of bears and ice. The same things she'd been sending him since he left the state fifteen years ago.

His father said, "If you love her, then you'll go see her."

He had a way of being honest and deceitful at the same time. It was as if honesty was a trick he could pull on you, get your head spinning around and around until you didn't know what was real anymore. "Fine," he said. "Fine. Fine."

So at the memory clinic they sit in a white room waiting for the doctor. "I'm in perfect health," his mother says. The doctor is charming, young, handsome, with three pens standing at attention in the pocket of his jacket. First, he speaks to them about their trip here. Was it a good one? What about Alaska. Is it true what they say about the Aurora? "It depends what you've heard," his mother says from her small plastic chair. She is as unsmiling as a shark. But the doctor grins and says, "I've heard it's beautiful."

"It is that," she says.

Then they talk about the names of presidents, the days of the week, and the birthdays of her children. "There's Peter," she says, with a nod in his direction, and she names his birthday, his job, the names of her grandkids. "And then there's that other one." She waves her hand at the air.

The doctor treats all of this as a charming eccentricity.

"I can smell urine," she says. "Urine and the stuff they use to clean urine."

The doctor asks her to recite the alphabet backward beginning with the letter Z and ending with A.

"Let me see you do it," she says, when she stops at R.

His laughter is generous and patient.

Peter tries it in his own head. Z. Y. X. W.

"Once more?" he asks her.

"Complete foolishness," she says. "Are you going to lock me up here?"

"Mom," Peter says. "It's not that kind of place."

"You're not going to put me in a home. You'll need my signature for that."

"This is actually not that uncommon," the doctor says to Peter. "Let's take a recess. I'll be back in a bit and we can start at the beginning." He turns and his voice softens. "Is that okay, ma'am? I'm sorry that this is upsetting for you."

"He reminds me of your father," she says when the doctor is gone and she is flipping through a book she's brought for the occasion. "That smile of his. It's like he wants to fuck me."

❦

The crying was the worst thing he'd ever heard and he was prepared to do anything to make it stop: bounce it, say sweet words to it, put it under a pillow or drop it out the window, pray to God or maybe even the devil. He wondered vaguely what his parents would do if he just let it fall to the grassy edge just outside the kitchen window. They were on the back porch talking. Yelling really, although he couldn't hear a word. Possibly he only remembers it as yelling. Maybe they were whispering in that way they used to whisper, through tight teeth, their faces close together with his mother's hand on his father's shoulder.

But the baby definitely cried and he bounced it and begged it. He gave it his thumb to bite. Its face squeezed and collapsed and turned red and still they did not come. He could see its pulsing flesh at the back of its throat when it screamed and he wondered if this was the foundation for something, if everything after would be built on this awful moment.

Eventually his brother appeared and said, "What the fuck?" He looked around the room and made a grab at his mother's cigarettes, slid three out and put them in his jeans pocket. "Dad's out there, huh? Did what's-her-name kick him out?"

"I don't know," he said. "They're having a serious talk."

"I think it probably wet itself," he said. "The little dude."

"It's raining harder," Peter said.

"It's sleet," his brother said. "Coming off the mountain. You can hear it on the roof."

They stood listening to it clatter on the tin through the wailing of the baby. He said, "It's traveled all the way from the mountains."

"Jesus," his brother said. "I'm the one who should sound stoned. What's the matter with you?"

Finally, his parents appeared, both of them soaking wet, his father running his hand through his hair. The baby passed around along with some towels. They all sat down again. "This is the situation," his mother said. "Your father and this little one are going to sleep over here tonight. The baby will sleep with me and your father will sleep on the couch. Then in the morning I'm going to go to work, you boys are going to go to school, and your father is going back to where he came from and have a good talk with his girlfriend. Isn't that right, Tom?" she asked, and she looked at Peter's father.

"I accept these terms," he said, and he laughed, but it was just a nervous titter, and he looked down at his hands. And Peter thought that if he could just keep them all together like this, under the clattering tin roof, then everything would be okay. First tonight and then they'd figure out something tomorrow, some new reason to keep them all here and out of the rain. The sleet, he corrected himself.

This is what he's thinking about as he moves through the letters in his head. JIHGFE. The test is over, but he's still answering one of the questions, and as he does this he's also able to consider, somewhere out on the edge of his mind, that odd family around the table. The baby has found his way back to him. His father is drinking a beer. His mother is holding a spatula. That's the picture he can't shake as they wind their way through the memory clinic. His mother is trying to find her way out past the numbered doors. "Mom," he says. "Hold on."

"I'm tired of waiting," she says. "These doctors think your life is nothing. They want you to die here."

They pass another doctor who gives them the once-over, then a place they might have been before. They are lost, lost in a memory clinic, and Peter wants to throw up his hands and laugh and laugh. He hasn't even found his way to A yet either. He keeps stopping and starting. Finally, he's there. The original doctor. They've journeyed back to him. "You wouldn't believe how often this happens," he says. "This place is a maze. Were you looking for the restroom? Down there and to the left."

"Right," Peter says.

In the bathroom his voice is shaking. "Nobody is going to hurt you. The sooner we finish this the sooner we can go."

"You need my signature to put me in the home," she says, "and you're not going to get it."

"I'm not going to put you in the home," he says, "and you know what? If I was going to lock you up I wouldn't need your signature. You don't know anything about it."

"I won't let you," she says. "Your *father* won't let you. Where is he? I want to talk to him."

"I'm doing this for you," he says. "Get back out there and behave yourself and answer those damned questions."

"Oh, please," she says. "I know what you're really mad about."

❧

The next morning, he rose for breakfast to find his father at the stove and his mother at the table with the baby. She was feeding it bits of mushed carrots with her fingers and its face was smeared with orange. Both of them, his mother and father, were smiling and laughing and the room was full of heat and music. Outside more rain. It had been raining all night and the truck was covered with a thin sheen of ice. He had never seen anything like this before, not in August, and he was a little afraid, but his parents didn't seem to care at all. The table was already set, plates and forks and even knives and napkins. He wasn't used to seeing knives and napkins.

"The first one is for you," his dad said. "Well, the second one. I burned the first one. That one was for the trash can."

His mother laughed at this as if this was something she really found funny and tweezered a glob of carrot into the baby's greedy mouth.

"No church today," his mother said, although they had not gone to church since the divorce two years before.

"I might not believe in much," his father said. "I certainly don't believe in the rule of law. But I do believe in God. And not the God in the Bible and not the God on the TV."

"This old horse," his mother said, but she was still smiling, feeding the baby.

And Peter did remember talks like this. Rants, his mother called them. Sometimes about the church and sometimes about the government. Back at the old house his father had kept marijuana plants in the chicken coop with the dirty-feathered chickens. He kept a gun in a wooden box under his bed and talked about how the CIA had shot Kennedy. "You don't remember it," he'd say. "You were just a baby. But they slaughtered him right in his car just because he was making this country better for the working class and for Catholics. Right in the brain."

But at that moment, as he made the second pancake, all of it seemed charming, a fairy tale he had told them once, read to them from a big picture book. "How's it coming along?" his mother asked.

"Almost there," his father said. "Maybe a little too far actually."

He held up the black thing and Peter thought, you did that on purpose. You think it's funny. But it *was* kind of funny. He found himself smiling too. The baby was funny and so was the pitiful black pancake. Even the weather was funny. You could see the ice pelting the porch.

"It's not a day for driving," his father said.

"Got that right," his mother said.

His brother was hiding out upstairs doing his thing. The place was small enough that if everybody stopped talking, stopped moving, maybe they would have been able to hear him. Except, he realized, the tin roof was clattering with ice and rain and it didn't seem like it was going to stop. It was getting worse. "Third time's the charm," his father said.

❦

The monorail had been his mother's impractical idea, involving parking in an expensive all-day lot followed by walking through a series of busy streets. He had said no four, five times, but eventually given in when she began to tear up. It was nice up there, he has to admit, although it gave the entire day a mood that felt celebratory when it should have been somber.

When they take the monorail back across the city the horse is gone, although occasionally he spots a kid holding a balloon. It's getting late and people seem to be walking home. They will travel this way as long as they can, to the end of the line, and then find their way to his car and he'll at least have the radio to fill the space, because his mother is silent for the first time all day. She's reading her novel and his legs are spread, hands on his knees, in a pose of concentration. Finally, she speaks without looking up. "You wanted me to be dignified," she says. But he doesn't answer. He's sick of speaking to her. One of his sons has a severe learning disability. His daughter has night terrors. She doesn't know a thing about them, doesn't even think to ask. "I just want to go back," she says. "It's my home. I know where my toothbrush is. I can find it in the dark."

He keeps his mouth and arms stiff. He's trying to pretend she's not there. The results will come by phone call, a more detailed report by mail. "Do you remember that we'd have to cut the lawn?" she says. "I always thought that was the most foolish thing I could imagine. That a person would move all the way to Alaska and still have to cut their lawn. I don't do it anymore. I just let it grow. Who cares? It's wonderful. Let it all grow. That's what I say."

He does remember. His father pushing the gas mower back and forth and then later, when he was gone, his brother. When his brother left at seventeen then it fell to Peter. His mother would watch him from the back window. Was she proud or just making sure he was doing a good job? He says, "It's not like we were living in a timberland. We had a lawn so we cut it."

"Timberland," she says. "That's funny," and he realizes that she's won. There's no way to return to his invulnerable silence. "Let me ask you something," he says. "How about this for a test? Do you remember when Dad came that time, and he had the baby, and he stayed for almost a week? What was that all about?"

"Your father and I have a very complicated relationship," she says.

"Yes," he says, "but you didn't answer me."

"You're remembering it wrong," she says. "It was more than a month. What do you think of that, smarty pants? I'm not denying anything. In fact, it's worse than you remember. He stayed for more than a month and we were man and wife again. And what's-her-name in White Horse, that idiot with the fetal alcohol syndrome, the slow girl is what I used to call her, she rang us up every night, and every night I told her that he'd be leaving the next morning. And she believed it. It's like she had never been lied to before in her damned life. So trusting. Like a little kid really, but built like a linebacker."

"I remember holding her baby," he says.

"You grew up too fast," she says. "That's on me. But what could I do? I grew up too fast too. Jesus, I was, what, eighteen when I had your brother." She smiles thinly. "Your father was something else."

But he remembers another thing, something he refuses to tell her. He's returned to his silence and found something more there: a strange kind of peace. The memory has returned to him as if it's a thing he's misplaced in plain sight, some eyeglasses or a wallet. Her voice has summoned it back through the corridors of his history and now here it is and it's as sharp as the thumping noise of the train. Soon he's going to check her bags, place her carefully on her plane, send her back to Fairbanks, but this thing stays with him.

"Is Tom there?" the voice asked, soft and little girlish, furtive. He knew immediately who it was. He held her child in his hands.

His mother was upstairs. So was his father. His brother, who knows where? He remembers the rain clattering, coming down harder and harder, but that must be wrong. It couldn't have rained that long. But it stretches through everything like the rail guiding the train car through the sky.

"Hello," he said. "I'm not sure where he is."

"Well," she says. "Has he left?"

He stroked the baby's head. He was getting good at it. He could make it sleep with a feathering touch, bring it back awake with a shifting of its weight to his other shoulder, watch it smile when he smiled, stare when he stared. "I'm not sure," he said.

"Please," she said. "You have to tell him I'm sorry. I'm not sure he's getting my messages. There's that woman."

"Yes," he said. "I know."

"She calls me stupid, but I'm not," she said. "I'm smart. I can raise the boy.

It's not hers. I don't even know if it's his. Who are you? Are you his son, the one with the drugs?"

"Yes," he said. "That's me."

"Your life would be easier if you let God carry your load," she said. "All you have to do is let His glory do its work."

"I'm going to tell him," he said. "I promise. You give me a message and I'm going to pass it along."

"Then tell him I love him," she said. "I do. I don't say that to everybody. I love him and I love my little boy and he needs to come back here and be with us. And tell him he doesn't have to compromise. He'll know what I mean."

"Okay," he said. "I'll tell him."

"Thank you," she said. "I can tell you have a good soul. Remember what I said about your burdens, okay?"

He took the baby into the other room and put it on the floor and watched TV. It made contented cooing sounds and its hand shook, making small grabs at the air, and his favorite show came on, the one his mother didn't like him to watch because the characters were always knocking each other around. But he'd watch it anyway, and then the one after and the one after that, until his eyes grew tired. The black-and-white figures poked and slapped but never actually hurt each other. No wounds or tears, no running away either, saying enough is enough and simply exiting the room. He remembers turning up the sound because of the noise of the weather, the ice and metal, the rain and tin. In his mind it is there when he wakes up and when he goes to sleep, there when he steps outside and checks the sky. His brother has gone, but there is this other one, this small thing in his hands, and there is a small voice on the phone telling him please.

❦

He imagines his mother moving through her house the way a blind person might. There is the couch, it's been there for twenty-five years, there is the fridge, her hand finds the handle. There is the nightstand and the alarm clock, the panel that slides back to reveal the circuit breakers, the closet where she keeps extra lightbulbs. It's the first time he's dialed his father's number in years, but he answers with a casual, "Hey, Peter."

All he can do is make a noise of hello. He sounds like an animal, and not a big one, something you'd find scuttling around in your kitchen. "You shouldn't have let her get back on that plane," his father says. "She's not going to last through the winter up there."

"Maybe," Peter says. "Maybe that's true." His wife is out with friends. The kids are doing homework at the kitchen table. He's up on the second floor trying to keep his voice down.

"Maybe," his father says. "You're always saying that. Maybe this. Maybe that. You should have told her, 'You're not getting on that plane.'"

"But I didn't," he says. "I didn't say anything." He's surprised to hear the swelling pride in his voice. He guesses his father can hear it too. "I told her she was going to be fine," he adds, "and then I watched her go. She turned and looked at me like a kid on her way to the school bus. Then she headed out." It's part confession, part boast. His children are already moving past him. Their math problems are getting just out of reach. He really has to concentrate on each solution. In a minute he'll go downstairs and get a glass of water and then stand a polite distance from them, waiting for them to ask for help. Or not. He's content to just watch. He'll drink the water and start at Z again. He's been doing that for the last couple of days and it's been a challenge to get to M without hesitating. He says, "That woman you lived with for a while in White Horse. What was her name?"

"Oh, her," he says. "Yes. Shit." Peter waits. He can hear the kids talking about a movie downstairs. There are potato chips in a bowl on the table. He knows because he put them there before walking up here to have this conversation. "You know what?" his father says. "This is going to sound crazy, but it's a blank. Leslie or something? Laura? Jesus, now I'm the one who's the jerk, huh? Is that your point? Is that what you're trying to prove here?"

He expected that answer. How long has it been? His brother is gone too. And the baby? The thing is, he doesn't remember its name either, although its warmth is still a living thing to him, a solace in that endless rain. "Let's not change the subject," his father says. "I'm still angry."

# The Gift of Flight

The story splits the room in two. She watches their faces change, some twisted up with disgust and others with laughter. The disgusted people, well, that's it, they're done with her for the night. The other half become her satellites, her acolytes.

It's as if she's rescued them, from boredom at least, but possibly something more nefarious: the creeping feeling that you might be as anonymous as all these others with their reasonable opinions and eighty-dollar haircuts. She knows what they're thinking: that a person who would tell such a story must be direct, honest, admirably demented. She lets this opinion enfold her.

To one side a cluster of people are talking about some very nice foreclosure opportunities south of the city. "Don't be afraid of taking risks," someone says. She's left her heels behind in some room or another and one of them is lucky enough to notice her bare feet. "Where are your shoes?" he asks, but he's smiling. Another sign of her uniqueness. They can count on a person like this to shepherd them through the tedium.

She shows them the size of the owl by spreading her arms wide, as if she herself might fly away. To show the size of the dog she moves her hands close together as if to cradle a loaf of bread, a newborn baby. Some of them are still chuckling.

※

Sheila B. had returned to Fairbanks for another summer, hitchhiking her way up through Delta Junction with a Superman backpack and a dome tent she had stolen from the open bed of a truck. Her body seemed a weight apart from her, a thing she had to lift and carry and then throw down when the day was finished. She hid inside it, her hair in her eyes, half-listening to the driver talk about the death of Jesus or the many ways oil money had destroyed the state. One of her sneakers was opening up slowly at the big toe, step by step, day by day. She could feel that too: the dirt and pebbles and shame. "How old are you?" he asked, and she pushed her age up a couple of notches. He didn't believe her—she could tell by the noise he made at the back of his throat—but he didn't seem to care all that much.

The best spots along the river were already taken by lean boys in groups of three or four. Long hair, patchy beards, dazed expressions, they all seemed like refugees from the same great shipwreck. She took a spot further away and hoped to spy a friendly face from the year before but there were none. An old man asked her, "Do you have any food?"

"No," she said without looking at him, but he hovered there for a moment, road grit on his vacant face, before moving on to the next campsite.

It would be cold soon. Even in the early summer the night brought in a chill that could sneak up on a person.

In the early evening she found the story in the newspaper she was balling up to set on fire. The owl and the dog were its two principal characters, but the photograph showed the two tourists. The woman held an empty leash dangling like a noose. They did not look pleased.

She did not set fire to that page. She folded it as neatly as if it were a letter addressed especially to her.

Over the next few weeks it began to disintegrate there in her pocket. But by then she cradled the best parts in her brain and shared it with people at the campsite. Some of them had heard the story already, but they still listened when she spoke. She repeated it again to store clerks as she worked up the courage to shoplift. She told the taxi driver she stiffed and the drunks in dirty hoodies trying hard to look sullen and dangerous in front of the Safeway.

Sheila B. remembers Katie's face, her wide hips and heavy breasts, her hair cut so close that you could see a bump at the back of her head where her skull became her neck. She remembers telling her the story from three stools over and then Katie taking her home to a warm shower and a bathrobe covered with yellow flowers. Or was it that Katie told it and that coincidence, hearing the story while she held fragments of it in her pocket, caused her to move over a couple of stools and listen to the rest?

She does remember this perfectly: Katie was the first one to laugh. Sheila B. hadn't noticed the humor in it until then, and soon they were *both* laughing and Katie was buying drinks with a sandwich bag of loose change. "Sometimes you just have to laugh," Katie said to the bartender, as if this were the wisest of wise things to share with a couple of strangers. She picked out the pennies and nudged them to a remote part of the smooth bar surface, then gathered up the rest. "Laundry money," she said. "My boyfriend is going to kill me."

❧

The people at the party ask her what it was really like to grow up in such a place. When did she leave and why did she come to this boring city, a city where nothing ever happens except heart attacks and traffic jams and parties like this one. She smiles politely. She agrees, it can be difficult here, but it's also comfortable. People underestimate comfort except when it's gone. She rattles the ice in her glass as a kind of evidence.

Of course, she's giving them just a crumb of it. That's part of the fun and part of her frustration. "Where are my shoes?" she asks, as if they might be anywhere at all, upstairs, in the yard, across town, back at the condo. She lifts a leg in mock surprise. Someone will go and hunt them down, return them to her as if performing a great chivalry.

"I wonder if it felt any pain," one of them says.

"Of course it felt pain," someone else says. "Jesus didn't feel any more pain."

Soon they'll be sharing their own small grotesques. She's pushed open the door for them.

Sometimes she forgets the story for months at a time. Not forget really, but it falls into disuse. Then it appears again at the forefront of her mind and she brings it out with a magician's skill, an actor's charm. In her imagination the dog is flying up, up, up. One of the tourists—the man probably—is confused at first, because just a moment before it had been toddling along the rocky edge of the road deciding on the best place to pee. Possibly it has run over the slope and is chasing voles in the wide field just now graying in the dusk. Or it's gone back inside the trailer. And then he looks up and all his questions are answered.

The whole thing has the kaleidoscopic force of a dream. A dream's logic too.

꙼

Sheila B. was standing at the fridge with the orange juice bottle in her hand when she heard the key in the lock. As one door opened she was closing another and she couldn't help feeling as if she had been caught doing something wrong. "Well," the man said, as he stepped inside. "Who is this and what have you done with Katie?"

His head was vaguely peanut shaped, although he carried himself with the air of someone who was good-looking, even glamorous. He leaned into the doorframe and tilted his head. And he seemed amused by the possibility of her being an intruder, a murderer even. Katie had just gone to take a shower. The water was still running. It was easy to hear.

"I'm Sheila," she said.

"I knew a Sheila once," he said. "She would eat anything for a quarter. Do you do that?"

It occurred to her that she might be the one in danger. But the man was thin, so thin that he positively swam in his button-down shirt, and he wore a knit tie to match his narrow chest—it was the width of a butter knife. Surely nobody had ever been hurt by someone wearing such a tie.

"My second Sheila," he said. "Katie? Are you here?"

"Hey, Eddie," she called out above the sound of running water. "Be nice, okay?"

He headed off into the other room and she thought of running to the door and out into the woods. But she was starving and she had glimpsed thick slices of bologna in the meat drawer, a brick of cheese and a bottle of ginger ale. She could hear them talking about his difficult day at work, about charity and surprises. She heard the click, click, click of the shower rings as the curtain was pulled aside. Was he climbing in with her?

"The thing is," he said later as they ate around the small table. "If you go out there and just look, you can see it. They're all melting. It looks like a retreat, like they are crawling very slowly back to where they came from. All you have to do is look."

He studied the glaciers. Or rather he assisted the people who studied the glaciers.

"Don't get him started," Katie said, and she rolled her eyes, touched her hand like they were good friends. The sense of danger still hung around the edges of the room but it didn't emanate from a particular person. It came from everywhere, from the configuration of the three bodies around the small table and the food she was trying hard to eat at an even pace. She reached across Katie for some more bread and butter.

"We're poor," Katie said, "but we like to share." She turned to Eddie. "Skin and bones, isn't she?"

"Skin and bones," Eddie said. He seemed distracted, poking at the debris on his plate. Maybe he was thinking about bigger things: the glaciers retreating, his own small place in solving the problem.

"You should see the dirt she left in the tub," Katie said. "Go in there and look."

Sheila B. knew what he was going to say before he said it. *Dirty girl.* She was a very dirty girl.

୬୧

The party will be over soon and the guests will leave in a swarm, silver Porsches steered by aging drunks, people shouting goodbyes from windows as they gun perfectly calibrated engines. More guests will stumble across the cul-de-sac and squint into the blaze of headlamps and the man next to her, her boyfriend, her whatever, will lean on the horn and steer onto the lawn, just for a moment, the sprinklers raining across the windshield. It's meant to be spontaneous, but it has all the calculation of a chess move. He's trying to show her something about himself. He can be reckless too.

Then they are alone, hurtling down the road and finally through the east side, where the stores have bars on the windows. Metal doors tagged with spray paint and boys slow-riding bicycles through the inching traffic. At the intersection ahead a man is making the sign of the cross at passing cars. Her boyfriend touches a button and the doors lock. He asks her, "Did you have a good time?"

She supposes that she did.

How do you tell the rest of it? Mumbled in his ear when they curl in bed, as they often do these days, with him on the inside, the smaller spoon, the sheltered one? Or should she shout it right now? The traffic hiccups forward. He's frustrated. She can tell. He wants to be home. He wants to be fucking her. "What's-her-name didn't seem to like you very much," he says. That's grudging a compliment. He likes when people don't like her. It makes his choice bolder.

When it's their turn the man blesses them just like the rest.

❧

That summer you could hear the story in all the bars and at the Chena River tent camp. Different people had different ways of telling it and when someone told it wrong, by forgetting an important detail or even sometimes twisting up the whole meaning of the thing, it was like they'd committed a personal crime against her. But like most crimes against her she suffered it in silence.

Katie sometimes asked her to tell it again and she did as she was told, feeling like two people simultaneously: a little girl obediently reciting the alphabet, but also someone telling a secret to her only friend. On the long languid afternoons, they put blankets on the windows and they ate in bed. Crackers and cookies and bowls of ice cream and then they fell asleep. Those hours blurred into a stream of minor pleasurable sensations: her body still wet from the shower, the taste of vanilla. A small TV often played silently in the background and she'd wake and watch the faces of the people on the game shows. They'd spin a wheel and jump up and down. "Eddie can be an ass," Katie said, "but he's smart. His family is completely fucked up but he's making something out of himself. Do you want some more?"

Always say yes because who knows when something might change.

"We should hang out at your place sometime," Eddie said.

"I live in a cabin," she said. "I don't even have running water. It's one room with a loft."

"She only loves us for our shower," he said. "Boohoo."

But if it wasn't love then it was something like love. She stood on the edge of the feeling, anyway, and could see it clearly. Just moving forward a few steps might cause her to arrive in that place. That's how she felt, at least, when she sprawled in bed with Katie and their bodies were warm from the steam, their hair wrapped in towels. "Sheila B. doesn't love anybody," Katie said. "She loves potato chips."

❧

Sheila B. was not new to that strange mix of kindness and hostility. People would give you leftovers at the back of their restaurants but then tell you to get lost. There were men who pulled their trucks over, asked you where you were headed, but looked disgusted when you told them you'd rather walk. It was best to be as invisible as possible. There was an art to holding your body and pitching your voice when you asked for change. It was the same shape and sound she would use in her dad's house when he was drunk and talking about the second son of God descending on America, so it was not that difficult. In fact, it was comfortable, and to change would have been as bizarre as, well, as bizarre as her current life. How could she have imagined?

She sat in a bustling coffee shop waiting for him and she was not disappointed to find him running late. Many of the traits he saw as unique to himself—his fumbling, arrogant lateness was one of them—she saw as part of a subset of traits shared by many, many men. He would apologize and offer an excellent excuse all at once. He forgets the time because he has so many important things going on. Making the world a better place and making gigantic mountains of money are not mutually exclusive. The entirety of his life is built on this principle.

It will be her job to say no problem. It will be her job to say well, what were you thinking about? Later that day they will have drinks and swim in the pool and maybe if she's lucky the thought of his lateness will cross his mind again and he'll grow tender and soft. The colored tiles of the pool bottom form a giant fish. She'll miss that fish when all this is over.

She thinks of the dumpsters with the black plastic bags, the occasional surprise of finding bread inside untouched by vegetable scraps and coffee grounds. The mind wants to tip everything in the direction of nostalgia. She's almost disappointed when he shows up.

"Your face," he says. "It looks different."

Because she's upset.

⁂

"This one never gets old," Katie said.

"It's on the verge," Eddie said.

"But this is the best part," Sheila B. said. She said, "The owl takes off from this big broken tree and sees this white fur ball peeing on the side of the road. The tourists, they look up, they're like, oh, look at the beautiful bird."

Eddie and Katie stood half-listening: the owl circling in a wide loop above the poodle dog and then descending. "They scramble for their cameras," she said. "They're adjusting zoom lenses. In fact, maybe one of them has his camera right up to his eye and he's ready to snap a picture when the owl plucks up their dog and carries it off. Of course, they start screaming. It's their beloved dog."

They sprawled in bed together eating donuts, her at the bottom like a cat. "They taste like Styrofoam," Eddie said, but that didn't stop him from twisting off pieces between his fingers and popping them in his mouth. The girls— he referred to them as the girls now—sometimes made a joke of throwing a piece at his mouth as if it were a basketball hoop. They were all naked except for Eddie, who still wore loose boxers and his dirty white socks.

They might let her stay all night, in the bed with them, curled to one body or the other. Or Eddie might sit up, clap his hands together, and say, okay, time to go. If she was smart she'd just shut up and pretend not to be there at all, that's usually what worked, but she wanted to tell them. She wanted to see Katie laugh again.

"So it lands up in the top of a tree," Sheila B. said, and she moved her finger through the air, the bird rising up and up until it perched far above the heads of the tourists. "And it just starts dismantling the thing piece by piece."

Eddie nodded to the music in his head, to the story. He had moved in closer. He opened his mouth and pointed inside but neither of them could be bothered.

What did an owl look like when it ate? She could see it dividing the dog into smaller chunks. As delicate as an old lady at dinner, but with blood on the talons. And just like that old lady it would take a long time to finish its work. First it would crush the skull and then knead the body. She said, "And this family with their big RV parked on the side of the road, they just stand there and watch."

Eddie said, "I don't think they would have watched. Why would they watch? They'd be horrified."

"That's *why* they'd watch," she said. "They're horrified. They're not going to just look away."

"Sometimes I think you're retarded," Eddie said. "What's with you and the dog getting killed?" But when Eddie stood up and headed into the other room Katie touched her hair while they listened to the piss spatter in the bowl. "He's so loud," she said. "Obnoxious. Do you ever think about dyeing your hair? You'd look good with short hair. Blonde, maybe." They smiled and hurried to eat the donut scraps before he returned. They could hear the stream stop and start up again. "Let's murder him," Katie said, and she laughed. "How should we do it?"

"Poison," Sheila B. said.

"Owl," Katie said.

Sheila B. laughed as quietly as she could. She didn't want Eddie to think they were having a good time without him.

"You know what I think?" Katie said. "I think you want it to end differently. That's why you keep telling it. You keep expecting it to end differently, but of course that's not going to happen."

Eddie stood watching them now. She thought it was strange that his half-nakedness could be so much sillier than these other bare bodies, but the fact of it was right there, standing in front of them with crossed arms and a confident smirk. "Well, I think the guy in your story didn't mind the dog dying," he said. "I bet he secretly hated that little yappy dog and when the owl picked it up he was like, oh dear God, is this it? Am I finally free? But of course, he couldn't tell that to the newspaper. He couldn't even tell it to his wife."

"Right," Katie said, "because there are things a man can't tell his wife. Dark things. Important things."

Sheila B. wondered why Eddie seemed so powerless there when he should have been anything but, standing above them in their nakedness. It was the bed. That was a kind of secret: as long as she and Katie lay in the bed with Eddie outside it then his words, his meanings, that particular spin he put on the world, were as laughable as stuff on a TV. He said, "Why are you two grinning like that?"

"Nothing," Sheila B. said.

"No reason," Katie said.

She thought again about murdering him. It was a funny little game you could play in your head. "Yeah, well," he said. "Time to go. Time to go. I have work in the morning. One of us has to do something with his life."

"He's entering data," Katie said.

"You won't be smiling when all this is underwater," he said.

"We'll just float away on our life raft," she said, coming up on all fours and perching at the edge of the bed. She looked over and it seemed as if the flooding had already come and that an ocean separated them from the man speaking. He seemed to float further and further away. Except that then he stepped forward and squeezed Katie's nipple and she kissed him and then he was in the bed, the life raft, as well, and everything was spoiled. Well, not everything, not really, because at least they had forgotten about her. She moved to the far corner and pulled the blanket around her shoulders. What would all of this look like from above?

✤

How to begin? Sheila B. considers this as she gathers her car keys, scans the countertop for her sunglasses. She is thirty years old but feels much younger. A child really, pretending at this life, but doing a very good job of it at least.

She's returning something to the store. She plans on bullying the clerk into giving her a cash refund. Him and whoever stands behind him in the store's hierarchy. This despite losing the receipt. Then off for coffee. She'll read a book at the window, the pages lit by sunlight.

She should begin with the owl and the poodle. That's the center of it. Or the outer edge. The trail that, when followed, leads her back to the rest. She does not recognize herself in that strange place but there she is, half her current age and expecting nothing from the world. If such a meeting were truly possible the younger would retreat into the forest like a furtive animal. Or perhaps she'd snarl before slinking off.

They know she was born in Alaska. They know her father still lives there. He sends occasional letters written in the tight block print of a former alcoholic. Records of his days, the health of his dogs and the weather. He sometimes encloses a twenty-dollar bill for her birthday or Christmas. Every couple of years he finds her in a new place and the mail starts up again.

She is in the car now. The bag is in the back seat, the strapless dress folded at the bottom. She won't even have to admit that she made a mistake. All she'll do is smile and raise her voice and ask for the manager. Would that all things be undone so cleanly.

She imagines the owl circling above her in the Arizona sky and then she is deeper, she is back in Alaska, and when she is back there why does she feel so free of worry? She could start from the beginning, allow the bird into the frame of her imagination again and turn herself and all the others into prey.

✤

"If we stayed at your place we wouldn't have to worry about when he's coming home," Katie said as she was brushing her teeth. She was always brushing her teeth, returning to the bed for a kiss, then hopping up to brush them some more. She had covered the windows with cardboard to block out the light.

"Then he'd really know we were hiding something from him," Sheila B. said.

"You're lying again," Katie said. "You shouldn't do that, especially not to me. Is it just because you're used to lying? You can't quit it even when it's just the two of us? Your place can't be that bad."

"I like it here," she said.

"He just really gets in the way sometimes. You know what I hate about him? You probably haven't noticed this but sometimes he'll turn off the light, turn it on again, and then turn it off. Like he doesn't trust that the light turned off the first time. I don't get it."

"I did notice that," Sheila B. said. "It's so weird." She moved to the edge of the bed to receive her the moment Katie came back. She didn't want to smile so big, she wasn't used to her face taking on that particular configuration, but she couldn't help it. "It was funny how you said you wanted to murder him," she said. "I could picture us doing that. It wouldn't be hard, you know. He's so skinny."

"Really," Katie said. "Are you serious?"

She didn't know if she was serious or joking. Nothing seemed to be purely one or the other here, so unlike her father's house. So unlike the tent city at the river. They withdrew from each other and Sheila B. patted around in the sheets for her bra but all she found was Katie's sock, stiff and shiny on one end. She thought of the time she had stood at the edge of her father's room and watched him in his drunken sleep, one of his hammers in her fist. Where had that hammer gone? She had lost it sometime last year. Someone had stolen it. "I mean," she said. "Don't you ever think about it? Does it pass through your mind when he's being a real asshole?"

Katie came up with the bra, the other sock, the bunched-up jeans. Her lack of laughter seemed a betrayal. She looked annoyed and disgusted instead. But that could have been part of the joke, a joke on her instead of on Eddie, but at least a joke. "You said so yourself," Sheila B. said. "You said that sometimes—"

"Right," Katie said. "He's going to be home soon."

It was early evening and the walk home was long but pleasant. She picked up change and trash on the side of the road and when she reached the gas station she threw the trash away and used the change to buy a hot dog, which she ate standing by the gas pumps. It tasted like sawdust and catsup but she liked standing there watching the dirty traffic.

ॐ

"We've tried to be nice to you," Eddie said. "We've tried to help you."

"Because of your *situation*," Katie said. "Whatever that is."

"Right," Sheila B. said, as if she were yelling at someone else right along with them.

"Sell your plasma," Katie said. "Do something."

"No more charity," Eddie said.

"No more anything," Katie said. "No more."

They were turning onto the block by the husks of old cars and piles of hubcaps and the confederate flag in the cracked upstairs window. The ghetto of tin roofs appeared in a tight cluster. There it was among the others, the one she had lied about. A truck sat in the driveway, although Katie and Eddie didn't seem to notice or care. Sheila B. didn't have a license but she could imagine driving a truck like that all the way back to Anchorage. She reached out to touch Katie. She said, "Please." And although Katie allowed the touch, that was all. She continued watching the small her in the rearview mirror until Sheila B. stepped from the car and slammed the door.

She walked back to the campground to find all the fires dead and black, the tents dark, and she crawled inside her own. All her things were still there: the two flashlights, the matches, and the jackknife she had stolen from her father, the jacket she used as a pillow when it was warm, the fast-food sugar packets and carefully folded map. The inside smelled of the entire summer, her sweat and bad dreams and stale Cheerios eaten by the handful.

ॐ

She is wondering what Eddie looks like now: a pale scientist in an office with a big window. On good days the Denali range comes into view and he pauses and gives it a surprised glance. Maybe he has a wife and kids. Maybe he doesn't. She knows that Katie is no longer in the picture. She had a hand in that. So it's some other supportive woman wrangling them at bedtime, listening to his diatribes about the stupidity of the human race.

But he loves that stupidity too. She knows it because that's what she used against him, against them. The dumber she acted, the more helpless, the more he liked her. She visited him at his lab, crying, and told him she needed to talk just once more. She wanted to tell him the truth.

He sat at his desk looking befuddled. A coffee cup full of sharpened pencils. She noticed that and the curtain of yellow Post-it notes covering the wall behind him. There were other men there, all older. How could he not show her some tenderness? She pleaded and he touched her and guided her to the door.

But the tenderness was real. The attraction was real. By the time they were at the end of the hall he was holding her tighter and he was asking her what was wrong—the words of a lover, a parent. In a way the tears were real too. She missed Katie terribly. "Please," she said. "Let's just talk for an hour. Not even an hour."

"I'm working," he said, but he was already halfway there. She just needed to push him a little more. She turned so that she was facing him and his hand on her shoulder became an embrace.

"I know I'm an idiot," she said. "Sometimes I even annoy myself."

He stood stiff and grinning. He was trying too hard.

"Is this a date?" he said in the car. "Am I going to meet your parents?"

First, they parked at the far edge of the Fred Meyer parking lot and he reached across her, flipped open the glove compartment, produced half a joint. In the middle distance people were marching to and from the store with carts piled high with supplies and she remembered her hunger. The last couple of days it had been a constant, a throbbing pain that she tried to imagine as pleasure. "Don't tell me you don't think about it," she told him. "You must think about it all the time."

"Think about what?"

"Leaving her," she said. "I mean, you're so much smarter."

"You wouldn't understand," he told her. "How old are you? Sixteen?"

"Yes," she said, a lie just an inch wide of the truth. So close that it didn't seem like much of a lie at all. She wanted to tell him that same thing again, the breaking apart of the flesh, the funny outrage. Eddie looked amused by his own boredom, but she could tell he was interested.

"You're high," he said.

"So are you," she said. "You're high all the time."

He said, "You have your head in the clouds. You *seem* high all the time. That's worse."

"You're making fun of me," she said, but she made sure to laugh. She'd be heading back to Anchorage soon, where the shelters were better, or in a pinch back to her father's house. She liked to imagine the look on his face if she appeared at the door, the story of the prodigal rolling around somewhere at the back of his head. She said, "Let's go down by the river. I'll show you."

A small city of tents and blackened spots in the dirt. Her city. One of the rules: don't talk to your neighbors. She unzipped the rainfly and showed him inside. It smelled of her body and the peppermint candy she had taken from a bowl at the front of a restaurant. The wrappers littered the ground. They crawled inside on their hands and knees, into the red light diffused through the polycotton. They stretched out as if to look at the sky, holding hands. She told herself not to like him, not even a little bit, no matter what he said or did.

"It's okay here," he finally said.

Her laugh came out as a cough. It was a cough. She had taken too big a hit.

She laughed because she was happy and she laughed because she was as angry as she'd ever been. Parts of that happiness emerged into the air in the shape of a few innocuous words and the rest, well, she kept the rest for herself. She had to keep the proportion right. A chip of willpower came loose inside her, something she had been holding in position for months, maybe years, and she became like that couple watching their dog fly up above their heads: a blubbering mess but funny too, ha ha ha, higher and higher. She was laughing at herself as she sobbed—the two became part of the same physical motion: a cry and a laugh, a bend and a lift, a chew and a swallow.

"Man, you are fucked up," she heard him say but he laughed a little too.

Sheila B. allowed herself to think of the dog rising in the air, that first moment when it must have thought it was flying but before its skull was squeezed to pulp. Was that where the comedy resided, in that moment of absurdity? Of fake triumph? Maybe even its owners, that disgusted man and woman, thought it was funny at first. One of them maybe, deep down inside, the one who didn't like the dog as much as the other. A place the person didn't even know about. A secret closet at the remotest part of the mind where a person could stack their resentments. But the other thing was this: their idiotic pain was funny, the sobbing and impotent anger, quotes in the newspaper about never, ever returning to this miserable place. They were mad at a *bird*.

And she was mad at a *dog*, a helpless ball of fur that couldn't fight back. For a second it really thought it was flying. That's why she hated it, that's why it was funny, that's why she is telling it again years later at a party in a beautiful house thousands of miles away.

⚜

She won the bed back. The food too, the cabinet full of teas and spices, the candy bars he liked to keep in the freezer, the potato chips she ate from the bag as she walked around the place. Everything but Katie, although there were still telltale signs of her former presence: the toothbrush, for instance, chewed up and dry on the edge of the yellowed sink.

Almost two months of living with him and then to Vancouver. Alone, of course, although she has always wondered if Katie would have gone with her. She can imagine them on the road together, although not in Vancouver during that very difficult winter. After Vancouver Montana and after Montana then North Dakota. Back then it didn't feel like running away from anything at all. Not even living with Eddie seemed like running away.

He'd say, "If people knew about this," and then he'd roll his eyes. He'd say, "I'm going to go to hell." That was part of the delirious fun but also, yes, he was scared. He was not nearly as unconventional as he liked to believe. After all, she had observed him with Katie for months. She knew what he liked and what he claimed to like. Two months and she hitchhiked her way west. A light snow was already beginning to fall. She took his gloves with her, his coat too. Too large, of course, but she rolled up the sleeves.

She did not loathe him. He was capable of occasional tender surprises: a gift of flowers or a sudden apology. So she returned the kindness by sheltering him. When Katie called she would tell him it was a wrong number, an old friend, anybody but her. "He doesn't want to talk to you," she'd whisper in the dark of the kitchen. "Don't you understand that?"

"I don't understand anything about this," Katie said.

It was strange to hear someone else's blubbering and wonder what percentage of it was genuine. Possibly all of it.

"Please," Katie said. "Just explain it to me."

She sounded like someone who didn't get the joke. Lay it out for her and she'd laugh dutifully but she still wouldn't get it. It might take years before she would.

Sheila B. is screaming at the clerk and even as she screams she knows that this is too much. Everybody is pretending she isn't there—they're looking at their feet, their phones, their pocketbooks, anything but her—and this makes her yell a little louder. The girl, she can't be more than twenty, shrinks into her body, pulls downward ever so slightly behind the desk.

There is a complication. They need the other credit card to run through, his credit card, and without it all they can give her is an exchange. It's the clerk's stupidity, her repetition of the words *I'm sorry, ma'am*, that makes the first swear word come and then from there it's easy enough to raise her voice, to become the well-dressed lunatic calling for the manager, calling for justice.

But really, it's over in, what, twenty seconds? And then she's pushing the bags into the back seat again, glancing into the rearview, spinning out backward and then forward in a satisfying arc of escape. When she gets home he comes up behind her, places his heavy palms on her shoulders and begins to rub. "What's the matter?" he asks, but she says, nothing, nothing, and arches her neck to kiss him from her sitting position.

They'll talk about her later. The other customers, the girl behind the counter, they'll head to their homes and share the story of the crazy woman vain enough to have her nervous breakdown right in front of them. Sheila, she was almost to the door before she realized she had forgotten her bags in the cart. She had to spin around and head back, lift the bags up and repeat the whole stupid thing.

They'd make a point of sharing that part. That was the comeuppance. That was the punch line. It would make everybody feel better.

# The Alaska Girl

September and he was still talking to the girl in Sitka. She was up there in her one-room cabin, playing with her dogs and occasionally texting him dirty, misspelled sentences. He knew what she looked like because there she was, eureka, in the background of the single picture she had sent him. In the foreground stood four dogs, all huskies, all from the same litter but one charging toward the camera, the one with the single blue eye and torn ear: the one she said she loved best.

In the photograph her face was hard to see, but she looked seriously annoyed with the person taking the picture. One of her hands blurred, as if she were bringing it to her face to mask herself. But then she shared it with him, along with a text that explained what she wanted to do to him, a couple of sentences as systematic as a grocery list, a set of instructions.

Spring had not been a time of renewal: divorce papers in April and then increasingly bad news about the house throughout May. And yet he had floated through the entire summer with the buoyancy he remembered from long ago, when he was fifteen and sixteen and the opposite sex was as new to him as the sudden strength found in his own body. In July he had made a promise to stop, and relented, and then rededicated himself to abstinence for a whole week before sending her a flurry of ridiculous messages. He had stood in the same indie record store he stood in today, waiting for his phone to vibrate in his palm, occasionally flipping through the musty vinyl, taking in the somber faces of rock stars. Then he'd send a burst of words to her across thousands and thousands of miles. It was a miracle, in a way, and he had used it to tell her she had beautiful breasts, the mouth of a porn actress. He was trying to convince himself. Possibly he was trying hard to become an unlikeable person, to don that invulnerable armor.

The last week of September and there was snow in Sitka, and not just a dusting. Although she didn't describe it to him—he longed for her to describe it in the same mechanical style she had described her list of sexual desires—he imagined it as a complete picture, down to the level of the ice hanging from the eaves of her cabin, the water collecting around her boots left by the heavy door. The dogs would run on trails, up ahead of her and then back, circling her shuffling body and then spinning out again. Was she thinking about him? Most likely no, but she probably wasn't thinking about any other man either, or if she was, it was a slew of men, their faces kaleidoscoping into a pleasant haze. Enough to be one of them.

*Rough times.* That was the last thing he had messaged her, in a moment of weakness, and there had been no reply. Indian summer in Massachusetts. People still wearing shorts, ordering iced coffees, it was like the good weather would never end, and the week before she had sent him a text asking if he could buy her a new winter coat. It was simple. Just go to this link. Click on it.

He had not known what to say, so he hadn't replied, and he wondered if this was the new pattern they were settling in before the whole thing developed rigor mortis. He thought of her slightly wild stare—the stare from the picture—and considered what it would be like to have those eyes on him, scanning his body and looking for flaws. And calling her up in his imagination seemed to make his phone ring, although of course, the caller wasn't her. It was the man from the bank, polite to a fault, always introducing himself by his full name and then saying, "Do you have a moment to talk, Mr. Flannigan?"

"Sure," he said, and he moved to the end of the aisle, where the records beginning with X, Y, and Z were displayed in one meager row: Neil Young's frown, over and over again, and a picture of a zebra standing in a posh bedroom.

He was only half listening to the voice on the other end as it explained that they were into the home stretch, and that there was more paperwork to fill out, but nothing overwhelming.

"You're going to get some very angry letters from the parent bank threatening legal action, but don't get too upset about that. That's just part of the process. They want to throw some muscle around, put the fear of God into you. It wouldn't be finished if you didn't tremble a bit by the end."

But the thick envelope of documents had already arrived yesterday and left no mark on him at all. He was a prize fighter dodging punches and even the big swings didn't hurt if they didn't land. The envelope resided, unopened, in the glove compartment of his car, and that's where it would stay, until all of this was far away and he could open it and look at it as if it were a postcard of a place he visited long ago. The Alaska girl would be a memory then too, although maybe she had always been that, in a way, even when she was talking to him more often. "You should also find a new place to rent soon," the voice said. "When this happens, it happens quickly, and you'll have to vacate fast. And you want to find a rental while your credit history is still solid."

"Right," he said. "I understand. Good advice."

The voice began talking about the specifics of the paperwork. There were forms that still needed to be signed and notarized. He was supposed to have signed them yesterday and he had completed one of his vanishing acts. "End of the day at the latest, okay?" the voice said. It was the first sign of irritation.

What had he been doing yesterday? He remembered driving right past the bank, sticking out his tongue as he made the turn, then eating tacos in a parking lot with his engine still running. He said, "What about tomorrow morning? Today is bad."

"Tomorrow is too late. Today is also too late, but we can't do yesterday or the day before, obviously, which is when you should have come in."

"Okay," he said, and thought of similar conversations he might have had with his grade-school teachers. So he played the part and he added, "Are you sure I can't just come by in the morning?"

"Do you think this is funny? Because this is your life."

It's not really my life, he wanted to say, but he lowered his voice to the appropriate level of gravitas and said, "I'll be there by the end of the day, okay? I'll be there soon in fact. And I'll be smiling. I want to get this done as much as you."

He stepped into the no-man's-land of soundtrack records and various artist compilations, some of them dog-eared and smelling of damp. The covers were especially interesting if you flipped through them quickly, taking in the general impression of psychedelic landscapes, film characters, cheesy images of half-naked ladies on beaches. Taken together, they made a complicated mess of a story, and just enough of a distraction that when the voice said, "Do you have any questions?" he had to catch himself and think about the meaning of the words. Yes, he had a lot of questions, and he thought of asking one and waiting for the scandalized reaction. "What do you think of a man like me?" he'd ask, after explaining what he was up to lately, pride and shame so intermingled that they formed a perfect soup of intense feeling. The anticipation of that feeling was enough to collapse it into some smaller shadow form, like a prelude to sex. He called it up and let it slide across his mind's eye, as slow and stupid-happy as a parade. Then he said, "No, no questions at all," and the schism between what he was thinking and the tedious outer world gave him a kick of gratification. His fingers had found a wonderful image: a girl covered in whipped cream, posed on a blank green background. Her expression was the opposite of the one the Alaska girl wore: compliant, passive, vaguely moronic. He had wandered into the discount dollar bin.

"Well, good talking to you," the voice said, and then it was gone, and he decided to text the Alaska girl while he had his phone in his hand. He began to type, *I am thinking of you,* and decided that it was a foolish thing to say. He had been infected by the talk with the bank man. A four-hour difference, which meant she was certainly not awake to receive it. She was curled up in her messy bed, dogs gathered around her legs. The world there was silent and empty as the middle of the sea. Whatever he held in his head seemed like static. So he erased it and sent the message to Shannon instead, because she lived in the same time zone and because she loved middle-class romance. *I'm thinking of you as I walk through a record store,* he typed. *I'm looking at the cover of a Miles Davis album, at a model with your haircut,* which he was not, *and I'm wondering when I will see you again,* which he also was not. He was actually heading to the exit, and the shrunken teenage clerk behind the counter gave him a dirty you-don't-belong-here-old-man look as he passed by.

The door shook open and then he was free from that part of his day, moving on to the next part, the part that didn't contain even the slightest residue of his previous phone conversation. He tried to think of his house, but all he could think of was the girl thousands of miles away, sleeping with the blankets pushed down to her ankles. The dogs were awake, watching over her. She sprawled in the middle of them like a princess.

Out on the street, he texted, *I'm going to buy this album because it reminds me of you. I bet it's beautiful music.*

The fiction he created tugged his feelings along in its wake, and soon he was missing her, and wanting her to visit again, even though the last time had not been successful at all. He would give her the album when he showed up at her door, and they would listen to it together, although he did not even know if the album existed except in his head. But he knew how it would sound: lyrical and old-fashioned, with an edge that came from loneliness. Did people listen to that kind of music anymore? He knew that he didn't. He waited for the walk signal and typed.

*The clerk told me the songs were written for his wife, and that they came out sadder than he had intended. One of them is called Shannon's Song. That's the one I'm most interested in. Guess why?*

He was digging himself a very deep hole, but it was a comfortable hole. The cars pushed across the intersection toward the center of downtown, stopping and starting, and he was apart from it all, walking through them to the other side of the street and then texting, *I'm sorry for the way I acted when you were here. I'll take responsibility for that, although obviously it was hard time for me, with my wife taking the kids to Florida. I didn't want to make you part of that drama though. That wasn't fair.*

He thought of typing, *I was nasty to you*, but he stopped short.

He would save that for the Alaska girl, change it to, *I'm going to be nasty to you.*

He joined the flow of traffic and became anonymous, still typing out words when the procession slowed or stopped, and then the words began to come back in a dribble. A twinge of disappointment that they were so passive and conciliatory. Was this the same woman who had made him sleep on his own couch, had thrown a box of Kleenex at his head, and told him he was a child? The exact words, actually, had been, "How can you have children yourself when you're such a child?" They hurt at the time but now, remembering them, he took them on as part of the puzzle that made up who he was, a confusion he presented to the world and made him as special as a complicated film. Because he did have children, and he was a good father, or at least passable, and here she was, telling him, *you really hurt me, you know.*

Of course, he had. It had been impossible not to hurt her, what her hair-trigger responses to everything he ever said and did. It was not that he was unkind—he had sent her flowers, he had called her sweet things—but he had to admit that later on he had made a game of poking at those tender places to draw out her anger and pain, the way a better person might have tried to coax out love.

He had used that word often, but she said it was a word she did not just throw around, she wanted it to mean something, and remembering that, he decided, it *did* mean something, it meant a lot. But he couldn't use it anymore, not honestly, so he wrote, *I've lost twenty pounds, you know. I don't eat the way I used to eat. I don't think about food at all. It actually feels good to be hungry. It's like any other little pleasure. It's like shaving or walking.*

None of this was true, but he wanted it to be true with surprising conviction. He could see himself at the bathroom mirror, inspecting a changed face, probing his own eyes. In his imagination he was a sorrowful man, a regretful man, but he was also thinking about what the Alaska girl had promised she would do to him if they ever found themselves in the same hotel room. And the mismatch between those words and the words Shannon was just now typing—tame, sentimental words—gave him a sexual jolt that made him drive faster. He was breaking the law twice over and it was pretty cool. The idea of being cool expanded his generosity to include first the people around him, then this silly little town, and finally Shannon, who at least had been passionate in her failures.

But by the time he was at Walmart they were fighting. At least as much fighting as a person could do while pecking at keys on a phone. He marched down the aisle toward kitchen goods, head bowed, his thumb twitching against the letters, and he was agitated enough that he passed the blenders altogether and had to make an about-face at bath goods. She typed, *there are people in the world who are like poison to me.*

He let that sentence hang there in the no place between send and reply while he sized up the kitchen appliances. They moved from cheapest to most expensive, from flimsy white plastic to perfect chrome, and buying *just* the right one seemed a very difficult task requiring an act of heroism and pure will. The wrong one—too cheap, too expensive—would cast judgment on his life. Its wrongness would be *his* wrongness. He wanted to explain this to her, or to someone, maybe the Alaska girl, but he knew the thought would lose something in its articulation. Its truth would come out all shabby and torn like a dollar out of the clothes dryer.

So he typed, *the clerk knows the band leader on this record. He says he was shot while taking a shower, by his girlfriend.* He passed the phone from hand to hand like a hot potato, reluctantly put it into his pocket.

The blender he preferred had seven speeds, a six-hundred-watt motor, sleek black and chrome finish. He touched the buttons and they felt good against his fingers. He didn't know what a watt was—the word called to mind black-and-white images of power cables and wooden radios—except that he figured six hundred of them was a very nice thing to have at his disposal. But more importantly than that, it was the weight of the thing he liked best. The box had real heft to it, like a bowling ball or hammer, and lifting it with both hands to his chest made him feel much more fully that he was part of the world of physical things. This was what shopping did to him, he decided. It made him closer to the earth.

His best jokes were private ones, often at his own expense. They made up the inner monologue that carried him through his days. This was one of them.

His phone buzzed in his shirt pocket. He could imagine Shannon standing frozen in the middle of a grocery store, the only motion the pecking of her fingernails. The neatness of the parallel images—him in one store, she in another—changed their argument into something a little more elegant, or at least it gave it a weird kind of purpose, like some pretty architectural symmetry. Before even reading her message he typed, *He died instantly.*

He felt bad for her, as if she was in trouble in some much more immediate way and she was calling for help. But he knew that he only felt this way for the person in his mind, the image he had created, and to say, "I'm sorry" to her would be to spoil that particular spell. He gripped the phone in one hand, blender under his arm. Teenagers down at the other end of the store were throwing shit around and laughing.

At the register he checked his phone again, and found two more messages from her, the first explaining that she never wanted to talk to him again, the second saying that she could at least give him the decency of a proper reply. There was also a message from his sister wondering what was going on with the house and another from her inviting him to dinner anytime he wanted. He could even stay with her for a week or two if he wanted. He typed back to her, *Thank you for thinking about me. I would love to see you during these dark days. But only if I can treat. You have to let me do things like that, even under the circumstances.* But as he was typing this he was thinking about the Alaska girl, the deep brown of her imagined nipples and her thousand-yard stare. What would it be like to sleep with her in that faraway place, to part her thighs and cope with casual indifference?

The clerk told him, "It's not accepting this credit card, sir. Do you have another one?"

Of course.

He produced another one from his pocket. The clerk swiped it, tried again, then a third time. That one didn't work either. The woman behind him, a teenager, really, holding a tiger-striped pillow, looked impossibly embarrassed for him, but the clerk was a machine. She asked him if he had any cash and he found two five-dollar bills in his wallet.

He knew Shannon was typing another message to him, one of apology, but that was just laying the groundwork for another insult. That was how they battled, like experts. He said, "Try this one," and he gave her a third card. This one she took slowly. He turned away and scanned the front of the store, watching the faces of all the morons with their shopping baskets and jelly-faced children. He was definitely included among their number, and when the clerk said, "Do you have another?" he looked back to her with real compassion. The stupidity she had to put up with, hour after hour after hour, as a procession of clowns and idiots moved their way through this narrow slot with whatever miracles they placed hope in. He was just the latest in that series, and if she had known the full expanse of his history it probably wouldn't have made him any more sympathetic to her. She gave him back his Mastercard and he held it and felt the nervousness in the crowd behind him, the monkey pulse of bodies nudging forward. Were any of them rooting for him?

"I've had a rough day," he joked, and he laughed because she didn't. "I feel like I've been all over the country."

"I feel like I haven't moved from this spot."

"Can I just leave it here?" he asked. He indicated the box with both hands, warily, as if it might be a little dangerous.

"You can do that if you want," she said, because she was already forgetting him, moving onto the tiger pillow. Although he had just decided to leave the box at the register, he picked it up and held it and the girl behind him finally said, "I'll be paying with cash." He set the box down again and thought of turning around, telling her to hold on, okay? But that would have just made him seem older and stupider than he already appeared, someone's fumbling dad venturing out for his weekly trip into the real world, fearfully bumping into everything newer and hipper than him. He told the clerk, "I don't mean to cause problems."

"You haven't, sir," she said, but she was sliding the tiger pillow across the barcode scanner. He moved forward and found himself escaping to the exit, empty-handed, and then he was holding his phone again, typing madly to the Alaska girl, *It must be getting cold there. I want to bury my face between your legs and listen to you talk. Write me back and let me know about what you've been doing. There's no reason to hold back. This doesn't mean anything.* Still no answer. He thought of her in her knit cap, her crazy unwashed hair, and that look born of many hard winters. Those dogs were named after the three stooges, the fourth most loved one christened Shemp, and she played folk guitar, fished in the summers and ate salmon all winter. She had a boyfriend but he worked for the forest service and was gone for more than half the year, living up in a tower and watching for forest fires through binoculars. Dating sites and message boards were the answer to that, she said when they first talked, and she described the weather, the ice at the window, at the electric sockets, at the seams of the cabin door. Her body, reclined on the sofa naked except for black panties, might be covered by a blanket, might not, depending on his mood. It offered itself up to the apparatus of his imagination without conceding an inch of who she was: completely impervious, not just to the weather, but also to whatever crap he might throw her way. But he did it anyway and he was still doing it. *Touch yourself and think about me,* he typed to her as the car engine idled, but the only reply was another message from Shannon, and then, as the car turned to the exit and out onto the main road, a single sentence from that woman he met a couple of weeks ago at the Yellow Door. *Are you going to be around this weekend?*

He could not think of a single detail to describe her face or body. She was simply that single sentence and the place where he had bought her a White Russian and there was a good chance he would see her there again, buy her another one, put his back to the bar and smile and make a joke about the crowd. To Shannon he wrote, *you're batshit, you know that, don't you?*

He braked quickly for someone backing out of a parking space and held the phone up, waiting for her reply to beam in. But it was the woman from the Yellow Door again who messaged. *It would be nice to bump into you again. I wasn't myself that night.* He toggled from her words back to Shannon and wrote, *this has nothing to do with me. This is just you talking to yourself.*

He thought of her ridiculous father, ex-hippie, ex-volunteer fireman, who had left her an old Toyota truck and six-figure debt when he died. Maybe she was talking to him too. Their first long talk had been about him, and he had shared the story of his own parents, married for fifty-one years. High school sweethearts and dead, one two weeks after the other, like it had been something they decided together in secret. Their marriage reminded him of a horse and carriage, rotary telephones, smaller diners with big-haired waitresses. It was all sliding into the past and good riddance, right?

He made a circle around the parking lot and pulled up directly in front of the ATM. Standing in the aquarium of the glass booth, he punched up numbers, glanced over his shoulder at his car idling at the curb, took the four hundred dollars as it tongued out of the slot. More than half his balance and it felt stupidly weightless in his hand. The other guy in the booth— he had entered just a moment before—stood a polite distance away, waiting for his turn.

"You look like you've seen better times," he said to the man, because the right side of the man's face, his nose and cheek and forehead, were covered in white bandages. The uncovered half looked completely normal.

The man grinned and said, "Melanoma. But they think they got it all."

He didn't understand what *got it all* meant. Had they taken a big chunk out of the bridge of his nose? The man was reasonably handsome, maybe in his fifties, with a full head of gray hair and he wore a nice button-down black shirt. They switched places, the man at the machine now, his own body held at attention near the door, but it seemed important to continue the conversation. He said, "It's not life threatening, is it?"

"Not really," the man said. His attention was on the keyboard. He was trying to remember.

"Well," he said, "you wear it well," because he did.

The man took his money and opened his wallet and slid it inside. He said, "Everybody who doesn't have cancer wants to talk about cancer. But if you have cancer you *never* want to talk about it."

And with that he was plucked from his very exclusive group of two—a pair of dignified men exchanging small talk in the lit display case of the ATM booth—and cast into a much less exclusive group consisting of nearly everyone. Another place where the idiots resided. "Look," he said. "I was just trying to be nice. Really. I saw a person with a chunk taken out of his face and I was curious. No, not curious. I was sympathetic. To a stranger. So maybe you could be sympathetic to me in return, right?"

"I didn't mean to insult you," the man said, but he seemed more interested in putting his wallet into the side pocket of his pants. He had the long body of a former basketball star, still lean, a curl of gray hair visible at the collar of his shirt. His overpriced watch was designed to simulate the cracked granite surface of a national monument. He lightly touched it with his left hand as if to guard it against philistine eyes. "We should both be going, don't you think?" the man asked.

"I'm sure you like to think of yourself as a man who doesn't make mistakes," he continued, "but some of us do makes mistakes, very bad ones, and we're worthy of notice as the rest of you. I might not be disfigured, but my year hasn't exactly been a good one." But as he talked on his anger fled him with every word and his voice lowered back down to the level of casual chat. He said, "Stupidity, maybe, hubris, maybe, but nothing a million other people weren't doing." And there he was again, back in the kingdom of idiots, each with their overpriced house. The man with the cancerous face stared ahead out into the parking lot where cars came and went, so impassive that for a moment he seemed to be in shock, but no, he was just waiting for the words to end and then he stepped forward to the door and pushed outside into the open air, as if nothing had been spoken at all. He must have decided that this was the best way to deal with a crazy person.

He looked at his own money, separated it, crumped it and smoothed it down and then put it away. Then he followed, head down, typing, *sorry to bother you but I can't stop thinking about you*. He wanted to tell her that he was forty-three years old and had never dreamed of pursuing a younger woman like this, but that sounded like something he should share with a therapist, and he wanted to tell her that if she just replied once to him that would be enough to sustain him through the entire week, through this whole ordeal maybe, but that sounded like something he shouldn't share with anyone. And he wanted to tell her that she was a tease and a whore for hurting him like this, for being as inert as a stone and impossible to understand, and then he wanted to follow that up with a string of bigger insults, but that seemed like something he should say to Shannon who—speak of the devil—was just now telling him that he should *go to hell and stay there*.

He wrote back the string of insults and capped them off with, *That's the final word, okay? Don't write me back.*

*Don't tell me when this conversation is over*, she said.

*Crazy crazy crazy*, he wrote, in all caps.

More symmetry. All caps right back at him.

He answered, *I'm going to spend some time with someone special right now, so I'm going to turn off the phone. So don't even bother replying.*

*Liar and if you're not a liar then I feel sorry for her.*

The Alaska girl was probably feeding wood into her stove, watching the flames rise up around the kindling. She had told him she chopped wood, and that birch was her favorite because of the white bark and the way it split, like the seam had always been there and each time you were finding it with your maul.

He liked to place her there at the stove, in his mind, her palms raised to catch the heat. Maybe she was crouched, squatting, with a knit cap on, or maybe she was sitting on a stool, but the image of her face lit by the fire was frozen there. It wasn't a beautiful face, not really, but he could tweak just slightly and make it beautiful, or at least even more interesting, and the mountains she might be able to see from her window were beautiful, right? That was more than enough beauty. Were there even mountains so close to her? He guessed not, but he put them there anyway, just like he put her in those black panties. He typed, *Shannon please leave me alone for Christ's sake.*

He entered the Walmart again, watching his phone for the next message, headed to the girl who had waited on him before. She stood with her back to her register as if waiting for him. Not a customer around. "I have cash now," he told her.

"Okay," she said. "Great."

"Where is it?"

"It's back on the floor," she said.

The text message from Shannon read, *Prick.* It read, *your face is fat.* It read, *you do not know yourself.* They came in fast and the second he had read one the next appeared. It was like eating cookies, that instinctive and unhealthy, and he was disappointed when there was no fourth. He found the display case of blenders and decided to buy the next one up the scale, thirty dollars more and twice as sexy, and then finally it was there for him. The message read, *I don't say this lightly but I want you to die.* He paused long enough to reply, *what did I do to you? Nothing that people haven't done to people since there were people.*

He wished he could stop but he couldn't, because even when he was carrying his purchase to the front of the store he was typing with his thumb. *Can't we be cordial?*

*No, we cannot be fucking cordial. What the hell does cordial mean anyway?*

He stopped to get his bearings and saw that he had wandered in the wrong direction: a million different colored bottles, shampoos and gels and hair dyes. Each box of dye showed a different woman smiling, a different shade of blonde moving brighter and brighter. Each woman impossibly happy, captured in her own pretend ecstatic world. He grabbed some shampoo, because he needed some, and then moved up the aisle to the aspirin, because he needed that more. He picked up a cart and threw it all inside. *You're scum*, she wrote, *you're practically a criminal. A criminal against women.*

He retreated to the kitchen aisle again and traded in the blender for an even better one, then threw in an espresso maker after that, a spatula, and a mixing bowl with a red clearance tag. He must have looked like a man moving into a new home. He felt like it too. He paused long enough to read the next insult and then spun away from the kitchen supplies toward the discount DVDs. He glanced some over, put some back, chose some others, and told the kid next to him, "This is a good movie," even though he had never seen it. There were more texts coming in—he could feel the vibration—but he didn't check them. He was talking to the kid about the Blu-ray players. Which one would he recommend?

"I don't know," the kid said. "I don't work here."

There was a line at the girl's lane now but he didn't care. Even when someone from an open register called him over he waved her off and stayed where he was. He wrote back to the featureless woman from two weeks past, *I'd love to see you again. I was just thinking about our talk. Are you going to be there tomorrow, because I might swing by and get you another White Russian.* He wrote to the Alaska girl, *I'm beginning to get a little worried.* He wrote to his sister, *What are the symptoms of a panic attack?*

The line cleared and he placed his box in front of the girl and she looked at him as if she had never seen him before. This was a good and bad thing, because he did want to be recognized, but not as the bumbling moron from earlier. And yet the only way for him to vindicate himself was for her to acknowledge his previous stupidity. It wouldn't take much, just a nod of the head or a comment about the blender as she turned it around, searching for the barcode. But she didn't do that. She just read the price off to him and asked him if he wanted it bagged, to which he said no, and then she dragged shampoo across the scanner, the aspirin, the dish towels and pillows and everything else. She held each thing but she did not even bother to recognize it as an object. She turned the box over and scanned it and the total price of his purchase doubled. Then he was making room for the next person.

Outside the message came in from far away, two sentences beamed off a satellite or at least a tall, tall tower and then appearing in the palm of his hand. It seemed to be just in time. The snow was already covering everything, she explained, and it had made her sad. *Paralyzed*, she said, and he imagined her with her knees pulled to her chest, watching the window. Just the beginning and it was already bad.

He didn't know if she was just making excuses or begging for help. Did she even remember who he was? They had not talked much. The wind was coming across the parking lot, sending plastic bags and other flotsam across his vision like it was all on the way to somewhere special. What did he have to tell her? Nothing at all, really, now that he had the opportunity, but maybe he was going to try anyway. Amazing to think that she was waiting just for him. He wrote, *did you get the check?* But of course she had received it. It had been cashed last week. He wrote, *what did you spend it on? Something sexy?* He wrote, *are you there?* But nothing came back except a picture of a dirt road covered in snow, a distant figure in heavy clothes holding something above its head. It was impossible to make out but maybe it was a gun or a branch. It might not even be her, hard to tell with the bulk of coat and hood. The hills behind the figure divided the sky into two shades of white. He wrote, *Beautiful.* He wrote, *Almost impossible to believe.*

Nothing.

*Where is that? Is that near where you live? Is that you?*

He waited for the blip and the flash of new information but the phone had become an inert thing in his palm, a piece of toast, a brick. He dropped it into the passenger's seat and clicked through stations. When had music become so awful? Each song, no matter the genre, had the same shouted chorus, the same desperation to please. He could not find himself in any of it and he decided that was probably because he was growing old, *had* grown old. When boiled down to their essence all the songs had one singular message: go for it, go for it now and go for it hard and go for *all* of it. As he pulled into the parking lot of Wells Fargo the phone rang. It was the bank, the man from the bank, calling from just a few hundred yards away, but he imagined the call coming from that frozen place in the photograph. The desire was so forceful that when he finally answered on the third ring it was with a crazy kind of joy. The voice said, "Where are you?"

"Don't worry. I'm almost there," he said. "I'm coming to you."

"Do you understand how important this is?" the voice asked.

He did. He did. But he sat in his car imagining the turning of pages, the repetition of signatures. His journey had not been a straight line but it *had* been a journey and this was its final stage. It would not take long. Then that would be that. He knew the inside of that house the way he knew his own mind, the slant of the dining room floor and the hairline crack on the back wall in the girls' peach-carpeted bedroom, the old paint stacked in the basement and the attic's sweet arboreal smell and exposed nails. They had only been there for two years as a family but they had been good ones. Well, at least that first year. He turned and smiled into his phone, the fish-eye lens waiting to make a record of his happiness that could be transmitted back to her. But he remembered the half-face of the bandaged man, his ugliness and his dignity, and he hesitated, although still smiling, thumb on the button. The phone made its chirping noise and he turned it around to look inside. Another picture: mountains rising in the distance, then hills, then a plain of ice with that same figure holding the same unidentifiable object aloft. Was it standing on a frozen lake? He could almost convince himself that he had just snapped this one, that it was *him* out there on the ice. *That is a human being in the middle of all that*, he reminded himself. The snow made peculiar windblown shapes on the surface of the ice, lines of force and motion curling in long arcs as if by premediated design. The figure seemed to strain to hold its position within the center of the space but it did remain, second by second, as he watched and thumb pecked and watched and waited for the next small thing. It was only a captured moment but the figure's willpower to stand steady within that frame seemed as immense as the jagged range behind it where people regularly died seeking adventure. He had never seen anything so beautiful in his entire life. That was the truth and that was what he wrote to her.

He also told her what he wanted to do to the nape of her neck, the fleshy inner thigh. But all of that had become lies, a pretend place sandwiched between his old life, the life in that four hundred and fifty-thousand-dollar house, and the new one waiting for him inside a third-floor office of Wells Fargo. In a moment he'd go in and write his name over and over, his *real* name, the one he had never told her, like a kid practicing penmanship until it was right. But for now, he held as still as the figure in the frame.

# Make Me Whole

I wasn't sure what I was seeing. A small crowd formed around what I first thought was a young child, someone about my age, but it was a fish, the largest fish I'd ever seen, almost as long as I was tall and shining silver-blue. I watched one man kneel as if to touch it, to speak to it. His hand rose and fell, just once and then more: a steady motion as if he might be hammering a nail, but he was clubbing its skull with a length of pipe. Four, five, six, seven times. His arm rose and fell. And when he did stop, after the eighth or ninth blow, he paused and knelt even deeper and clasped at its mouth with his other hand. It seemed that after killing it—after making very sure it was dead—he would now lean deeper, put his lips to its mouth, breathe deep, and try to bring it back.

He forced it open and looked inside its throat, searching for something down in there, his forearm disappearing down into its guts. I glanced up at my mother to verify that she was still with me. She was watching too, but with that same look of judgment she sometimes cast in my direction if they sent me home early for fighting, as if she put this in the same category as my black eyes and bruises and notes about detentions.

I followed her sight line. She was not looking at the fish, but at another man, standing a little further away and holding his hand. Twenty years have made the sight beautiful—the long spiral of green hose and the rainbow of diesel covering the dock as it mixed with thinning blood. They were washing it away, but it seemed to be coming up from between the boards. That was not the case, of course. The blood came from him, the man my mother was watching. It ran down his arm, his leg, and pooled around his black rubber boots. He gripped one hand with the other to make a double fist. That's where the wound resided, somewhere in there, but his face didn't register any pain. He seemed more curious than anything, expectant, as if he might be wondering what the other man might find down there in the throat of the fish as he crouched in close.

Two men in white jogged down the steep plank to the dock and I saw their ambulance behind us strobing red. The two men split, one to the injured man, one to the man kneeling, and they spoke as if they might be commenting on the weather. The kneeling man produced a knife. He ran it down the length of the fish and then dug in both hands. After a moment he held something up—a ring or a jewel—and then he handed it to the paramedic who cradled it in both palms. I had the sense that this ceremony had been conducted before, many times, although of course I knew that was ridiculous even then. The crowd had grown larger. I heard someone say, "That must have hurt."

"Hey," my mother said. "Let's not talk about this with your father, okay? There's no reason for him to know we were here."

I think I might have said okay, or maybe I just kept looking. They were taking the injured man back to the ambulance and the rest of them stood on the dock. I think they were waiting for something else to happen. A few minutes passed without incident, and eventually the crowd began to disperse, although a few people remained. They seemed disappointed that it had all ended so soon. Then my mother did a very strange thing. She took me by the wrist and walked down the plank, down to the dock, and moved up to the men, and her attitude—carefree, almost girlish—was as surprising as what we'd just seen. "Did somebody do something stupid?" she asked.

She seemed to know them, or at least one of them, the man closest to us, the one who had hammered the fish and cut it open. His wide face was red and pockmarked and his long hair whipped around in the wind. "Hello, Marlene," he said, but he didn't seem happy to see her. He glanced at me and then away, out at the bay. All the boats turned in the same direction with the tide, clinging to their moorings, and out past the jetty and the white triangles of a few sailboats. I looked down at my feet and noticed the blood was almost gone already. They were letting the water run it away.

"My kid is sick," she said, "but I couldn't stay away. Glad I didn't either. I would have missed all the drama."

"Just an accident," he told her. "Like you said, somebody did something stupid. I suppose you wouldn't feel any pity for someone like that, would you? A stupid person, I mean."

"I didn't say that," she said, and now she was the one who looked annoyed. Her hair whipped around her head too. She reached up and tried to tug it out of her eyes, but the effort was useless. "Harold," she said, "this is the man I told you about. Bobby. He's a friend of mine. Say hello to him but don't shake his hand. You're sick, after all, and he's filthy."

"Right," I said, but I couldn't remember her telling me about anybody. All she wanted to do was leave the house and watch the ocean, get the hell outside and breathe some real air.

"Nice to meet you," he said. "Marlene told me about your exploits. You going to be a boxer when you grow up?"

I made a sound of dismissal, false humility, and watched the water for traces of the blood. But it was like nothing had happened. Even the hose had been curled up again. "That's nothing to be proud of, you know," my mother said. She had been holding my shoulder, using that grip to guide me as she walked, and squeezed—squeezed so hard it hurt at the place where her thumbnail pressed against my collarbone—and said, "The child is the father of the man. Have you heard that expression before? Every decision you make is an important one."

"I'd agree with that, Harold," the man said, and he laughed, and she laughed too, and for a moment I thought they might touch.

"See, Marlene?" he said. "You can't help but have a good time with me."

But all it did was make me think of my father, who was at work about an hour away in Kingston, New Hampshire. I felt sorry that he'd missed everything and sorry that he had to get up early before I was even awake. I would find traces of him, bread crumbs on the table, his dirty coffee cup in the sink, a *Popular Mechanics* left open by his chair.

They had taken the fish away when I wasn't looking. I felt like I had been tricked, distracted from the important thing by all of this back-and-forth between my mother and this man, the thoughts of my father rising before the streetlights were off. I heard my mother say, "Oh, don't flatter yourself," but she was still laughing. "Do you think this is going to change things? We're still the same people. It's not like you're some kind of hero now."

They grew quiet then and I figured this was it, my mother had said everything she had planned to say. Possibly we'd stop for food on the way home, cheeseburgers that we'd eat in the parking lot, and she'd remind me not to mention anything to my father. She'd ask how I was feeling and I'd tell her good and that would be that. There had been other men. I had seen them too, had them slap my shoulder and smile at me, speak my name and make a joke.

The man must have noticed that I was looking at the boats because he said, "Fantastic, huh? It quiets the mind, looking out at all that. Of course, all of those out there piss me off a bit. Seems like mockery." He indicated some of the biggest sailboats anchored further out in a shoal where the water grew greener and calm. One of the boats had a double hull and it reminded me of pictures I'd seen of manta rays, alien and beautiful. I couldn't picture myself ever stepping foot on a boat like that and that made me a little angry too—and angry too that the man had snuck that feeling into my heart against my will. "Lawyers and doctors down there," he said. He pointed at the very biggest boat. "That guy is a real piece of work."

"Hey," my mother said. "Quiet mind, remember?"

"Sure," he said, and put his hands on his hips. He was lean and he reminded me of a gunfighter standing that way, a gunfighter watching the distance for enemies. I decided that I was his enemy and he didn't even know it. I was standing right next to him and all he could do was watch way out there at the prettiest spot in the bay and get mad. This was in Newburyport, Massachusetts just before all the boats became like those boats out at the shoal and people like Bobby had to move on to Gloucester and Ipswich. At the time he seemed so confident that he was going to win and it wasn't that hard to be tricked by his confidence, the way he looked out at the water or smashed the head of a fish. I guess that's one thing my mother liked about him. I could tell because I liked it too.

On the way home, my mother shouted into the backseat above the music, "Hey, how are you feeling?"

"Pretty good," I said.

"Well, don't tell your father about this trip today, okay? It's important for people to have little secrets, and he wouldn't like that I kept you home. You've missed so much school already, you know?"

"Sure," I said.

"Good," she said. "Now would you like a snack?"

A few days later, after my latest fight, my mother picked me up at school. She didn't seem angry though—she was grinning—and she reached over the seat to open the door for me. She didn't ask me what had happened. Instead, she pulled away from curb and said, "You know that man who had his finger bitten off by the bluefish? They surgically reattached it. Can you believe that?"

"Finger?" I asked.

"Yeah," she said. "The one in the fish."

She seemed to be tickled by the whole thing. More than that. The news had made her giddy. "It's incredible," she said. "I saw it today. He could even move it." She raised her arm and wiggled her index finger in a small dance. "That's the time we live in. Your kidney fails on you and they just slap in a new one. You lose a finger and they pack it in ice and reattach it and it's like you never lost it in the first place. Boom. All fixed."

"That *is* amazing," I said, although it felt strange not to know what was *really* going on.

"And then," she said with a wave of her hand. "They ate the fish." She paused for a moment as if considering the next piece of news. "I ate it," she added, "and it was delicious."

"It didn't taste funny?" I asked.

She glanced at me and I felt even more like an idiot. "Why would it taste funny?"

I shrugged. "I don't know," I said.

The next time I saw the strobing lights they flashed across our house, across my face as I stood in the living room window, and I'd think of my mother's words and tell myself everything would be fine.

❧

I don't remember much about my father: the sound of him taking his shoes off in the bedroom, the way they would clatter on the floor and wake me up; his face illuminated by the television as he clicked channels; and the size of him filling our small kitchen. He was tall and heavyset, ponderous, a victim of a heart attack at the age of thirty-three. The second one killed him at thirty-eight, when I was ten. It was like a door had been kicked open. My mother and I left a few weeks later for the Southwest.

"This is a new start for you and me both," my mother said. "Try not to break anybody's nose at the new school, okay?"

Except that I only stayed in the new school in Santa Fe for two weeks before we moved out of our small adobe house in town to a circle of trailers on a stretch of land in the hills. Fires burned at night and the people there sat in circles and discussed politics. Warheads aimed right at us, right at our children, they said, and everybody would nod. This was the open secret of the world: that we could all die at any moment. My father had proved that.

They seemed to be planning something, something important, but what it was could never be directly stated. We often ate together outside, gathered around two doors set end to end on sawhorses. Good food, especially when it was summer, although as we moved into October and November the portions grew smaller. By December my mother saved things for us in our trailer, cans of soup, the heel of the bread. She said, "It shouldn't taste so good, but it does, doesn't it? I think it's because it's just you and me."

I wondered what my father would have thought about a place like that, but he was already growing dim to me, a thing that moved around the edges of my mind but no longer seemed to occupy it. In the mornings I woke before my mother and expected to hear his car in the driveway as he headed out. Then I'd reorient myself and the length of the trailer would come into focus, the plastic curtain hiding the toilet, the hot plate and the burned-black toaster oven.

My mother would be homeschooling me from now on because she didn't want teachers filling my head with nonsense. That, she said, had been the problem on the East Coast, that and a couple of poor choices she would take responsibility for now that she was past them. "There are all kinds of violence," she said. "I'm reading books about it. Sex can be an act of violence. Fast food is a form of violence. And education can be violent. So I don't blame you and you shouldn't blame you."

Some of the books were stacked outside along a little wall we had made of stones in a half-circle at the front of the trailer. Stickers along the spines bore the name of the West Newbury, Massachusetts Public Library. The inside covers were inscribed with the names of people who had used them before and the dates they had checked them out. That was the thing that had impressed me most: that these things had come through the hands of others and found their way to us.

In that place there were other children about my age, most with long hair, so long that at first, I couldn't tell if they were girls or boys as they stood in the bright sun. Sometimes we played with metal cars in the dirt, but mostly we walked the perimeter of the camp along the old barbed wire made for cattle and tried to find things: arrowheads, old pieces of pottery. People had lived here hundreds of years before, one of the kids said, and left behind some ghosts. Good ghosts, my mother told me later. The kind you can learn from if you listen carefully. She tied her hair in two thick braids on either side of her head. Her skin darkened. She wore dresses made of yellows and browns, loose fitting in the heat, and her arms grew ropey with muscle. My skin turned red along my arms and the back of my neck. I'd peel it off in small patches and sometimes taste it. I felt like a snake, hard and still in the heat. "Your father's bad influence," she said. His complexion, his eyes, his laziness. "But biology isn't destiny," she said, and she laughed like it was a joke I couldn't understand, might never understand.

"Let's pretend we're monsters," I'd say to the other kids.

But they'd have none of it. They knew it meant rolling around in the dirt with me, headlocks, a twist of the ear and a pull of the hair. They were all thin as sticks and I had my father's bulk. "Cowards," I'd say, because that was a word I had heard my mother use. I'd try to laugh like my mother too but it was difficult to capture it exactly. Her laugh was animal-like and deep, a smoker's laugh, the bark of a dog.

Sometimes my mother would wake me and say, "Hey, why don't you go look at the stars for a while, okay? They're beautiful tonight." Which meant I needed to pull on my jeans and vacate the trailer for a while. There was always someone else with her when she did that, and I knew I shouldn't ask if they wanted to come with me. I'd head out and the stars would be beautiful and when I saw them I wouldn't mind being out there at all.

The man who came to our trailer most often reminded me of the children: blonde hair and small wrists and an untested confidence. He was the one who spoke most around the fire but something about his voice lulled me into calm, even when he was speaking about war. I imagined myself as the survivor scrambling through the rubble, finding treasures in the cracks. Sometimes my mother was with me, but sometimes I wandered alone. "Five megatons," he'd say. "That makes Nagasaki look like a firecracker." His car sat on blocks on one end of the property so sometimes he borrowed my mother's to head into town for supplies and he'd come back with a secret thing for me: Twinkies or fruit pies, sometimes a long stick of beef jerky I'd eat while wandering the fence. As the weather grew colder he talked more and more about the missiles and one night he grew so angry that he stood up and began shouting, waving his hand. It seemed kind of funny, as if he were trying to conjure something out of the fire, but everybody else sat there gazing up at him. My mother turned her head sideways away from him and out toward the flat land where the sun squatted red against the horizon.

"We keep going around and around," she finally said. "Around and around and around. Like a fly stuck behind a windowpane."

She made a light buzzing sound and I smiled in the dusk.

"This is important," the man said, but his confidence had already abandoned him. I could hear a crack in his voice. He looked out at the horizon too and maybe he saw our future there in the red ball disintegrating at its edges. Maybe he meant everything he said.

"Men try anything to get laid," my mother said, "but this has been a new one. It really blindsided me." She looked at a couple of the other women around the fire and then she laughed her barking laugh. "You don't know what working class is," she added, as if this might be the worst insult she could imagine.

"What's that?" he asked.

She sat back on the stump with her arms folded and said, "I've got the only functioning car in the commune. One of the key things about being working class is the work part, don't you think? Winter is coming and we haven't even started the building you were talking about."

Another woman said, "So true. You guys are too busy planning a revolution to dig a decent well."

"Let's start the revolution at home," my mother said. "Let's start by having some of the guys do the dishes tonight."

Their eyes met across the fire and they smiled at each other—these two women, my mother and a stranger with pigtails just like hers.

"We're learning as we go," the man said.

My mother was still looking at the other woman. They seemed to communicate to each other in a way I couldn't understand and they seemed to be enjoying it. I was enjoying it too, but for different reasons. I wanted to be away from that place and I thought there might be just enough force in this argument to send us spinning back to our neat adobe house in town.

"My husband, he was working class," my mother said. "That was a real man." She had a smirk on her face, as if she were mocking her own words as she said them, but as she spoke her voice grew louder. "He worked his ass off. All he did was work. He wouldn't fit in here very well."

She had started a debate. The man sat down.

When she spoke again she sounded more forlorn than angry. "Some of you had other lives, but not like me. You never lost someone like that. Divorce isn't the same thing." She paused and let that settle in. She smiled and said, "Fishing is one of the most dangerous jobs in this country, you know, and it's most dangerous on the East Coast. You wouldn't think that, but it's true. He loved it though. It was a choice he made every day. It put him at peace."

She seemed to be describing the man on the dock and not my father. I could imagine his hand rising and falling in that hammer motion. I remembered the ambulance and the blood and for some reason I said, "Tell them about the fish, Mom."

She turned her head to me as if surprised by my voice. But then she nodded and said, "This is a good one. He lost his finger once. And then it came back to him."

She held up her hand and wiggled her finger again, just as she had done in the car a year before, although I guessed that she didn't remember doing it then. In the moment it must have seemed an original and funny thing to do, to hold up her own finger as an example right then and let everybody imagine it being severed. She said, "He caught a bluefish and it took off his finger just below the second joint. Not his fault. You have to club a fish like that, really beat its brains in, and the guy who was supposed to do that didn't hit it hard enough." She looked at the man who had been speaking before and for the first time I realized he was maybe a good decade younger than my mother, maybe in his midtwenties. His face was sunburned, his eyes marked by crow's feet, and he seemed older most of the time. "They had to gut the fish and get this. He reached in himself and took out his own finger. Would you be able to do that?"

I decided I would have the courage, I'd kill it and open it and remove that small piece of me without thinking twice. For a second, I saw myself as the center of her story and it made me listen harder to find out what might become of me.

"They packed it in ice," she said. "And rushed him to the hospital and stitched it on." She wiggled her finger again. "Almost as good as new, although he didn't have much feeling in it anymore. After that he called it The Deserter." She laughed and the woman across from her smiled. I laughed a little too. I knew we were done with the trailers and the desert, the red sunsets and talk about death by fire.

Later that night she woke me up and said, "Sorry about earlier. Sometimes I go off on a tear, you know? They just get me going. But this is a good place. You like it here, right?"

"Sure," I said. "It's okay."

"Good," she said. "Do you want to look at the stars?"

"Okay," I said. I threw my legs out of the bunk and found my jeans in a small bundle on the floor, belt still attached. I pulled them up my legs and began putting myself together. There was the woman from the fire standing just behind my mother, except this time my mother put her hand on the back of my neck, very gently, and stepped outside with me. The woman followed and the three of us walked a bit away from the trailer, looking up at the dome of the sky. "The Deserter," I said, and laughed again, but my mother didn't respond.

After a while she said, "I'm still very young, you know. I met your father when I was nineteen. I've never told you that before. I know nineteen probably seems old to you now, but trust me, it's incredibly young. Too young to have to make certain kinds of decisions, you know? But I had to make them and I made them fast."

I considered the moment that always separated the insults from the first punch. I never grabbed or wrestled like the other kids. I made the decision fast, and the other person was always surprised by the sudden burst of pain. Did they think we'd just stand there arguing, strutting around? No, go for the face with everything you've got. Someone had told me that once, but I'm not sure who, definitely not my father. Maybe I had heard it from the TV. Regardless, I thought I understood what my mother meant by having to make a quick decision and I said, "Sure."

She rubbed the back of my neck and said, "You're a good kid. You've already led a full life and you're ten years old. You know more than all the men here put together, don't you?"

"I don't know about that," I said.

"Well, I do," she said.

The next day I felt stronger and out at the barbed wire I knocked one of the other kids down hard to the ground, stood above him and watched him to see how he would react. His hair fell across his eyes but I could see that he was afraid of me and that seemed like a good thing. I kicked him, small kicks that sent him scuttling backward in the white dirt, and then he scrambled to his feet and ran. "Coward," I hollered after him. "Liar."

꘎

My mother said, "New Mexico was a mistake. I admit that. But in another way, it wasn't a mistake, because it brought us here. It made me realize I needed a more radical approach to my life." She paused. "To our life. Together."

"Right," I said.

"That which doesn't kill us makes us stronger. Which is not true, just tell that to the person who's had a debilitating stroke, right? But it's as good an illusion as any. Remember in California when the transmission exploded? That's what I was telling myself then when we were standing on the side of the road with our thumbs out. It sounded really good then."

We lived on the west side of Anchorage in a nest of apartments that used to be off-base army housing. Icicles hung from the roof, some of them as long as me, and at night we'd walk outside and check for the northern lights. We hadn't seen them yet, just the smallest flicker of blue that might have been nothing at all.

"Light pollution," my mother said. "There's nothing we can do about it. Too many people. Even here." Then we'd head back inside.

My bedroom wall was spotted with fist-sized holes. Each one had been covered up with spackle that didn't match the paint. I decided that something bad had happened here but I couldn't imagine what. One or two I could see but a dozen seemed like something else entirely, something beyond me. My mother spread books on the kitchen table and sometimes lifted her head up to share a quote with me. "Listen to this," she'd say. "'Labor is the father of material wealth and the earth is its mother.' That's pretty clever, don't you think?"

"Sure," I'd say, and her head would go back down as if into deep water.

She wore flannel shirts now, heavy boots with double knotted laces, and tied her hair back in a single braid. Her eyes had sunken into her skull and she liked to mumble to herself, to the writers she was reading. The table became a complicated puzzle of dishes and books and scraps of paper bearing small notes. When I stepped outside I could walk out to the main road where the traffic was heavy, then look up and see the mountains all around. Sometimes she went with me and we walked through the slush on the side of the road on the way to the grocery store. Everything was breaking up, melting and coming loose, and the cars were all covered in dirt. Ours had made it this far but had died and we were waiting to raise some money to fix it.

"If you're going to get stranded somewhere," she said, "it's best to make it a beautiful place, right?"

We'd walk back from the grocery holding shopping bags. Sometimes the cars would honk at us from behind and my mother would hold up her middle finger without turning.

"Just give me a little time," she said.

She didn't talk about school and neither did I but we'd go to the library and she'd stack more books up in her arms, in my arms too.

But I also remember books about vampires and werewolves. She'd read parts of them to me aloud and then tell me to continue while she spread out the other books and took notes. Numbers and measurements and the names of plants. "You're growing strong and smart," she said to me. "It's better not to be too dependent on others. What's happening in your book now?"

"He's arrived at the castle," I said. "I think he's going to go inside. And then he'll probably get killed."

"I don't know about that," she said. "He's the one telling the story. But keep at it."

My mother no longer talked about the missiles but that strange sense of imminent danger had stayed with me, with us. I even felt it in the quiet of the library, so silent you could hear the turning of our pages, the water from the fountain when someone bent and drank.

We slept in the same bed and late at night she'd sometimes push my shoulder, a nudge, and I'd wake up and she'd whisper to me, like there was someone else around, a parent in the other room maybe, still awake and listening for us. "Years from now you're going to write a book about me. I swear it. That's how I see you. You're a deep thinker and you're going to write a book."

"And it's going to be about you," I said.

"Yes," she said, "I think so. And this place, I think. We're going to go to those mountains, you know. The best is yet to come, as they say."

"Biology isn't destiny," I said.

"What?"

"Never mind," I said.

And then she'd talk about what she was going to do for work. She wanted to become a nurse. If you were a nurse you were always needed somewhere. She'd take classes soon and there was plenty of work around. "What I'd really like to be is a doctor," she said, "but that ship has sailed." She'd tell me that eventually we'd buy some land and if I wanted to pee I'd just walk in the woods and go against a tree.

Doing something like that somehow seemed like the height of indulgence to me and I liked to hear her talk about it.

Then as the weather warmed up I began sleeping alone some nights. She said she would still be in the building, not far away, and if there was a problem she would know about it.

"I don't believe in love," she said one night. "Not in the way most people think of it anyway. But I believe that two people can line up in the right way for a while."

"Can I meet him?" I asked.

"That's probably not a good idea," she said.

I remember the night she nudged me awake, roughly, speaking my name, shaking me. "Hey, Harold," she said. "Tell me. What does it feel like to be a man?" I felt her moving in the dark, her leg shaking. "Because I'd really like to know."

"I don't understand," I said.

"Tell me," she said. "Give me all the secrets."

That same hoarse laugh. I thought of telling her about the holes in the wall, how I sometimes could imagine myself doing something like that, but then I decided that's not what she was looking for so I didn't say anything. "Tell me," she said again in a raspy whisper. "How does it feel to be a prick?" She took a deep breath and turned on her side away from me. "Sorry. You wouldn't know, would you? That's why I like you. You're not one of them yet."

She kicked her legs out over the edge of the bed. I could hear her shallow breathing and I stayed awake for a long time listening. I could tell she was still awake. I said, "You're a very good mother. Sometimes you just get angry."

"You too," she said. "Sometimes you just get angry too, don't you?"

"No," I said, because at that moment I felt as distant as the scenery around us. My own body was just another thing apart from me and I wanted to keep it that way.

I met him the next day. He appeared at our door, his face in the gap allowed by the chain lock, and then my mother said, "Let him in. Let him in. Let's have breakfast. I'll make sausage."

He sat at the table turning his coffee cup around as if he was trying to wind it, forward and then back, forward and back. He looked like a lot of the men I saw around there, unshaven, heavy, slow to smile. I sat on our couch and turned on the radio and listened to a song playing out from the Lower 48. My mother called out from the stove, "Tell him it's true. He doesn't believe me. You should believe me, Toby. I have a reliable witness."

"What?" I asked.

"He doesn't believe what happened to your father. Remember that? Isn't it all true?" I turned from the TV and saw her hold up two sausage links. She opened her mouth in a circle, fish-like, and made a feint at them, as if to swallow, as she watched the man. "Just like that," she said, and she laughed. "What can you do with a man who doesn't believe in things?" she asked. "Everything I tell him he looks at me like we're playing poker."

"It's all true," I said. "Everything."

⋇

In the early evening the moose would come down the hill, usually one large one trailing a couple of calves, their heads lowered in a way that seemed almost shy. I'd watch them from the porch and as long as I didn't move they'd come closer and closer. It was something I was good at and sometimes it seemed that they'd come so close I could touch them. Then something would happen—the smallest of noises—and they'd lift their heads and recede back into the trees. It was early June and everything in Fairbanks was turning green again.

Often my mother sat inside reading her books. She had transitioned to how-to manuals, things about building your own house, vegetarian cookbooks, home remedies with small drawings of leaves and herbs. We were living with her girlfriend Bianca and my mother was talking about building another room onto the back of the place. Sometimes the three of us slept in the same big bed, me on the far-right edge, my arm dangling to the cold floor. Although often Bianca patted my back and said, "Okay, now. Go on and get," and I'd head off to the couch in the cabin's only other room.

We brushed our teeth outside and spat the toothpaste onto the ground. I remember that for some reason and also the smell of the wet lowlands, decaying leaves and fallen branches and sometimes the smell of a rotting animal coming in from a long way off. It was not a bad smell, it was just nature, and late at night we'd sit outside and Bianca would tell us stories about working the pipeline. It was tough, she said, but the money was fantastic and as long as you didn't weaken—as long as you didn't spend the money on drugs and booze—then you could make a good life for yourself. Which is what she had done. Now she worked sporadically as a river guide.

She reminded me a little of my father because she was slow speaking, slow moving. She wore a black hoodie most of the time, even when the weather grew hotter, and smoked cigarettes, dropping the butts into a Coke bottle she kept on the porch. "Never do this," she'd say, as she finished one off, and then she'd tell a story about someone falling out of her boat or a guy busting himself up because he did something foolhardy while working on the line. She'd tell us about the parties afterward, men running through money on cocaine, snorting it right off the table at a local diner between mouthfuls of pancakes. All of it seemed to have happened a long time ago but it was just a couple of years.

I was twelve, almost thirteen, and my mother told me, "This is it. Wasn't it worth it?" She cut her hair short and took to wearing a knit cap. In the morning she'd be the first one up and I'd hear her outside splitting logs. By the time I was out of bed she was already inside, smelling of birch, slivers of wood on her T-shirt, putting dishes down on the table. We ate dried salmon and eggs for breakfast, the same thing for lunch on weekends.

I was going to school again and although I was failing a lot of the work, I had made a few friends. We'd roam around the halls, skipping classes, and it felt like innocent fun, like we were just exploring. I would spit in the drinking fountain, kick open a door and head outside. "We should be careful," one of them said, and not long after I rifled through a closet of art supplies they began to avoid me. I'd see them up ahead and they'd act like they couldn't hear me calling out to them.

"Nice shirt," I said to one of them when I finally caught him alone in the hall. "Nice new pants."

"I got to go to the office," he said.

"I'll walk with you," I said, but I trailed just behind him, sometimes kicking the back of his foot. "I've been missing you," I said.

"Cut it out," he said, and stopped and stared me down.

I went right inside and knocked him into the lockers just to hear them clatter. When I came away again he was hurting, holding his face, and I felt sorry, not for him really, but for myself and mostly for my mother, because I thought I knew what would happen next. This was a long time ago and a teacher could grab a kid by the back of the neck and shake him. That's what happened to me. The burly shop teacher gripped me hard and I almost came off my feet.

"Wait," I said, as if I had something to say in my defense, and he loosened his grip.

"Don't spoil this for me, Harold," my mother screamed at me in the car on the way home.

"I'm not going to spoil anything," I said.

"You spoiled his smile," she said. "You knocked out two teeth. That's money I don't have right there. Is that all you know how to do? I swear sometimes. Maybe you are a man. Maybe I should start treating you like one."

"I don't know what that means," I said.

She stopped because there were moose ahead, just before the turn to the dirt road that led to our place, to Bianca's place. I liked to believe that I could tell the difference between two moose and these seemed familiar, a family that lived close by, maybe. She twisted her fists on the wheel while we waited. By then we were used to them and they could just be an inconvenience. Their slowness now made me think of the elderly and they seemed fragile out there, especially the three smaller ones.

"Fuck," my mother said. "I was just starting work this week. You're going to have to stay home by yourself. Can you do that?"

I didn't say anything. The last calf moved down into a rut and then off into the woods and my mother picked up speed onto the dirt road, past a long row of mailboxes. All the streets were named by miners. Grubstake. Hardrock. Each name a kind of boast. I looked out the passenger window away from her at the white trees flickering past. "You know what?" I said. "There's reasons for what I do. Good reasons."

"Oh yeah?" she said. "That's just great. There are reasons for what I do too. You can't stand that I'm happy with Bianca. And don't look at me like you don't know what I'm talking about. I know more about what's going on in your head than you do."

"You drive too fast," I said. "Someday you're going to get us killed."

"Shut up," she said. "Just shut up. We're five minutes from home. Can you keep your mouth shut that long?"

I made a sound of agreement, guttural, somewhere from my insides.

"I said shut up," she said. "No more about her."

A few days later Bianca returned from Homer smelling of salt water and my mother smiled for the first time that week. We cooked up caribou from the freezer and Bianca stood apart from us smoking while my mother worked the grill. "What's news this week?" Bianca asked.

"Nothing much," my mother said. "Pretty boring. The cycle of life continues."

"Well," Bianca said. "A Cessna crashed into the Beluga Lake while I was there. I mean, I wasn't there. I didn't see it. But I heard about it, and I met the guy who was flying the plane. He just walked away from it."

"Swam away from it," my mother said.

"Yeah, swam," Bianca said, and she smiled.

"Did he do something stupid? All your stories have someone doing something stupid. But you're never the stupid one."

Bianca shrugged and looked out at the line of forest.

"Everybody but you," my mother said.

"Is the food ready?" I asked.

"We need you around here more," my mother said. "I have a son, in case you didn't notice."

Bianca shrugged but she rubbed out her cigarette and moved closer. "Don't touch me," my mother said. "I'm not in the mood."

"Okay, okay," Bianca said, and she held up her hands in surrender. I remembered my father making a similar gesture but I couldn't place it in a moment. I could recall my mother telling him to stop but not the exact words. And then it was gone, wiped away by my mother's voice.

"I've had adventures too," she said. "I'm as strong as you."

My mother held up her hand as if to show off a ring, but there was no ring there. "Yeah, I know, I know," Bianca said. "The fingers."

"Right," my mother said. She seemed on the verge of screaming again, just like in the car, but her voice stayed low. "Alaska isn't the only dangerous place in the world. You don't have a monopoly on that."

"C'mon," Bianca said. "Why are you being this way?"

My mother wasn't even listening. "There's no bluefish here. We had to gut it down the length of its body and pull it out. I said before that there was no pain but it was very painful. It hurt like hell. And there were people there who thought it was funny, I could tell, even though I was missing a finger. They weren't smiling but I could tell, they wanted to laugh at the dumb girl who got her hand too close."

"So we're picking up where we left off?" Bianca asked. "Is that what we're doing? Why are you in such a bad mood, for God's sake? I thought me being away would help." She looked at my mother and something hard came into her face, a look I couldn't read. "This is for shit," she said, and she went into the house. I could hear her marching into the back room.

My mother turned to me and said, "What? Haven't you seen a lover's quarrel before?"

"There's no scar, Mom," I said.

"Yeah, well," she said. "If you look close enough."

"Mom," I said.

"Look," she demanded, and she put her hand to my face.

I've learned that things seldom end in one moment. We stayed there for a couple of more months but one day in early November Bianca met me at the school bus, her hands shoved into the pockets of her hoodie. "Hello, kiddo," she said. "Just thought I'd have a walk with you."

"Sure," I said. "Nice to see you," because she had been in Sitka for two weeks.

"Great," she said and we began our walk home.

"Your mother will say some bad shit about me," she said, "and some of it's going to be true. I just wanted you to know that I'm not usually the one who breaks it off. I'm the one who sticks around. Really. And I like you a lot, kiddo. You know that, right?"

"I do," I said, because that's what I was supposed to say. I knew that even then.

"Good," she said. "I'm not going to give you piles of advice, but I will tell you one thing." And then she stopped because she saw my mother up ahead, standing in the snow. She was wearing Bianca's heavy parka and she looked small and strange and for a second, I thought she might turn and run. I suppose she looked frightened, that's what I'm trying to say, but I don't know why I would think that. She was too far away to see her face. "Man," Bianca said, when she saw her coat. "For a second I thought that was me." I tried to laugh a little but I realized that I had thought the same thing, and not as a joke. For a moment I had thought Bianca was out there and also standing next to me. We stood and waited for my mother to do something, to come closer or go away. Finally, Bianca said, "Just take care of yourself, okay?" And she reached out and her hand touched the back of my neck and I was the one who wanted to run.

I reached up and slapped her hand hard, hard enough that she made a noise and pulled it back, the way you do when you touch something burning. It was that fast. I watched her hold her hand close to her chest and then I moved in, striking at her body until something hit me back, so strong that my feet came loose beneath me and I hit the ground. I heard my mother yelling, "Leave him alone. Leave him alone." And then I rose to my feet. "I'm fine," I said. "It's nothing."

❦

"It's all coming back to me," my mother said. "Look at this. This is where I would hide." And she slid open a small door, bent down, and looked inside at the square hole. There were blankets in there, a small box that I thought might be a mousetrap. "I used to get a pillow and a flashlight and read books. I wonder if there are any books still in there. What do you think?"

My grandmother sat downstairs in the living room, a shawl across her lap, watching the TV. I had never met her before. I hadn't even known where she lived: only an hour from our old house on the coast, in Haverhill, Massachusetts, a place we used to drive past on the highway.

"I wish I had a flashlight," my mother said. "You probably have better eyes than me. Come down here and look." She knelt and pushed herself half into the space. I leaned down above her but I couldn't see anything. "Hey, hey," she said. "A discovery." She pulled some dust-covered books out and something else, a pair of black leather gloves. "For some reason I used to like to read with those on," she said. "I don't know why. It felt nice, I guess."

At dinner my mother raised her voice loud to speak to my grandmother. "I'll do the dishes," she said. "You just show me where to put things. We don't want to be an inconvenience."

My grandmother said, "We used to call your mother Mouse because she was always underfoot."

"Mom," she said. "Please."

"I'm sorry about your father. I didn't know."

"We've been over that, Mom," she said. "That's ancient history. This food is pretty good, by the way. You still know how to burn a meatloaf."

My grandmother looked at me across the lazy Susan. I could tell there was more that she wanted to tell me. "Pass the catsup," my mother said, and I gave it a spin.

At school that week the kids asked me where I was from and I told them

Alaska. They stood around me in a half-circle, sizing me up, and the more they looked the more I looked back. I could feel my hands ball up in my coat pockets. "Nobody's from Alaska," one of the kids said. "It's just glaciers and polar bears. What were you doing there? Living in an igloo?"

"You don't know anything," I said.

That afternoon my mother picked me up in my grandmother's Chevy Impala. Her hair was styled, pasted down across her forehead, and for the first time I saw the connection between them, something I couldn't identify, but hoped ran through me too. She opened the door for me, slammed it hard. It seemed a perfect car to escape in, much better than the other one we had owned. That one made rattling sounds when you brought it out on the highway. This one smelled like butterscotch. "I can't believe this," she said. "What are you trying to do to me?"

I sat watching the front of the school. It was early afternoon and the rest of the kids were still in there at their desks. "They didn't believe me," I said.

"Believe you about what?"

"It doesn't matter."

She pulled away from the curb and I imagined that we were going someplace else other than home. "You've got to listen to me," she said. "I know things have been rough, but they're going to get better. A lot better. Don't become a stone on me. Look at me when I'm talking to you." But I was staring at the houses gliding by, the fences and porches and squares of lawn. She was going fast and it was starting to stream together. I put my hand to my face and closed my eyes and I could feel the vibration of the car engine in my body, the car moving beneath me. She said, "Tell me what they said. You want me to understand, don't you?"

"I guess," I said, and I felt like I might be flying. Or pushing through the water. The tires *sounded* like water passing under us and then when I opened my eyes I realized that it *was* water and it had started raining. Had I fallen asleep? Everything had become different. The car up ahead glowed in our high beams. My mother was still driving fast, even faster, through a place I didn't recognize.

It's easy to just fall asleep again and then wake up somewhere else.

This is how we moved through the world back then, and even now, when people ask me about my mother I don't know where to begin and where to end. Newburyport, or Alaska, or northern Montana or the others. I have not talked to her in a long time and I imagine her in each of these places and then I am there too. What would I tell her if I had a voice? That they didn't believe the story of the fish that took my finger.

But that's not what made me throw the first punch, the second punch, and the next and the next. They didn't believe the next part, because I told them my mother didn't miss a beat. I told them how she pulled out the knife and slit it open and found the stolen thing there, and now look, here it is, returned to me, my hand made whole. Watch it move. Watch it open and close. The same as it was before. See it open up in a wave. See it close into a fist. Isn't it amazing? Isn't it so strange?

# Marriage or Wolves

Talking roosters. Farmers and their dullard sons. Princes and princesses. At some point red eyes almost always appeared at the forest's edge. Then the beasts would enter the plot.

Nobody was spared.

In a way that was the point, the point of the stories. Jaws would rend the bodies of sinner and virtuous alike, then vanish as quickly as they'd come. Or a single beast would find its way into a home, a village, a life. Someone would open a door to find a muscled presence in the dark, sometimes masquerading in the form of a friend. Was it any wonder, Alexis would remark with a smile, that she had become the person she was? All those Russian tales ended with either a wedding or a mauling. Alexis was always saying that back then when they lived in Alaska, calling up that internal landscape as an answer to the unforgiving one outside.

Alice took it as meaning, *don't try to change me, I have powerful forces on my side.*

❧

On the night Alice proposed, the air grew warm and heavy and the snow began to blow sideways across the valley. Alice had never seen anything quite like this before, but Alexis seemed relieved. "This is not a good thing," Alexis said, and was soon rewarded for her insight when the electricity began to cut in and out.

"Where are the flashlights?" Alice asked. She had no idea.

They moved upward from the basement into the living room and then to the bedroom above that, stepping like children, hands on the walls for extra guidance. "Slow down," Alice said, or at least she *thought* she said it. She kept so many of her protests inside back then that it was sometimes hard to tell what spilled over from her head into her voice.

"It's not where it should be," Alexis said. She was standing at the back of the walk-in closet, digging in a cardboard box.

Alice remembered the storm with a clarity that alarmed her. Everything would go dark and then, just as Alice thought, *ok, that's it,* everything would go bright again, and she'd spot Alexis positioned just a little differently, here, then there, then over there, like a series of photographs. In each one Alexis looked grim and determined, her usual look, her usual attitude, except caught like this she seemed *more* grim, *more* determined, more *Alexis*.

The closet stood in disarray: sweatshirts and scarves and the old sweater she hated, the one she had knitted when knitting still seemed like something she might contribute to the collective household. Alexis was always calling it that with a slight Marxist flair, a man's sense of macho determination. Sometimes Alice thought of politics as men fighting men in opulent rooms. When the voices grew too loud it would all spill over onto a battlefield. Alexis rifling through the closet meant only that Alice would have to clean it up later.

"Hold on," Alice said. "Let's talk."

"We have more important things to do," Alexis said.

Because it wasn't just the night of the storm. It was the night of the proposal, the night when Alice slipped the collar of reality for just a little while.

"You didn't have to answer so quickly," Alice said.

"So I should have lied then," Alexis said. "For what? To spare your feelings?"

She muttered the word *feelings* the way she usually said *shit* or *fuck* or *action movie*. To be polite, Alice wanted to say, but that word, polite, would have sounded even more ridiculous than feelings. It was so strange how it had happened, as if Alexis speaking the word *no* had brought about the snow and wind. Although maybe it was Alice's words that had really done it, the stupidity of asking such a thing of a person like Alexis.

Down they went, as if the photographs were flipping backward, Alice's fear balanced by a kind of detached amusement. It was sort of fun to see Alexis unprepared, hiding her confusion. Was she afraid too? Alice remembered her once capturing a bat in a dishtowel, holding it up to watch the mouth open and close as if it were begging for food. "It wants to bite me," Alexis had said, and then she had puckered her lips into a fake kiss.

When the place finally went dark for the last time it was more of a relief than anything else. "Well, that's it then," Alice said.

Yes, all the talk of love and commitment had somehow caused this. She had summoned it all, as if those words were a kind of spell. "I'm going outside," Alexis said from somewhere in front of her. "Follow me."

They were a long way from true danger yet, but they seemed to be walking casually in that general direction.

﷼

Alexis never talked about the other stories, the ones that ended in white instead of red. She seemed only interested in disaster, and she spoke about it as if the blood on the farmhouse floor, the vanished children, all of *that* was the happy ever after. Of course, danger is here too, right in the room, squatting on the floor beside Alice's bed, underneath the bed, or deep inside her brain and belly. She is sliding in and out of something a lot like sleep. And she wakes to this thought—the thought that doom is the inevitable happy ending—as if from a perfect, complicated dream. But it's not a dream, it's just a question that won't leave her alone, and for a moment she thinks she's back in Alaska and the body next to her belongs to Alexis, a shape as lean as a bone with a birthmark like a button in the small of the back.

Except it's a double mistake, because there's no body at all. She's *alone* in this bed, this room smelling of flowers and sweat and even the apple juice on the nightstand. It all has the pungency of magic, the randy old quality associated with roots and dirt. She swears she can even smell the thirty-year-old wallpaper. Her fingernails and tongue. *I'm the body*, she thinks. What had she said exactly in that long ago? That they should *make it official and tie the knot*. Such a silly way to put it. And then the storm had rolled in and the power had gone out. When she woke early the next morning she found the whole north side of the house covered in jagged ice. Through the windows she could see a soft impression of trees and snow and the truck. It appeared as an impressionist painting, a blue shape floating in white. And not just now, but then. This was not a trick of memory.

She could not read the thermometer and she could not open the door when she tried. Even when she braced herself and tugged it wouldn't budge.

She blew out a stream of fog and felt again like the little girl she once was walking through the snow on the way to school back in New England. Except she was an adult and she was worried about the pipes in her house freezing, about herself, and—she realized this with a rush of guilt for not having thought it earlier—about Alexis still sleeping, a faceless mound beneath heavy blankets. For a moment Alice imagined that she might be dead. That seemed the only thing that might stop her from nursing the stove all night, from taking care of things.

On the other side of the house she could see the yard clearly, the swing set left by the last family who had lived here and the tree line beyond that, the long garden beds covered in tarps. Sometimes she and Alexis sat out there on the swings and simply hung suspended while they talked, occasionally nudging the swing into motion with a foot in the dirt. They had done it enough that each one had her own swing, Alice on the left, Alexis to the right. Last week they had sat out there and talked about something, but now she couldn't remember the nature of the problem or if it had been solved, just that it had been important, was *still* important. Alice braced her knee against the doorframe and pulled and pulled and finally she was outside and part of the ice-covered countryside. She stood there for a moment breathing hard—she could hear her breath thrumming in her head—and then she reached back inside and grabbed her coat.

Not *her* coat. The coat Alexis wore when chopping wood and it smelled of a particular mix of birch and sweat that made Alice think of sex, the sex she realized she had been dreaming about in her fitful sleep. She could at least play around with the fake recollection of it as she moved through the cold. That was enough.

Years later and carnality has tiptoed back into her life. The source sits deep in her body, but she finds the deepest pain and frustration in small things—the way her tongue sits stiff in her mouth, her dry hands cracked at the knuckles, and the tedium of her own discomfort. She has been sipping at the dregs of that long-ago moment for hours. If the flashlight was a comfort then so were her lover's small breasts, the slope of her belly. Alexis is ageless, and even now that small body resists her will.

❧

"There are no American men," Alexis used say. "Not like in the South. In

Uruguay farmers read Borges. Your car mechanic in Uruguay, yes, he likes football, he likes to drink, but he will at least talk to you about Marx while he looks at your tits. In America they are boys."

Alexis had lived in South America once with a man, a painter and sailor, and she sometimes liked to bring it up as an amusing little story. Her Spanish, she said, had been terrible, and the sun had burned her pale skin. At parties men would ask if they could touch her hair.

But Americans, she'd say, and she'd laugh.

That was part of the seduction when they met—

This talking about men. Alexis presented her experience in South America as a courageous and foolish thing, a kind of depravity, and Alice had no equivalent. She had never been with one. It was as if she had never tasted a boiled hot dog. Alexis would bring up this or that one, most often to disparage, but also to compliment some animal part of them: an appetite for sex bordering on gluttony, a disregard for social codes, an especially memorable part of their anatomy. Was she saying that she would never return to that world or that she might? Those conversations seemed like small threats, like the fairy tales—the same exotic worlds, the same strange beasts.

Instead of saying *tie the knot* she should have said *you are mine*.

She remembers shimmying across the changed landscape. By the time she reached the truck her arms were extended airplane-style to keep from falling. The driver's-side door was sealed shut too. Icicles ran down from the undercarriage to the ground. And the power lines stretching down into the gully. They had been ripped loose. She began to walk up the driveway, but her progress was disheartening. On the road she saw the long line of mailboxes encased by ice. No cars coming either way, but that wasn't unusual. She stepped into the road and began to make her way. It felt like she had landed on a different planet, that she might encounter anything out here. And what was she doing anyway? After twenty feet she stopped and took off her shoes. It was easier to slide in her stocking feet. She was wearing wool socks so the cold didn't touch her immediately, and she held a boot in each hand and moved as if skating. Although she had no destination in mind she moved as if she did have one. She even thought, *I'll be there soon*, as she reached the intersection with the bullet-spattered stop sign. Once they had almost gone off the road there after an evening of too much wine back in town, but Alexis had reached out from the passenger's seat at the last second and given the wheel a twist. *My hero*, Alice thought, remembering the gesture with a mix of irritation and lust. She thought about falling on the long downward slope, but it didn't happen. Thinking about it seemed to ward it away, one spell against another, and then she was on the main road and yes, she was almost there.

Alice remembers the clouds above like a great ornament, but of course, that would be a deception of the mind, because the sky would have been dark. She came to this memory seeking a small, warm body and instead she's moving further into the cold, into the ambition of her remembrance, her imagination. Yes, she took off her shoes. So much easier to just slide your feet. And yes, she laughed for the first time in a long time at the damage the weather had brought. But did she really slide so easily across that glacial surface? *I am the first*, she remembers thinking.

The window is dark and so is the television. A kind of secret triumph. She feels it even now.

Because what would Alexis have said if she had told her? That such things were not possible? No, not that, although of course anybody would *think* that. No, Alexis would have sighed as if Alice were trying to *upstage* her, and then she would have told her own story of someone back in Sortavala who had died from walking in such a storm. In the town where she grew up people always seemed to be dying as a result of their own foolishness. For some reason Alice found this charming. There was a justice to it, a moral neatness, like a glutton dying of starvation, and it was especially pleasing because she did not think the stories applied to either of them.

⚜

Up ahead something like burned logs fallen from a truck.

Not logs. Not bats. Birds. She knelt and tried to pick up the first one, but it was frozen to the ground. A raven and its eyes were open within the chrysalis of ice, one of its wings fanned open. Then the next and the next, each one a perfect statue, the same and also entirely unique. Finally, she found one she could tug and free and she held it in two hands. Another dozen or so awaited her further up the road, a trail of them leading into to the main pass where she had to tilt her feet sideways to make it up the hill. She didn't feel a thing for the ravens. They seemed as much a design as the clouds in the sky. She could feel the sweat pooling in the small of her back. If anything, she grieved for her own dignity as she crouched low and made apelike movements up the hill. Just a few minutes before she had been traveling so effortlessly.

At the hilltop she found another half dozen, some with their wings splayed full open. The storm had hit with such incredible force that it had caught them in full flight. Except that such a thing *was* impossible, wasn't it? She did not really know this place she lived in. What was possible and what wasn't. Alexis would know except she was still asleep. Alice saw this as a fact as solid as the hard shape she cracked free from the ground. Its eyes were so black it made it hard to imagine that it had ever been alive.

Except it did not seem dead either.

She put it in the pocket of her jacket. Alexis's jacket.

Then she found another one and pried that one loose as well. It did not feel as if she were saving them, not exactly, but it was more than collecting them. She found a third, the largest by far, and freed that one as well.

She went down the other side in the same ape crouch and at the very end of the incline gravity forced her into a spastic run. In a moment she was on the ground and for the first time she truly felt the cold and stillness. She stared up at the sky and thought what the birds must be thinking. It was like a sheet of music she had seen once as a young girl, that beautiful and inscrutable, and then it was gone just like the memory of where she had seen the music and with whom and the song it granted you access to if your fingers knew how to make the right motions on the piano. She did not think about moving for a solid minute and when she did her knee hurt badly enough that she made a sound of protest. Tomorrow Alexis would call her an idiot. No, not that word, but something like it, something well-chosen and unique. Even in that exotic landscape, this place of pure imaginings, she could not conceive what it might be.

Except maybe there wouldn't be a tomorrow. Over the ridge some of the trees had fallen and taken out still more trees in a vast wave of motion now so absolutely still that it held her like a great painting. Trails of ice moved down the broken power lines to shallows of bluish ice she could see clearly through some mechanism that eluded her. It shouldn't have been this clear, this indelible. It was just for her. So she moved deeper into it. She had to pass under the largest tree and then over another. She flexed her fingers in a vain attempt to warm them. If she lost one she'd never hear the end of it.

Just the day before it had been autumn. The leaves were preserved in webbing of ice. As she pushed through them they made a soft breaking sound. She emerged again into bright daylight and there it was, the other side. One of the ravens had fallen loose from her pocket and she bent to pick it up, its wings splayed like a fan. She smoothed the feathers, stroked the head. She remembers all of this. She is not creating it. It was hers, is still hers, as much as the warm apple juice and the smell of the sheets.

꽃

Inside Ivory Jack's the men sat at their usual places. Of course, she thought, of course they'd be here. One of them—the one she recognized—slumped at the bar with his face in both hands as if he had been crying. She knew him by the slope of his back and his long mangy hair and the bright orange vest he wore over a heavy work shirt. Once he had said to her, "Excuse me, ma'am," but his face had worn a look of irritation. Now he seemed almost beautiful.

Alexis liked to come here and sit at the bar and then, after two beers, slide an arm around Alice's shoulder and pull her in shoulder to shoulder. A few heads might turn in their direction. She always looked back, made hard eye contact.

Another leaned against the stove. His eyes were open. He seemed ready to say hello, but he stood motionless. In the kitchen—she knew she was an intruder here, but who would stop her—she found the sink full to the brim with ice, a single air bubble beneath the surface, that and eggshells and on-ion scraps in the drain. Behind her the double doors stood open and snow blew in and out of the place in a tidal motion. She had to slide across the floor to reach the other end of the bar. Three men sat in a row with food and drinks in front of them. The first man held his drink almost to his mouth. The beer ran up the bottleneck and down around his hand. It seemed like a second long-fingered hand was holding his own. She swore she could hear, if not a heartbeat, then something from inside him.

The men reminded her of the ravens and she wanted to touch each one, look into each still life. She did not want to save them—she knew they did not need saving—but to sit with them a while, that seemed a neces-sary thing. She was moving slower. Her hands were not cold at all and that seemed a bad sign. Her toes too. Why had she come here? To push up close to the man in mid-drink and watch the changing inner world of his iris. She saw it again: a flicker of a foreign idea. His shoulders glistened. His hair fell in icicles.

She moved her face in closer, as if to kiss him, but definitely not to kiss him. She just wanted to see. Touching him with her bare hands would have caused her harm so she moved as close as possible, until she could see a thin white scar running from his eye to his ear, as thin as a pen tip. And then she noticed it continued, interrupted by the left eye, across the bridge of his nose, where it stopped just short of the other eye. She tried to imagine the source of the injury and came up with nothing except for some kind of machine a man like this might use, a heavy cable or sharp something, but she knew it might just as well be a fishing line, a child's toy. It was most likely not visible unless in a moment like this. Not even a lover might see it, insulated as they were by the dark and the narcissism of attraction.

She thought very quickly of listening to his chest but not out of any kind of concern. She simply wanted to know what it sounded like, or what its silence might sound like, so she bent her head in without touching. She could only hear her own breath, watch the shapes it made against the man's opened face. His lips were too large and his fingernails were as white as china. She did not feel sorry for him. She did not even like him, really. Normally he would be full of grunting energy, boasts, sardonic humor, but now the best parts of him seemed laid bare: a kind of helplessness usually disguised by the engine of his will. And she did like his hands. Big hands with ugly oversized knuckles. He wore a bracelet but no rings. The top half of his thumb was missing. So different from those other hands.

She found the two rings in the coat pocket, just where Alexis had placed them after the failed offer. They were so cold now that they seemed to belong to him. Silver rings, less than a hundred dollars each. She had thought their cheapness might tip Alexis into saying yes. Trick, she thought, not tip, not convince, their cheapness a mockery of the institution even as they entered it. She coughed and her cough echoed to the far corner and back again. It seemed to rouse something in the eyes of the men, but they did not move. Could they hear her? She thought that yes, maybe they could, and that if they could then she should say something. But what? It seemed important to get her words exactly right. Once Alexis had told one of them, or possibly a man a lot like them, to shut up, and she had pushed back the barstool and sent a drink spilling across the bar. What had that been about again? Alice couldn't remember. She couldn't remember lots of things Alexis had done, but they remained somehow. She lowered her head a little bit more to the center of his body, the flat of her palm against the ice. She thought she did hear something, a kind of low throb pulsing into her arm. Her hand ached, but she kept it there.

A person discarded so much of it as they went along. She couldn't remember what Alexis had done for a living in South America, or if her hair had been long or short when they first met, or which summer it was when she ate too much ice cream and grew momentarily chubby, so that at night in bed she called out in mock pain in the dark. She couldn't see that sleeping face in her mind's eye or rather, she could, but only long enough to get the most general impression.

Here was another face, this other sleeping figure, and she raised her chin again to take it in. She watched the scar and it seemed to grow into a sharp white thread running right through the staring eye. Shut up, Alexis had said, but the man had laughed quick and sharp like it was all just a bad joke. It was this man. She was sure of it.

The more she looked the more she noticed, and the more she noticed the more she wanted to look. It cured nothing—not confusion and not old love—but she wanted to look. The nub of his thumb reminded her of a child's penis or maybe an eyeless little sea creature. She decided it was beautiful. She decided it was ugly. She was right there, right up against it, and then she was coughing—she is coughing—and she hears the thrum and click of the air conditioner and the name of this place—Page, Arizona, like the thing you read and turn—returns to her. One of the children has refilled her glass and one of the grandchildren has placed a small stuffed dog in the crook of her neck, but that could have been an hour ago. It could have been yesterday. They are all trying their best. Friends, family, even the ex-husbands—they've tried to make her comfortable.

Alexis and her stories, they had been right, but not in the way she had presumed. Or even in the way Alice had presumed. They were not warnings. They simply presented a clear choice between two opposites: the mystery of the forest and that other thing: the life Alice has been living since then.

❦

Cold felt worst as the body warmed. Alice stood first on one leg and then the other, tugging at her wet socks, and the pain radiated from her toes into her heels and up her legs. The socks looked like dead animals and she laughed louder than she had in a long time and even that did not bring

Alexis up the stairs. To wake her she had to push her own cold body against the other one, the warm one wrapped in blankets in the powerless house.

"Jesus," Alexis said. "You're wet."

"And freezing," Alice said. It was a boast, but it was also a secret, and it felt good to share it with this person she loved. "Here," she said. "Let's do this," and her hands pulled the other body into a rough tug. She could feel the sharp tailbone against her tummy. Sometimes Alexis seemed like nothing but bones and skin and a stern voice. Even with Alice on top of her holding her body down Alexis spoke directions: just a little bit that way, faster, slower, fingers right there, yes, no, yes. When speaking like this the body lost its wholeness. It became a series of parts, a jigsaw puzzle of breasts and ass, leg and neck. The man had become that too, in a way, first under her scrutiny, and then again as the ice broke apart. The ravens in a row along the bar and maybe the two rings next to them? Or had she never made it out past the tip of the driveway? She is trying to remember it all, to birth it out of this hot bed and body.

She is cold and she's hot and she's the muscled thing creeping into the house when everybody is asleep. She's the one who can't be trusted despite her constantly saying *love, love, love.* She is grabbing this small woman and holding her down and why *this* story right now after all this time? The body is in her arms and she is telling it that everything is okay, that it is safe, but it buzzes with alarm. For a moment she is sure. Her touch is causing it harm. But it's also a deep solace. After all these years to not be comforted by the thought of her own grown children, but by this woman, always this woman. A woman she had not forgotten about, but at least had reduced to a size she thought appropriate, manageable. The first couple of years after their separation Alice had expected a letter addressed from some faraway place. She had braced herself for it appearing in her mailbox, the unfolding of it, the kind words, the inarguable proof of resiliency. Gradually such a gesture seemed impossible. By then the words would not have harmed her in the safety of her new coupling. It was as if Alexis had said, *do what you want with our story*, including those last embarrassing moments.

Once when she was fifteen Alice had been caught masturbating. She had simply forgotten to lock her bedroom door. That last sex with Alexis felt like that too: the same shame, the same annoyance at having one's privacy violated, this time by the squirming body beneath her. "Yes," it said. "No."

"Quiet," Alice told it back.

Their bodies had slowed to an occasional spasm.

"I love you," it said. Alice could hear the sobbing.

It had been surprising, surprising and disappointing. Alexis had begged in the most ridiculous way. She seemed about to shake apart. And the sounds. The more sounds she made the more resolute Alice grew as she explained why things weren't working out, how this was best for both of them. Did anybody ever make such sounds before or since? A low keening wail as if up from a deep hole inside herself. Even then she seemed unreachable, as if this were just a performance delivered from a stage. Not all that different from Alice's ongoing performances in this bed. Who knew dying could be so embarrassing?

"Get up," Alice told her, with a kind of shocked disgust.

And Alexis *did* stand up, and wiped the back of her arm across her wet face, and said, "I'm sorry," the voice a tiny little thing in the dark.

Alice had disregarded that moment, had nudged the memory away because it did not fit inside the frame. Because without that moment—that very real thing—Alexis could fall into myth.

But not myth, not really, because Alexis had moved past that stage onto the next one. She had been mostly forgotten until resurrected by boredom and pain to enter back into her life like the wolf into the plot. A punishment, in a way, a revenge, but also an unexpected gift. It was the wolf that made those stories interesting. Its appearance saved those old Russians from happiness, from the clarity of unforgiving sunshine. "Get up, get up," Alice had told her lover, but she had been secretly pleased. She feels this pleasure again years later, as if it is a thing to swallow and savor.

She decides to stay in this world a little longer.

# Fare Forward Voyagers

We paused in our work and stared down the tree line, waiting for the dog to appear at the bottom of the gully, a black shape cast against the winter. "Stupid thing," Nate said. "He's off to find some shit to roll in."

But then the lean figure appeared, head down and running fast, transmuted into an arrow of pure joy, his target the vole he chased through the underbrush. The dog's body arced up and forward through the deep snow. The motion looked like swimming, the breaststroke maybe, and all that frozen land had become ocean. The black arrow vanished behind the trees, then appeared again even further out, part of *that* world now—the gulley and broken birch trees and moose trails—and definitely not mine. "That's a dog who knows his own mind," Nate said, and he shoved the boxes into the truck bed.

"It's really going to come down," I said, because the sky glowed dirty silver.

We were walking boxes back and forth from the cabin to the truck and I was wondering why I had waited so long into October to do the crazy thing I was doing. But the idea of waiting until summer rolled back around seemed even more crazy. Two troubled daughters waited for me in Seattle, one with a bad job, the other with a bad marriage, both with kids. We were going to be together for the first time in years. "I think it might, Mary," Nate said, as he inspected the sky. "I wouldn't be surprised anyway."

He carried two boxes to my one, all books, all heavy, but he had a point to make. Fifty-six years old but he could still do this kind of thing. Brokenhearted too, from a recent difficult split, but that wouldn't stop him. His face was still boyish, I decided, despite the mangy beard and dark circles, all the flaws I noticed when in a particular frame of mind. The dog shrank to a speck now, out where the telephone lines stretched over the hill and toward the city. Nate didn't even bother calling after him. I said, "I'm a little worried." But by my next trip to the truck the dog was back, right there in the driveway, his whole body shaking with triumph. It was one of Nate's new dogs and I didn't remember his name, so I just called him *boy* as I ran my hands up and down his body. I knelt and felt his warm breath against my face and I knew he had just killed something. "God," I said. "You smell like death," and I laughed.

He broke away from me and back down the hill.

I found Nate inside, sitting on a milk crate drinking black coffee from a paper cup, and I made a joke about his laziness, a second one about his dog, but I sat down too. I did the math in my head: six trips for each of us, six boxes for me, twelve for him, maybe twenty books in each box. I saw each book as a decision I had made. When taken together they were as definitive as a marriage or crime. This was a life of sorts and soon it would be somewhere else. "I'm going to sit down too," I said, and I collapsed on the floor. My stomach was calling for something, anything, to fill it, but I had emptied out the pantry cabinets yesterday. Now there was nothing but some milk and cans of beer in the fridge, a box of Cheerios I would eat by the handful when driving. "We really should get some food," I said.

Nate made a noise like it didn't matter to him one way or another. "You're going to like it there," he said after a while.

"This from the man who thinks every state in the union but two are hellholes."

"And Hawaii is on its way too," he said, and then, when I just smiled instead of laughing, "Did I ever tell you about the time I spent on the Big Island?"

"Of course you did," I said.

"Yeah," he said. "That long-haired guy out there, I must have told you about him, the one who played the guitar and sang those songs about fish and birds? Christ, he was amazing. Except for the songs. Birds. Always with the birds. But I would have done anything for him."

His face had sharpened, grown younger, and I knew he had remembered something. A kind of accident of the mind, the equivalent of finding a folded dollar bill on the sidewalk. "From the sounds of it you did," I said, and he grunted, just like before when I had asked him if he was hungry.

"And then I wrote him that letter."

This surprised me. I had never heard about any letter.

I said, "Yeah, the letter," because I didn't want to put even the smallest ripple into this perfect little moment. He added something about it being a different time back then, when people actually sat down and placed their thoughts on paper, one after another. There was something fantastic about that, even when those thoughts were designed to maim. He made a motion with his hand as if placing each thought carefully on the empty air. He was trying to be funny again, sort of, but also serious. He had a way of living in both of those places simultaneously, like a lot of men I knew and had known. I had never understood it, not as way of being, not as a survival tactic even, but it could be endearing. I said, "I've never done anything like that. I don't think I have it in me."

"Too nice."

"Too lazy."

The snow had come. I noticed it over his shoulder through the cabin window. The truck cap was open and the boxes exposed. The dog had probably charged back down into the gulley or was just now hurtling out of it. Nate smiled and said something about the letter again. Apparently, he had found an old wound, or some combination of old wound and funny story, that he wanted to pick at. He said, "Once you know someone for about a year, that's when you have all the ammunition you need. That's all it takes. One year." A shadow had moved across his face but he was grinning, and I wondered if he was in pain. I had suddenly remembered him telling me, a few years before, about a bad back, how he was always pushing through soreness when chopping wood or even bending over his truck engine. This forgetting seemed like a pretty horrible thing to do, but at least I was patient as he tried to remember the words he had used in the letter. One of them was *compromiser*, another *thief*, because of a missing jacket. Worse than that. *Talentless Faggot. Wannabe rock star.* A bad driver, a bad lay, a bad cook. A hypocrite. A folk singer.

"Yeah," I said. "I never did anything like that. How long was it?"

"We dated for about a year."

"No," I said. "The letter."

"God," he said. "It went on and on. Ten pages."

"It was a gift," I said. "It settled the deal. You showed yourself to be an asshole. It made everything easier for him."

He made his little grunting sound for a third time.

"An act of kindness," I said.

"I never thought about it that way before."

"Wait," I said. "I do have a story like that." I didn't know if it was a good idea or not, sharing it, or just another rash decision like moving here, like moving back, but I decided, then and there, that an occasional rash decision could keep the blood pumping, and so I told him, "It was with my ex-husband."

"I figured," he said. "The famous painter."

"And the physical therapist."

"Sure," he said. "His new muse."

"He wasn't really famous until much later," I said. I didn't know why that seemed important except that I remembered many long talks about money, bills spread on the kitchen table. I had been working part-time as a schoolteacher and trying to paint myself, little studies of rocks and trees laid down on small squares of canvas and then stacked in the pantry with my other projects: empty canning jars, gardening tools, knit blankets, and scarves.

"I wonder if they're still together?" Nate asked. I had told him about them before, of course, at first as jokes at their expense, and then the jokes changed and I became the target, my innocence in the face of hard realities. And then the humor drained away and it all became serious, after we had moved through a whole cycle of seasons in Alaska and Nate had lost a lover to cancer. Walking through the hill trails I looked straight ahead and told him the details like I was reciting them from a page tugged fresh from the typewriter. I was still feeling the effects, more than two years later.

We sat there and I considered pushing myself into motion, back to the boxes and then to the chairs, the kitchen table, the rugs rolled up and stacked along the wall. The snow outside had picked up, but it was nothing terrible. I knew it could stop as quickly as it started and leave the world outside transformed by whiteness. A bad time to be leaving the state though, all things considered. I said, "Talentless. That was never the problem with Jason. Too much talent. That was an issue."

But now I was fumbling. I said, "I don't know how to explain it," and then I tried to explain it. Even as I opened my mouth I knew it would come out wrong, but I reminded him about things I had told him before: the series of affairs, the occasional crying confession, and then Jason's busted ankle and his weekly visits to the physical therapist, where light exercise and ice packs evolved into lust and love. A woman fifteen years younger than me and four inches taller. I remembered her bouncing ponytail as she jogged around our small town.

She was the last one in the series, and it did not seem like love so much as a switching of allegiances from one infidelity to the next, as if all those other women had been betrayed too. Also, a compromising of his values, because the others had been intellectuals, chain-smokers, a sculptor, a photographer, a woman with a history of mental problems. I would stop at a traffic light and suddenly this girl would be there, ponytail bouncing, running in place at the crosswalk, looking both ways and then off again and out of sight. I allowed myself to imagine her body naked, stepping into the shower, her mind even and clear from her runner's high, hurt and guilt burned away as easily as calories.

Nate matched those details with his own. He remembered the paintings filling the living room, what would have been our living room if not for the paintings, the sheer desperation in them. This was before Jason's work grew smaller and more refined. Would they embarrass him now, or would he just see them as a necessary stage?

Nate had seen none of these but he knew them through my eyes.

"You know how hard I worked to stay friends with him," I said.

"Sure," he said. "For the kids."

I took a breath and decided that this was it. "I still had keys to the old house," I said. "It had been almost a year, but I still had a few things there. My paintings, mostly. I had abandoned them. We'd have coffee in the kitchen sometimes and talk about art and he'd say, hey why don't you take a painting back with you, and I'd always say no. Then he'd keep talking about this or that. Like a teacher talking to a student, I guess. That's what we had become."

"I can't imagine you that way," Nate said.

"That's the way I was. I was content with that, with being that person. At night the girls and I would sing and read books aloud in our new house. We painted the walls bright colors."

I considered what I thought of as the old house. Those walls had been brightly painted too. I hadn't been aware of it at the time, but I had tried to duplicate it. I said, "I couldn't bring the barn with me though. I told you about that barn. Falling apart, but it was beautiful."

"Sure," he said, and I remembered the sight of it on the horizon, splintered open and leaning to the south like the dogwood trees. The barn led me to the other memory of destruction, and I withheld it for a moment, recalling the weight of the porch boards underneath my feet. It had been raining lightly and my hair was damp, my glasses speckled with water. Jason and his young bride were nowhere to be found. I knew she had an apartment on the other side of the valley.

"So you went there," he said. "What for?"

"I don't know," I said. "I just found myself there. I'm serious. I just wanted to talk to him."

"And then what did you do?"

"I went inside."

I could have told Nate that I was outrunning myself, as a desperate attempt at improvement or just to see how it felt to be her. I could have told Nate that I was bringing by a small gift, because I did do that sometimes, as a spur of the moment thing, or when I was lonely. I would have looked equally ridiculous in running shorts and sneakers and a wet sweatshirt or holding a tinfoiled brick of banana bread. But I didn't remember. I was there as I often was and they were not.

The door was unlocked. I stepped into the living room.

Nate smirked. Now we were getting to the good part.

I remember running water from the tap, tilting my head sideways and bending and drinking. It seemed wrong to open a cabinet and remove a cup. I remember walking to the back of the house and staring down that hideous barn. When I returned to the living room I noticed new paintings, no more than sixteen inches across, all browns and yellows. I'd like to say that I saw something in them, and that's what caused me to do what I did next, but who knows? Once when I was small my friends, two neighborhood girls, and I had pulled back a large rock from the earth and found a centipede, writhing as if in pain, though I knew it wasn't in pain, that pain was something it might not even experience, at least not in the way I knew it. We took turns jabbing at it with sticks, turning it over the way a person might an egg, the way I had seen my mother turn eggs, with the slenderest attention. Then we poked the sticks deeper until the writhing mass became two pieces, then three. This was like that. There was no feeling in it, just a methodical sense of obligation. That was the right word. It was something that needed to be done. This is the only feeling I can find in my past that corresponds to the feeling of moving through that house. "I wasn't angry," I told Nate, although he looked skeptical. But it was true.

I was ready to stop right there.

I think his silence urged me on. If Nate had said a single word I would have said that's that and gotten back to work, laughed the whole thing off. But he didn't, so I pushed myself into the silence, like I was talking to myself. "You're not going to believe this," I said.

I could only recall what happened next as an outsider. I am that person, of course, but I also wanted to believe that I was someone else, and that the person telling the story had very little to do with the person in it. The person *in* the story, she was watching the barn. She was looking at the new paintings and then she was rifling through the cabinets. The pots and pans clattered as she pulled them out. That made everything else easier.

Nate wore his usual smirk but he was silent.

I told him about the jars of spice. I emptied them into the sink and then dropped them to the tile. The glass was thick enough that they didn't shatter. They broke apart like eggs into two or three pieces and then I picked up the shards and dropped some of them. I told him about the gardening gloves I found in the back room, my old gardening gloves, which I put on as I tore the curtains from the dining room windows. "Fingerprints," I explained.

"Crazy," he said.

The story had its own gravity now. All I had to do was keep going, let myself be drawn to its weight.

"Get this," I said. "I'm not making this up. On the VCR there was a videotape. A tantric sex tape. It's like it had been put there especially for me."

He laughed and so did I and I told him about beelining through the house to the back where I found something new: a dog chain running from the back porch to the storage shed. It was being used as a clothesline. Two towels hung from it like white flags. I took one, balled it around it around my fist, and smashed the back-door window, first just one pane but then the rest, six, seven, eight, nine. I made sure to stand outside and smash the glass inward. I was thinking that clearly.

"Oh God," Nate said. "Wow. In your gardening gloves."

"In my gloves," I repeated.

"Are you trying to show me how tough you are?" he asked. "So I won't be worried about you making this trip alone? Because I already know you're a tough lady." Half-joking, half-serious again, and I ignored it.

I pulled the cabinet from the wall and heard the plates clatter down, the silverware chime. Behind it was a small space where secret things gathered: dust, a few marbles, a paperclip, nothing that raised my interest except a piece of paper with phone numbers on it. No names, just the numbers, and so I returned it to the floor and then moved to the cabinet again. It took some shoulder muscle to get it up and against the wall again and when it did I walked to the kitchen, stood there at the sink and waited for the other moment, the moment back there in the dining room, to be over. "Then what?" Nate said. "Did you burn the place to the ground? Pee on the floor?"

"Yes," I said. "I peed on the floor."

"Christ," he said. "Really?"

"Nate," I said. "Of course not," but why did I think that was so ridiculous? I did run a knife across the kitchen table and then push it through one of my own paintings. I spilled a bag of rice on the carpet, pushed over the TV, tugged the phone from the wall. And then, when I was finished, I stole one thing, the videotape—no, two things, the videotape and the hammer—and I used one to smash the other when I returned home. "It wasn't satisfying," I said. "I don't know what it was."

Nate fell back and made a deep whistle. What could he say?

"I'm not finished," I said. "Two days later I got a call from the police."

"Damn," he said.

"My heart almost stopped. That was it. I don't know how to describe it."

"Try to describe it."

"I don't know how. But it was just a second, because this cop, he was extremely polite and concerned. He said, 'There's been a break in at Jason's house. They stole some jewelry. They stole some money. What a world, huh?'"

"And then what?" Nate asked.

"That was it. We talked about other things. It was a small town and he was just calling to gossip. Checking up on me. Maybe he thought I'd find some pleasure in it? After the divorce there were men in that place who were interested in me. I'm not sure."

"They liked you there in that town, didn't they?"

"They did."

"And Jason not so much," he said. He seemed to consider the whole thing as he might contemplate something in a store, an expensive coat or a piece of furniture. He smiled and said, "And you told me you didn't have a story."

I didn't know what to do with my hands so I put them on my knees.

Nate said, "You know what? Fuck it. I'm just going to tell you this. That letter, I never sent it. Okay? I wanted to but I didn't. Jesus, Mary. I don't know. What the hell. What the hell."

He said it twice, what the hell, what the hell, and then he coughed. I told him that it was okay, not to worry about it, he was telling me now, right? I told him I understood completely.

Because there's a part I didn't tell him either, and not just an omission: a substitution, a hack's magic trick, one card for another when nobody's looking. It felt necessary to turn Jason into a certain kind of person, for the sake of the story. For my sake. So what about this? No video placed in plain sight on top of the television, and so no hammer smashing down, no satisfying splinter of plastic. Which is not to say that tapes like this didn't exist. A number of them could have existed somewhere in the house, under the bed or in a drawer or even unnoticed out in the open. Certainly, there had been tapes like this when we had lived together, a couple I found ridiculous in their mix of spirituality and depravity, and one which I quite enjoyed. We both enjoyed it, had purchased it together actually, and so I called it up from my memory as if at the end of a long, gray rope and then placed it in my old house, my new story. I held it in my mind like a treasure, then I smashed it to bits and watched Nate's smile.

A substitution. Because I was not afraid, not rushed very much at all. I spent more than an hour in that house and when the cabinet was pulled from the wall and the dishes shattered on the floor, I wasn't finished. I moved upstairs and found the unmade bed, the sheets and blankets pushed to the bottom, a pillow on the floor, and I paused before picking it up and placing it back on the bed. Stupid, of course, considering the destruction downstairs, but that's what I did, and then I sat on the bed's edge and then I reclined and looked at the ceiling, up through the skylight and through the dark.

Possibly I was waiting for them to return and the shock—the punishment—that meeting would bring. There would be a scene. There would be consequences.

After a while I moved to standing again and made my way to the bathroom, where I washed my hands, listening to the reassuring sound of water in the porcelain. I was coming back to the world, or at least I was able to pretend that's what I was doing. I stood at the mirror behind the sink and noticed the water stains and flecks of toothpaste. I don't remember my own reflection, although of course that must have been there, a serious face: impenetrable even to myself. I found the latch and the mirror became a door leading even deeper into their private lives: bottles of shaving cream and dental floss and an arrangement of medications. So many medications actually, each with Jason's name, one for depression and one for anxiety and one for the side effects of the first. This was new to me. One read, take one hour before conducting sexual activity. The word conducting, that would have made Nate laugh, the image of waving arms, a tuxedo, a pompous crown of gray hair. The orchestra rising in volume. But I held all that back. Instead I said, "This is the thing. Months later we talked. Jason and I did. I was giving him a gift for his birthday, just a little trinket, just expensive enough not to be insulting, and we were standing on the porch. I'd like to say it was my first time back since the incident, but it wasn't. We had eaten lunch there a couple of times and once I had dropped by unannounced to give him a different gift for some other occasion. Anyway, everything was repaired by then. In fact, they were building an addition at the side of the house. The workmen were pounding away at the frame but there were no voices, and I remember thinking that it was a little strange that there were so many people, four or five, and not a word between them. Jason took the gift from me, small enough that he could put it in his pocket and wrapped with the same care I had always spent on gifts, on the ones I would give and the ones he would give too, when we were together. I am sure he noticed that—I wanted him to notice that. He said thank you and then he stopped, he still hadn't unwrapped the gift, and I could tell he was thinking hard about something."

Nate stared at an invisible point on the floor but he was listening hard. His face was tight as if concentrating on some desolate thought, but I knew that at any moment that face could break into a grin. I looked at the floor too, trying to match up my gaze with his own, and I told him about Jason looking tan and fit. Maybe he had taken up running.

"He said, 'Mary, last summer when we were away, was it you who broke in here?'

I gave him a look like, how dare you ask me something like that, and I said, 'Jason, I've never lied to you. Never.'

I let that come to rest in the air. Then I added, 'I did not break into your house.'

We measured each other, looking into each other's eyes. My open face, my sensible haircut and conservative makeup. I don't know what he saw. Finally he said, 'Thank you for the gift,' and he began to open it at one end."

Nate was measuring me too. Everything had stopped.

"Christ," he finally said, and he exhaled. He shook his head, greedy for more, and I could have kept going. But we returned to the heavy lifting. He picked up first one box, then another, went back for more. After a while he added, "And you told me you didn't have a story to tell. Christ, Mary. That was a million times better than mine."

He shouldered the boxes into the truck, shook them around until they angled just right against the others. I knew the story wouldn't end with him. There would be a night with a new lover or an old friend—Nate had many of both—when the well of his own experience would go dry and he'd say something like, "There was this woman I knew. A really sweet little thing. I had never seen her angry."

Which would miss the point, wouldn't it? Because it was not a story about anger. But when that new person imagined my face they'd color it red with blind rage. I could see it that way so clearly that I wondered if I had lied to myself too. Nate said, "We've been good to each other, haven't we? It's been a good few years."

"Sure," I said. "What are you getting at?"

"Don't know," he said. He shrugged. But I knew. I looked deep into that face the way my husband had into mine and I could tell he was holding something back, a cold judgment usually reserved for people you read about in the paper. And as I assessed it the dog appeared again, bulleting toward us. I heard him before I saw him and then there he was, a noise exploding in the dark. He was past me before I thought, *the dog*, because I had forgotten that he was out there, forgotten *everything* out there. He threw himself across the snow and the sight of that black shape striking forward almost snakelike caught me and brought me back and maybe it was the dark or the snow but I was frightened of that place I found myself in. Not a place, really, but the slenderest position in between places. The dog rattled off into the woods again and Nate threw a few curses at him and then I was all the way back, squarely in the now. The crunch of snow, the sharpness of the frozen air, the heft of those last boxes—it felt like I might stay there forever. But all of this happened a long time ago. I pulled out of the driveway and the nameless dog chased me down the road, barking at my tires. Nate headed in his own direction and took my life with him, possibly to share with others or just keep for himself. By the next day I was already at the border, gloved hands gripping the steering wheel, jaw set tight. I took the possibility of danger and placed it to one side, like a meal I preferred to eat a little bit later, and pushed myself down the road for a few thousand miles.

An idiot's journey. That's what I think of it now, but I saw incredible things, and then I shared them with my daughters.

# The Black Bear Month

Forty-two to forty-two and the big blonde chick kept mumbling Eskimo. She'd bump Heather's hip and say, "Eskimo." She'd drop her shoulder and push off and say, "Eskimo." She'd give her a secret shove when the ref wasn't looking and say, "Eskimo." Any word said that much began to lose its meaning, but with this one it was different. It was definitely getting more and more meaningful every time. "Aren't you getting tired?" Heather would say. "Don't you want to quit? Look at that belly on you. How much Kentucky Fried did you eat today? How many Big Macs?" The chick had thirty pounds and four inches on her, but you had to give back what you got.

"Eskimo," the chick would say without even looking in her direction, and then their feral cat point guard would lob pass her the basketball at the top of the key.

"You should be sumo wrestling, not shooting hoops," Heather would say. "And what's with the nose? I wouldn't fuck you if you were the last girl on earth." It was like talking to a wall except that the wall moved and sometimes knocked you over and tried to break your heart. "We fuck dogs up in Barrow," Heather said. "We fuck our snow machines. But even I have to draw the line somewhere. I'm so sorry, but there's just no attraction."

Heather knew she'd find bruises on her body in the hotel shower that night. Her mouth guard tasted of blood and lukewarm Gatorade and half the crowd had Tourette's. Delinquents and half-wit grandmas stomping their feet and waving Styrofoam number one hands. And they all loved that big blonde girl, number twenty-six, and they especially loved it when she backed Heather in with that meaty ass, held up her hand to receive the ball, and spun with the hook. Ugly shot but it kept rattling around and dropping in. Then the blonde chick would backpedal and give the nastiest little fist pump you ever saw and even though the crowd wasn't shouting the word—they were shouting the chick's last name—it was easy to imagine their chant as the reverberating echo of her enemy's voice repeating that one word over and over.

><

When Heather's team started the season with two solid home victories, her mother asked, "Why are you so excited? You know how this ends." But when she returned from the first road trip with three more victories, her brothers were waiting at the landing strip on their mud-spattered ATVs and Jason, the youngest, called out to her, "Five-o, Five-o," above the sound of the engines, as if they were calling her new name to her. Her team dissolved around her, splitting off and meeting parents and grandparents. Heather had scored thirty-two points in the blowout in Anchorage, including a half-time buzzer beater that even the home crowd had cheered.

But once she unloaded her bags and said goodbye to her teammates, all her brothers talked about was the stuff they always talked about. They gave her shit about her too-short hair and her smelly sweatshirt and Jason said the state troopers had arrested Kyle Shandy for shooting the new stop sign. They all thought that was pretty funny, although the only thing they did to show it was a bunch of sullen nods. A few weeks ago a story about anyone shooting anything—even a dog—would not have deserved retelling except to maybe just say, "He went on a bender again." Did they think she had been gone for years?

They took the ATVs down through the center of Barrow, going slow with her on the back of the lead vehicle, her arms wrapped around Jason's waist. People called out to them as they passed in their miniature parade. Then down to the beach, where they rode along the water, tires spitting up chunks of broken shell and rock. They slowed down to walking speed where the water met the sand and let the waves clean their tires. It was late but Charles Bekoy was still down there tying off walrus skins and throwing them back into the water. She smelled him first, the scent of death and fish, and then she saw him. He was bent low tugging on a knot. "Old fucker," Cody said to her with a tilt of his head.

"Back into the sea," Heather said. That was something Charles said as he did his work. Back to the sea, back to the sea. It was almost a song he sang, a lullaby to whatever he killed. He'd ease them out and then pull them back in, clean as a whistle, after the sea had done its slow work. The fog felt cool and wet on her bare skin—she was dressed in just a T-shirt and jeans and she was cold but she didn't care.

"You've got a split lip," Cody said.

"Yeah," she said.

"Good for you. I remember scoring forty with a broken hand."

The number and the injury had changed in response to her games. It used to be twenty-eight with a sprained finger.

Charles Bekoy stood behind them now. She couldn't hear his song but she could imagine it and she could imagine the skins floating beneath the surface, pulling the ropes tight. Her brothers liked to come down here and build fires out of plywood and branches and whatever the tide brought in. They pulled the ATVs around the blackened remains of their last party and spoke over the idling motors. In the nest of charred wood she could see some crushed beer cans and something else made of melted plastic. Sometimes they could get rowdy out here and other times they just watched the mist pulse across the water and envelop the boats at their moorings. Now they were talking about a pack of wild dogs they had seen earlier that morning up on the east side. Little scrappy things with open sores and broken ears. One of them had tried to sneak into someone's trailer and steal bologna off the counter. Bologna and mayonnaise. It trashed the place and got the jar stuck on its head. "A ten-dollar photograph," Jason said, because the trailer's owner had taken a picture, because mayonnaise cost seven ninety-nine at the local grocery. But the brothers just nodded their heads as if he had said something profound. Then he added, "Heather, do you have it all out of your system now?"

"Winning?" she asked. She gave some of the wreckage a light kick. It shifted and collapsed in on itself and she realized that the melted plastic was one of her old Barbie dolls. Whatever. She hadn't even touched it, let alone played with it, in years. She spun away from it and back to her brothers.

"C'mon," Timmy said. "Don't be that way."

The others nodded in agreement.

"When I came back from Portland five years ago I came back humble," Cody said.

Down the beach Charles Bekoy was casting out the first of five skins, moving into the water with his waders, scrambling sideways in a low crab walk. You had to bring them out far enough for the ocean to catch them and bring them down and then leave them dancing out there for a couple of days. From this distance the water looked as deep gray and hard as gunmetal and Charles seemed to be sliding across it on his knees.

"I don't know why you have to do all this shit," Cody said, but he didn't sound angry, he sounded sad. His arms were folded across his chest and his head lowered and shaking back and forth, a heavy thing he seemed to be trying hard to work loose from his shoulders.

Timmy said, "It's like you're showing off."

Jason added, "You don't know how much Mom loves you. You should see her back at the house. It's crazy."

"Don't mess this up," Timmy said, but she didn't know what they were telling her, or even what failure and success were anymore. She walked up the beach to the hill, her brothers following her slow on their ATVs. But when she reached the pole with its signs pointing every which way they motored past her down the slope, three across like bandits on horseback. From there she could see them getting smaller and smaller and then the trailer, the plume of fresh smoke. She wanted to tell the girl something important she had discovered: that luck was a thing you could grab and grip and hold and use just like any other tool.

"Mom," she said when she came in through the back door. But she couldn't think of anything else to say. Her mother stood at the stove making potato pancakes, her hands white with flour. She stepped forward and touched her chest to chest in an almost hug, her mother's hands raised like a surgeon just before going into the body.

Her father came into the room in his Carhartt overalls and pulled her in for one of his slap-back hugs. He smelled of the ocean and Old Spice. "Where are your brothers?" he asked.

"Coming," she said, because they'd roll in sometime, knock into things in the dark and laugh. Her mom returned to the spitting grease. She picked up a pancake and slapped it from palm to palm. "I'm going to see you on TV someday," she said. "When you're in the NBA."

"That's not even possible," she said. "Dad, tell her."

"Maggie," he said. "It's no women allowed in the National Basketball Association. They have their own thing, the women do. It's on TV too though. It's actually pretty good."

"There's always a first time," her mother said. The faint residue of her old accent like the tasty guck at the bottom of a cup of instant coffee. Heather loved to hear it creep into the edges of her sentences. It felt like a small branch she could follow down into the roots of her mother's history.

She still spoke of the beauty and harshness of New England winters by saying, "Seasons put you in your place. Like here." But other times, during a cold spell, the water of the Ikpiarjuk and the land formed a seamless blank vista, you could tell her mind had taken her back to a red farmhouse in New Hampshire and that she had decided this place was *nothing* like that. She'd screw up her face in disgust and turn away from the thought and back to her family, the work in front of her.

Always work, much of it involving grease or blood. They kept rabbits in wire cages on the back of the house. The children were forbidden from naming them. Heather and her sister did it anyway, things like *Sugar* and *Cupcake* and *Bugs* when they were younger, and then names like *Toby Keith* or *Michael Jackson* when they reached their teenage years. Heather had once fantasized that finding the exact right name—the one that would melt her mother's heart—would spare the rabbit's life. When it was time, her mother would pick a rabbit by some hidden rule of selection and grab it by the back of its neck. She'd hold it up and look it in over, the matted fur, the weight of the still object. Then she'd shake it out the way she might a damp rag, a flash of the wrist and it became something else, a thing to put on the table with instant mashed potatoes.

Her mother's right eye leaned slightly outward, a defect from birth, and as her fingers brushed across the backs of the rabbits that eye looked off in another direction, as if she were worried she might be caught in the act. That day in the kitchen after the road trip that expression had vanished. Even her eye seemed normal, kind of. "It's not like that, Maggie," her dad said.

Her mother patted down the first pancake with a rag. "The universe is full of possibilities," she said. "Anything can happen. Don't snuff out the magic in things."

She had never heard her mother talk like this but her father sighed as if he had heard it all before. She said, "The Angakkuq were the doorway between the spirit world and this world. They snuffed them out. We did. But not all the way. I think you're a new kind of Angakkuq." She looked at Heather and smiled without breaking the motion of her hands at the spitting pan. What was this except maybe happiness?

"Maggie," her dad said. "If you're going to talk that way, at least get it right."

Heather stood waiting for something to happen. All her confidence had left her. She could hear the engines coming up alongside the house, the footsteps behind her. Her sister had come into the room at its edge but her mother did not seem to notice. "I'm telling you because your father won't," she said. "The Angakkuq could run as fast as caribou. They could fly. And if you had a hard life you could become one and sometimes you were called on to visit Sedna the Sea Woman and comb her hair."

"Cut the shit, Maggie," her dad said, and his face had become a hot mask, a fake imitation of the smiling man. There were flecks of gray in his hair, in the braid running down his back and down his collar into his heavy jacket. He turned to Heather and tried to work the smile back into his features, but it didn't look right. "Don't listen to her," he said. "Just find your spots and shoot the damned ball."

❧

Forty-four to forty-four. Heather raised her hand like she knew the answer for the first time in her life. Then the ball appeared there on the tips of her fingers and she was turning. She could take this chick all night off the dribble so she faced her square up on the left side, a simple isolation move, and then stepped past her with a wide crossover. Because even when a wall moved it couldn't move well and no way was she going to let her team lose to West Valley like last year and the year before. How many now? More than a decade, flowing back into the lives of her brothers and cousins. Heather, youngest of five, one of two girls, saw it in the way they entered a room and how they smiled. It seemed like the typical shyness of tall men, but of course that wasn't it. Forty-four to forty-four and she could do this all night. She could do it tomorrow too and the day after. They had won in Portland and won in Anchorage and won in Juneau. They had even won in Seattle and then toppled through the city laughing and dizzy.

"Don't get cocky," Coach said but it was just a chip on her shoulder, an angel giving her advice.

At the end of the second half she changed hands and watched herself from outside as she did something she didn't think she could do: a finger roll from the left side above two defenders. The ball arced up and then in and she felt the contact, hard, to her face. She hit the court, but she could hear one of her teammates say, "Wow."

That shut up the crowd, at least for a moment. The big blonde chick walked away from the fallen body. But even then Heather could hear the word, "Eskimo," from the other side of the court, or maybe that was just an echo of the last time. She spoke from the floor looking up at the lights in the ceiling, the conference champion banners and stained tiles. "I could fuck something right now," she said to the open air. "I'm really in the mood. But not you, fat girl. Anything but you. Do you know why? I don't fuck losers." She was still talking as three teammates helped her up. "We don't fuck losers. We might fuck a moose once in a while, if it's a pretty one, but we have standards."

"Your nose is bleeding," Clarice Dickens said.

"How many fingers am I holding up?" Megan Powell said.

"Get off," Heather said, and she shook herself free from their hands. "I'm fine. I'm just speaking in tongues."

At the other end Heather crouched down and the blonde chick's ass kept pushing, pushing, pushing. And then again with the hook and the word. It was like the chick was digging a very narrow hole, as small as the shovel itself, but digging it very, very deep. The same thing over and over again, the motion of her arm, the word, the fist pump. Her hair was tied into a ponytail by a red rubber band and the ponytail bounced when she ran and it was getting to the point that Heather was seriously considering giving it a pull. Forty-six to forty-six but she had a lot left in the tank, she'd talk herself through this, and then she'd go home and never stand on the hill again. She decided that the pole itself was a kind of sign pointing down into the ground, to Barrow, the place where she lived. She tongued blood from her upper lip. It tasted pretty good.

"Want to hear a good joke?" the blonde chick said after another two. Was that the hint of a smile? Suddenly they were coming together. A tangle of arms and legs, a double foul, the ref between them.

Coach yelled, "Do not get kicked out of this game."

Someone in the crowd yelled, "Kick her out."

Her dad yelled down the long corridor of her imagination. "These mashed potatoes look like something you'd smooth over cracks in drywall."

"What's worse than an Eskimo?" the chick said, and then a pause. She answered herself. "Half an Eskimo."

Someone in the crowd stood up, cupped both hands to his mouth, and let out a throaty holler. He was calling the number on the back of her jersey, but she refused to look up there, even when the number transformed into her name. They knew her here. They had read about those other games and wondered how she had done everything she had done during this brief season. He seemed to be calling out to her for some kind of acknowledgment, a recognition that maybe she knew his name too. As she stood at the free-throw line her mother whispered in her ear, "Don't name them. All it will do is break your heart."

The evening of the eleventh win Heather crashed in through the back door to find the house empty. She found a mixing bowl and filled it to the brim with corn flakes, crushed the box and left it on the counter like an open book. Milk was too expensive—they never had any—so she put the bowl under the tap and ran cool water into it. Maybe they were still looking for her in the frenzied pulse of the crowd. She had slipped out through the locker room and across the back parking lot, running all the way home. She was upstairs in bed when Ashley entered the room. "Are you in here?" she asked.

"Yeah, I'm here."

"That was amazing."

"What was?"

"Don't be funny. You're always being funny. Are you eating something?"

She tried to chew as quietly as possible.

Her sister liked to sweep her hair across her face and then occasionally wipe it out of her eyes and smile as she talked to boys. She imagined her doing that now in the dark. After all, she had taught herself to do it when speaking with hunky sports heroes and that's pretty much what Heather had become, right? *Was in danger of becoming*, she thought, as if reading it from a sign displayed at the back of her mind. She said, "Do you know where my September issue is?"

Heather said, "It might be under my bed."

"I saw you up on the hill," she said. "By the signs. Whenever anybody stands up there it's a bad thing. Remember when Ashley kept going up there and then she overdosed?" Ashley had been a classmate of Heather's who had been especially good at English. She wrote stories about dragons and fair maidens with names as long and flowing as their gowns and hair. Sometimes she spoke of moving to California, the hole from which all these fantasies seemed to spill. "Yeah," Heather said. "It's not like that."

"I bet you're going to go to one of those places one day," her sister said. Paris. New York and London. If Ashley had a sign it might read *married with six kids*. But Heather tried to snuff out all her mean thoughts with more cornflakes. Maybe her mom's sign, long ago in New England, had read *Barrow*.

Her mom cracked open the door and spoke into the dark. "Where'd you rush off to?" she asked. "We were worried."

"Why would you be worried?" Heather asked. "You said it yourself. I'm not even a real person." The silence stretched on long enough that for a moment Heather thought her mother wasn't there anymore, had never been there. She closed her eyes and let the dark inside her. It felt like water. She was standing at the bottom of a lake for three, four, five days and soon they would pull her out and the initiation would be over. But no, she let the darkness, the freezing water, out with her next breath. She was still dressed in her uniform, sweat cooling on her skin. She was falling asleep with food still in her mouth. She could hear her sister fishing around under the bed and then she heard her father's voice saying something about exploring, like she was a mountain climber or jungle hunter. He was speaking to her mother in the hall but then something shifted and he was speaking directly to her from some place beyond the dusk of her brain. "You've heard about my teenage years before I found your mom. And your mom found me." He liked to say that Heather's mother had poked a pinhole in his heart. The anger had bled out over the years in a barely noticeable dribble like oil from an old engine. He still liked to walk to the outskirts of town and smoke a doobie, sure, but he hadn't sold anything in two decades.

"It's not the same thing," Heather said. "You were in jail for almost a year."

"Your father likes to tell tales," her mother said. "That jail was nicer than this place."

"Right," Heather said.

"We have no objections. It's not like we're religious people anymore."

"Thank God for that," her dad added.

But really it was just the hand sliding under the bed, searching for the magazine. It was just her parents arguing in the hall the way they did, about God and geography and tradition and marijuana and a hundred other things. It was just desire and fantasy. She stood beneath the signpost positioned at the center of town. Two dozen signs and one of them pointed as far as Paris and showed the number of miles to get there: more than four thousand. If you followed the arrow you couldn't see the educated city, of course, just the gray ocean so still it seemed you might be able to walk across it and through the wall of sea fog as if through a veil in the world. If she looked the opposite direction she could see the small trailer park at the bottom of the south slope. The girl didn't come outside until noon at the earliest, but she was clearly visible when she did, and she'd make coffee on her stove and then sit in her plastic lawn chair and think her small hippie thoughts. If she saw her outside then Heather could join her, maybe bring her a little pot from her father's hidden stash and they'd talk about how beautiful everything was in this incredible place. How lucky that Heather had lived here all her life, although luck did not exist, luck was just a name you sometimes gave to unexplainable things, of which there were many. At this the girl would smile hazily and make a motion of her hand to indicate the two bodies, one in the lawn chair, the other squatting and tensed as if to jump: Heather's body, waiting. Heather had to listen to a lot of this kind of talk before the girl's mouth would finally run out of things to say and they'd head into the dark of the trailer together as if into a damp cave. It smelled of grilled cheese and blueberry incense sticks and the complicated alchemy of the other girl's unwashed body. Always when she stood to enter she thought of the pole up on the hill and arrows pointing in all directions at the world's greatest cities.

❧

Forty-eight to forty-eight and the blonde hair chick set up for another barrelhouse hook, squatting like she might take a dump, hand waving, hey everybody look at me as I am about to take a colossal dump right here at the foul line. The crowd was throwing stuff: paper cups full of lemonade, balled-up candy bar wrappers, even a box of tissues smashed flat and landing just on the periphery of Heather's vision. The crowd threw baseball caps and popcorn and a flattened tube of toothpaste. They threw old telephone bills and a broken baseball bat. A number one foam finger and a baby pacifier.

"You wouldn't believe the things I've fucked," Heather said. "I've made love to trees. Permafrost birches. The kind you can push over like movie props. I've fucked old ladies with fish breath. But I know when to say no and I'm saying no to you right now no matter how many times you beg." Making love to a tree didn't seem like such a bad idea. It was late October in central Alaska and they had already missed the blazing yellow of the valley. She had seen it only once, when she was ten and her mother had moved to Fairbanks with her and her sister. That had lasted just a year and during that time her mother had talked often about going even further south to cities like Seattle and Portland where you didn't have to struggle just to survive. But what Heather really remembered from that time was the sound the wall-to-wall made when she slid her feet across it, the divided highway splitting the town in half, the smell of wildflowers.

"Keep your head in it," Coach yelled, a fifty-four-year-old woman with a buzz cut and a skeleton tattoo on her forearm. Sometimes after a win she gathered them at half-court and told them they were special and they just needed to play the game of life the way they played out on that court. Then they would all be okay.

"My head is in it," Heather said. "I'm all the way in."

Fifty-two to fifty-two. They were draped over each other waiting for the inbounds pass, faces practically touching. If Heather turned her head she could speak directly into the chick's ear. "Not ever. No matter how much you plead with me. And I have no taste. There's this girl in Barrow I fucked, she smoked reefer. She even huffed paint, she could hardly string two sentences together. She was my first which shows you where I set the bar. But not you. Not if you were the last girl." It occurred to her that the girl in the trailer park *was* the last girl. At least that's how she had seen her: as her only choice, sitting out there on a lawn chair in her raggedy trailer covered with spirit catchers. She walked around town with a boyfriend now, skulked around the edges of the town, really, looking for shit to steal.

"Lesbo," the blonde chick said. "Eskimo." And then she threw the hook and the crowd cheered. They were throwing new and more dangerous shit: plastic soda bottles, pens and pencils, aviator glasses, wadded up gum and spit and even a toupee landing center court and sitting there like a sleeping schnauzer. The ref kicked it off the court with a sideswipe of his foot and Heather looked left, looked right and decided to do something crazy. She backed in, wiggled, set herself, and then she did the hook. Nobody was expecting that, not even herself. Everything rained down: sweatshirts and belts, hats, a couple of beer cans, old love letters and poems, paperback fantasy novels and an old flip phone, until they had to stop the game again. Heather strode to the three-point line and picked up a couple of loose pages.

It was a badly spelled drunken note to someone named Krystal and it was full of promises. A promise to never stop loving her, but also a promise to get over her, a promise to forget and a promise to remember always. Her teammates waited for her at the bench, but she kept reading. The letter reminded her of something her father would have written to her mother in their younger days. It *was* that thing. Even the penmanship. She wanted to put it in her pocket, but she didn't have a pocket so she looked up to see if maybe she could spot the person who had thrown it.

Coach said, "Six minutes left. Just keep doing what you're doing. I'm so proud of all of you."

"There's dust in your eye," Heather said.

"Right," Coach said, and she laughed.

The blonde chick said, "Eskimo Lesbo."

Heather said, "Sometimes I'm in the bathroom reading an issue of my sister's *Glamour* magazine. She has a subscription and they come almost a month behind. I look at the pictures and I touch myself. I might do it tonight. I don't need the magazines because I remember. But if I think about you even for a second everything will be ruined."

But she *was* in it. There were the bodies, all shapes and sizes, and the blonde chick had somehow found her way between the girl from Algebra II and Nicole Kidman or Alicia Silverstone or Kelly McGinnis or whoever-the-fuck in *Top Gun* with the big eighties hair, but wearing Tom Cruise's army green jumpsuit. Right there. And also holding the ball, passing it out to the three-point line, getting it back for the layup.

Sixty-sixty and just under three minutes left. The crowd threw hats smelling of the empty heads that wore them, wine bottles, and car keys to beat-up American-made trucks, children's drawings of popular superheroes looking pumped up and pissed off, and even a quarter striking her right on the top of her head and infecting her, just for a moment, with the spirit of George Washington. It met that other spirit there—the one placed there by her mother—and they twisted around each other in a swirling knot made of smoke and old disappointments. Heather closed her eyes and opened them and found the ball in her hands. Fourteen seconds left and she willed the world into slo-mo. As the double team turned into a triple team she ducked and faked and the bodies rose in the air, all three as if diving in reverse, and then as they came down she was on her way up, and the net puckered to accept the ball. Nobody cheered except for Coach. She was pumping the air with her fist, screaming, and what was the look on her face? It was a kind of joyful rage. Heather had seen it before, *felt* it before, but she couldn't remember when. Possibly in the trailer of that girl back home as she worked the other woman's body with none of the grace she had just shown on the court. And as she luxuriated in that filthy thought the blonde chick took the pass in the far corner and let it loose. A completely open shot because Heather wasn't charging fast enough to the outside. Five hundred people stood and stomped their feet. Heather didn't even bother looking to see the shot go in. This was what her mother had known until she forgot it. The ref pointed down the court toward the other basket and everybody followed the direction of his hand like animals let loose from the harness. Now was the worst part: the time for compassion and pity. No more trash thrown from the stands. Everybody would talk about that upstart team from nowhere and their miracle run. The buzzer sounded as the inbound pass careened over her head.

"Good game," the blonde chick said because everything, every bit of it, was supposed to vanish. She even held out her hand for a slap. So Heather slapped it and even said good game right back.

"Rough one," Cody said when she returned home. It was two in the morning but they were all up. Her mother had made macaroni and cheese and her brothers were already eating it in big mouthfuls. They looked like what they were: three big men camped around a small kitchen table eating their mother's cooking. They were happy and they were sad and they were full, but still eating like it was a race. Someday she'd think of this moment and miss them. In a way she missed them right now.

"Tomorrow let's go out on the ice," her father said as he ate. "You always bring the fish running, you know?" He laughed at his own odd turn of phrase and she laughed too. She remembered once, not more than a year ago, seal hunting with him, the shining faces popping up through the hole in the ice and then vanishing, the waiting for the next face and the next. The first one had been big and fat and her father was waiting for it to return. "That's the one we want," he said. "This is a waiting game." He had held a spear across his lap and sometimes he checked his calculator watch and nodded as if he was playing a second little game with himself. "I guess it's not coming back," he said later in the day. By then no faces at all, just the empty hole, and they went home with nothing but a story.

She had never seen anything like it before. Not the seals. She saw that often enough. No, the thing she saw now from the couch. Her mother came around the corner with another bowl filled over the brim and her eyes were red and enflamed. At first Heather did not recognize this woman who had taken her mother's place. A split second of animal fear, of feral confusion, and then her mother spoke and everything was normal again. "Eat this," her mother said. No speeches, no spirits. Her father looked out across at his wife as if from the pole on the hill. The distance was that intimate and that vast.

But Heather wanted to tell them. She had not been defeated, or if she had it was just a number on a board, an article in a newspaper. That night in Fairbanks she had slipped away into the city, down to Cushman Street, and that's where she found the row of western saloons, the strip club, the two ramshackle dyke bars. She had never seen things quite like this before. It was easy to get in, easier to smile and nod her head to the pulsing music. None of these people gave a shit about some stupid game.

Funny how easy it was. So many faces just like in her father's fish story, and some of them with that same blonde hair, the same chunky ass. She wrapped her arm around a shoulder and kept all that crazy talk going as if they were still trading baskets back and forth, up and down. Just a few hours before the flight and Coach would let her have it bad, but for now let's make out in the back corner. Let's see how it feels.

"What's with the black eye?" the girl asked her between kisses.

She touched herself there. It was a surprise, a thing just forming.

"Don't worry about it," the girl added. "You're super beautiful."

They would never see each other again, but she at least had to know her first name, so they exchanged them like little secrets. By the time she had returned home she had forgotten it, but not the perfect fit of her mouth.

Of course she couldn't tell them. She was supposed to take the bowl and eat. She was supposed to show them that she had learned a lesson. And then tomorrow they'd go out on the ice. Her father would let her hold the pole his father had made from wood and iron, raise it above her head and bring it down into the shining neck. If you did it right then no sound at all, not even the splash of water. Only if you did it just right. The light would come spilling across the sheets of ice and everything not within arm's reach would be lost in the heliocentric haze. This was the only time her father still prayed, although not really to God in heaven so much as the shape below him. It was as much a reflex as the shudder in the dying body. Its unmoving bulk held a different kind of strength, a strength demanding acquiescence. So he crouched and mumbled something she could only half understand, words paired carefully with objects like the arrangement of silverware at an extravagant meal. When the heavy knife appeared, it was as if all the hardest work had already been completed.

# The Wolves Again

In those last days my mother seemed to rally on the stage of the damp mattress, rising up and pushing at the blankets and speaking about the past as if it were a thing living in the room with us, sleeping right beside her like a loving husband. "Mom," I'd say. "You have to calm down. Drink this," but she'd twist her head away. For her it was 1975 again and she was stuck at Thompson Pass in a difficult Alaskan November. She seemed unsure what might happen next, but I was very sure. Her matchstick legs were cold to the touch.

Her story began at the end, after hundreds and hundreds of miles already crossed. Proud union men with neat collections of boasts gathered up from work in Texas and New Mexico and Colorado but when they stared at the mountainside they were as tentative as boys at a new school. They'd look and then look away and then look again as if that might change something about the altitude, the hard slant of rock and ice. All that was needed was one volunteer but the men would swear and laugh and shake their heads and then go sit at one of the big portable heaters and open a pop-top of peaches.

She watched the mountain too, but she made a point of telling me that she watched it for different reasons. The snow blew across the ridge in unpredictable arcs, and it reminded her of play, the swirl and trickery of it all, although she knew it could carry a human body along as easily as it might the tides of snow. The wind came across the ice field so hard you'd stop whatever you were doing and brace yourself, close your eyes tight and try to focus on all the money you were making for just sitting here and listening to them brag.

"Eat," I'd say. "It's good."

I'd push the cup to her mouth and she'd shake her head no, no, no. I could appreciate being stuck somewhere and I decided it made us closer even though her eyes turned inward. She'd say, "Get that away from me."

Maybe she wanted to address them privately—the men she had shared the journey with—but it seemed important for me, her only daughter, to understand it all. "We ate like kings," she said once. "You wouldn't think that, would you, but we did. Not like that slop you're trying to give me." They ate steak and eggs in the morning, more steak at night, drank peach syrup from the can like it was soda, set their plates on the ground so the dogs could finish everything off. They listened to talk about disasters nearly averted, big paydays, idiots and greenhorns lost to bad ideas. They were tiny though, all of them, including her, but at least she knew it. For the first time she felt stronger listening to them, small, yes, but stronger, like a hard, little stone. She smiled at this turn of phrase and her face tightened into a pale skull, unadorned by anything but her bright eyes. I went to kiss her forehead, to show my courage, my devotion, but she twisted away from that too. I didn't mind. After all, I was the ghost haunting her present, always calling her back from the real thing into this shadowy place, the sweaty bed and the boring food.

She made her fingers into a tweezer shape to show the size of the thing. Her hand shook and if she were holding anything but that imaginary rock, her imaginary self, she would have dropped it onto her blanket.

For a moment I almost believed she was handing me a real thing. I almost held out my hand to take it. "Mom?" I asked.

They all agreed that the project was insane but the extent of that insanity was the subject of much deliberation. Often, they argued about it. They were boys talking in the schoolyard, pushing each other around, testing each other with feints and jabs. She had brought three cartons of Marlboros and they would give her a couple of bucks for a cigarette. "This when the dollar meant something and smoking wasn't a crime," she said.

They camped for three days playing cards and finally it was boredom more than courage that pushed her into saying she would do it. She was the smallest one, just touching five feet, and she'd rappelled before, in Colorado, and she was disgusted, both with herself and with these others. Even an accident, a tumbling blur of arms and legs, would have been a relief when compared to playing another game of rummy. They only had two decks and one was missing a jack and an eight.

So that was that. They'd put her up the mountain to the pass with thirty pounds of welding equipment strapped to her. The rest would watch from below. Except that she had broken the back of their fear, or replaced it with a greater one: the possibility that she might reach the top while they stared up from below. The runty guy with a Texas slur said he would go instead, then the big one with the missing thumb. Another man and then another. As if their fear had never even existed, that it had been some kind of trick they had played on her.

"Mom," I said, but this part of the story was very important. It needed to be understood so she repeated herself. She pointed her finger at the air as if addressing those men, now much older and helpless. She liked to joke that they were all back in Oklahoma wearing adult diapers. The fact that many of them were probably dead did not seem to cross her mind.

In 1975 she was twenty-eight years old and had forty thousand dollars in the bank from this crazy job spreading pipe across frozen wilderness. The sky dwarfed her, the land dwarfed her, but no person could make her feel weak. The land had done that, yes, and that was fine, but not a man. She loved it all. She spotted lynx playing in the snow, moved so close they stopped what they were doing to look back. She walked alone waiting for the next incredible thing. Forty years later and Alaska continued to surprise. Just the other day a moose appeared as she was checking her mail.

Of course, that had been *last* winter, when she could still make the walk down the road to the intersection.

At the next part she slowed her voice to a crawl.

She might not have been the first to the pass, the first to light her torch, but she was the first to say yes. They couldn't take that away from her. "Understand that," she said, "when you look at me now."

Almost three thousand feet to the ground below, down black rock slick with ice, to the rest of the men, the circle of military tents, the comfort of the small fires and generators and cans of salted pineapple ham. She clung to the metal and lit her torch. It hissed and spurted and then showered fire up from the contact point. They yelled to each other above the wind, all attention on the work now. She did not think about dying or even injury. She didn't think about the cold and she did not think about her past in the Lower 48. She seemed to be floating. She could do this forever.

"Just have one sip," I said.

At the end of the week she spent five hundred dollars in a bar in Fairbanks, drinking and laughing, chasing that feeling, but it never visited her again, not even once, not even when she told the story to her daughter: just the outline of the experience, a thing she couldn't quite trust. It was that night, the night in Fairbanks spreading money around, when she met my father, and I'm guessing that he was one of the first people she told about that journey across the interior, and that he was impressed, even amazed, by what she had done. Although the thought has occurred to me that he simply did not believe her, but he liked her reckless smile, he liked all that cash and the way she spread it around.

❧

It is 2015, another bad winter, and when I get home from the club my mother is sitting in the dark watching the TV. She calls out, "Is that you, Tamara? Did you get it?" even though of course it's me. Who else would it be?

"Sure," I say, and I put the paper bag on the table. I open the fridge before I even have my parka off and begin eating cold cuts right from the drawer. It's not even that I'm hungry, although I'm starving. I want her to turn her head, notice me, tell me to stop, she'll make me something. My uniform smells of smoke. At the club it's all flashing lights and ancient hair metal, shouted choruses, jumping bodies and guys yelling out drink orders. Here the TV is turned so low I can hardly make out the voice. If I sit down, or even stand close, I know she'll slide into her story again so I stand in the glow of the refrigerator light rolling a piece of bologna into a tight cigar shape.

"Can you be a dear and make it for me?" my mother asks. "Not much ice."

"Sure," I say. "Just give me a minute."

The kitchen table is littered with the week's mail, including a familiar letter from Local 798 in Tulsa, Oklahoma. My mother still pays her dues even though she hasn't worked as a welder in almost two decades. I drop in the ice, pour in some milk, take the Kahlua out of the paper bag. The bottle is Hawaiian-themed, bright and festive, with the image of some kind of jungle spirit on the label, open-mouthed and staring. I still haven't taken off my coat and my boots are making wet marks on the linoleum. My hat is still on my head. I'm still eating while I finish up her drink. This is what I've been doing all night anyway—serving people—so it's not difficult to do one more. I walk it over to her and she reaches up. She doesn't say thank you but she nods her head to acknowledge me.

The house is cold. The fire's almost out. That's the next thing. So I grab a strip of birch bark. "Come over here," she says.

I can predict her words the way I can predict the plot of the detective show on the TV. Everything a rerun. Hundreds of miles of frozen ground, the arrogance of thinking you could snake a pipe through all of that, that the things you learned in Texas and New Mexico and Colorado could actually be applied to a land like this. Amazing they had succeeded but a little sad too because it meant that the land had yielded and she was partially to blame. She swirled the glass and sipped from the rim. Moving slow, trying to be careful. That meant she was already standing on the edge of drunk and ready to step over. I decided to start first, cut her off before she had a chance to begin. "Good tips tonight," I said, "but that guy was back. You know the one who asked me on a date?"

I don't know why I lie about this. He hasn't been back since I said no the second time. I guess I just want to share something.

"Yeah," she says, and then, "That's the murderer. Right there. That one. I figured it out in the first five minutes."

There's another letter too. This one has been opened and put to one side beneath an apple. I know what it is without opening it. It's from the doctor in Anchorage explaining that my mother's cancer is in remission. But there is no celebratory mood, not even a smile, because it's an old letter, from the first round of chemo half a year ago. Sometimes she likes to take it out and reread it while she's waiting for me. She says, "Eight hundred miles. I don't know if you can imagine that but try to picture it. In weather like this. Worse than this."

And then something unexpected, something I've never heard before.

"The first time one of them climbed into my tent and thought he'd get frisky with me. Have I ever told you about that? I punched him right in the nuts and then he must have told the others because they were more polite after that." She ruminates on her drink for a moment and adds, almost as a joke, "I should have done the same thing with your dad, but I was always a sucker for a sweet talker."

That last part I've heard before, the stuff about him being a sweet talker, although that's as far as she'll go with it. And then she's back at the ridge, in the field of ice. She says, "Wolves followed us for days. You could see their eyes in the woods at night. Red points like hot coals." She holds up her hand flat. "Scout's honor they were out there, a dozen of them, watching us, and you know what? I wasn't afraid. You know how dolphins follow ships at sea? It was like that."

I've never heard talk of wolves before.

"Hundreds of miles. They were just curious, I guess. That's all. Although they were hungry too. Maybe they were curious if we'd make good eating."

She laughs and her face becomes all skull again. Despite myself I am back there with her watching the points of red light at the forest wall. It's like a fairy tale and she is Little Red Riding Hood and the wood cutter all rolled into one. The wolves follow her all the way into the interior and then, finally, they leave her at the edge of civilization. That's when she steps into Fairbanks, that's when she finally has a chance to spend some money and meet my father. I am not even a possibility then, of course. I come much later, after a series of ups and downs, angry goodbyes and sheepish hellos. But at the time I must have seemed like the latest in a string of victories.

He's impressed when she takes out the roll of cash and he slides a couple of chairs over and she likes his curiosity, his almost effeminate leanness. She wants to show off for the other welders, show them that she's not a dyke or a prude—that none of them were worthy—so she puts her hand on his shoulder and laughs at his jokes. That's how I imagine it.

⚜

My mother did not celebrate her remission. It was as if she expected it. She opened one letter and then she opened the next: an overdue notice from the library. My fault.

Possibly my mother did not celebrate her remission because she knew that her illness would return, that the cancer slept in her skull. It would wake up again at the tail end of October as she stepped outside in her pajama shirt and rubber boots. I found her there when I returned from work, belly down in the mud, her head turned to one side so she could see the house twenty feet away. She must have watched it for hours, unable to rise, occasionally yelling out to see if someone might help. She was naked from the waist down. I could see that from the car, in the glow of the headlights.

For some reason I sat for a moment, perplexed by the sight of her in this condition. Then I pulled her up to my shoulder and walked her back onto the porch. When she reached the threshold, she raised her chin and said, "I don't want to be tracking dirt in there. Get me a towel."

She hissed this as if I were to blame.

The next time she talked about the pipeline she spoke about it from her hospital bed. The wolves again and something else: a stupid man who raised a gun and shot in their direction. Sent a bullet into the night and the red lights vanished. She heard the gunshot from her tent. Or she saw it all and couldn't believe it. Her mind played tricks on her because of the meds but she remembered the rapture on the man's bowl-shaped face, his pride in being the group's protector. I sat and held her hand. "It's all so jumbled up," she said. She needed to get out of here, get some fresh air, get the stupid needle out of her arm.

For some reason I wanted to lie again, tell her something interesting about the club. I had the drink prices memorized by now, knew all the regulars by name, but that didn't seem worth sharing. She settled back again, took a deep breath, and said, "Naturally I was upset."

So she climbed from her tent and across the camp and cursed him. He still held the gun in his hand, an old Sears catalogue kit rifle, a toy gun, really, and she wanted him to point it in her direction as if she were another danger. Then she'd have an excuse for breaking his nose.

And then just the act of *imagining* the gun pointed in her direction granted her license to step forward and strike him hard with the flat of her hand. And then again, her fist balled now and knocking him back into some of the other men, who caught him, lifted him up, and gave him a nudge forward. Some of them were smiling.

No more shooting at them, she said. No more.

She stopped speaking at the sound of the dinner tray's wheels. "You didn't touch your food," the night nurse said.

What did she overhear? I was afraid the woman might see my mother's story as ridiculous, and that she might make me view it that way too.

My mother said, "My throat is so dry."

"Then drink," she said, and she pushed the plastic cup into my mother's face. A big flat-faced woman with a tight red perm and reading glasses hanging from a chain around her neck. She seemed suspicious of something, as if we were children up to no good. When my mother twisted her head away she simply put a couple of fingers on her chin and pivoted it back to the rim.

Many women took an instinctive dislike to my mother: teachers at my school and other mothers in our neighborhood. The nurse was most likely one of those. And she had broken the story in half. Because when she finally did leave my mother began complaining about the ache in her back, the smell of the room. The wolves vanished as cleanly as when the rifle had been fired.

That night I called my father in Detroit and told him the news. Or rather, I spoke the news into his voicemail. "I thought you would like to know," I said. "Mom's in the hospital again. She's going to Anchorage tomorrow for more tests."

He called me back a minute later while I was stoking the fire. "Tamara," he said. "What happened? I thought everything was fine."

It was past midnight in Fairbanks, later than that in Detroit, and I could tell I had woken him from a sound sleep. "I guess they were wrong," I said. "That happens sometimes."

"Yeah, well," he said. "You should sue."

Money again. He had fallen from a ladder while painting a house a few years before and he had talked about suing then too. "I have a weird question for you," I said.

"I don't want to talk about that," he said.

"About what?"

I fanned the flames with a strip of bark, watched them glow brighter and stronger. Soon the stove would start to click and rattle from the heat. I was planning on staying up all night feeding it and I wanted to talk to him all that time, keep him up until the sun bled around his window shade.

He said, "You know. All of that. It's ancient history."

I suppose he meant my mother giving up her work to stay in Alaska, her long days at home with me as a baby, his jumping from job to job and finally his big jump to the Lower 48, first to California and then Michigan. He was still doing odd jobs at sixty-nine despite a bad knee and a worse heart.

"You know what?" he said. "I always thought it would work out. Even when things were really bad. I thought we could just hunker down and get past it. Not because of me or anything. I know who I am. But your mother is an incredible woman."

I let his voice unspool. If I listened long enough, if I let the silences stand until he filled them, then he would keep going.

"There you go," he said. "You got me." I could hear a crack in his voice. I thought of the men at the club, all bravado and hoots and hollers until the end of the night when the house lights turned on. The stragglers always looked so strange in the glare then, bloodshot and confused. "Dad," I said.

"What?" he said. "What are you blaming me for now? I didn't make her sick."

I made a noise of agreement.

"I just had to get out of there," he said. "You don't understand how it was then for us in the tribe. My father was always talking about the Athabascan people this, the Athabascan people that, pride this, pride that, and meanwhile he'd shit all over my mother." He paused to let that sink in. "He'd shit all over every single one of us. Do you know how many of your uncles committed suicide?"

"Okay," I said, because he was right, I couldn't understand. I couldn't feel even a small part of it no matter how much I tried. He was talking faster. His voice sounded like something that had got away from him, escaped his control, and now he was rushing to catch up to it. I wondered if he was alone or if he had someone there to say, hey, take it easy, a person to touch his back and rub in circles after this phone call from his old life. He said, "Even when your mother met me I was thinking about it. She was on her way in and I was on the way out. It just took me a lot longer because, you know, things happened."

"You're right," I said. "It's ancient history."

"That's what you should be thinking about too. Get out of there. Do *something* for God's sake. Don't live alone in that house after she's gone."

"Okay," I said. "Enough. I need to sleep."

"Now you're tired," he said. "Right."

"I have to go."

"One more thing," he said, but I was saying goodbye.

⁂

The week my father left my mother said, "Things are going to be a little different now."

She walked into the local Safeway holding me by my hand. "Now just keep your mouth zipped," she said. "This is important," and she walked to the service desk and asked for an application and a pen. I remember her clicking the ballpoint, testing it on the back of the single sheet, and then writing her name. The girl behind the counter, a teenager, watched us the way the nurse would watch us twenty years later: that same suspicious gaze hidden behind a half-smile.

My mother handed the finished sheet back to the girl and said, "I can start tonight if you want." There were people in town, friends of hers I could stay with while she worked. Days would be better but she'd take anything. She said to the girl, "I'd like to do what you do, but I can stock shelves. I can grab those grocery carts out there. That's something I wouldn't mind doing."

A union card from Oklahoma didn't mean much in Fairbanks with the pipeline long since finished and the economy flatlined. And I think my mother had lost the ability to envision a fresh future for herself. She took what was easily available, which meant applying at some of the newest stores in town: the Safeway, the McDonald's with its golden sign, the Kentucky Fried Chicken. She took my hand again and led me deeper into the store and bought me a candy bar for being so good. Outside she snapped off one end and handed the rest to me and we stood there eating our lopsided portions. I remember feeling annoyed that she would take some of it for herself and strangely happy that my father wasn't there. After all, he would have taken the lion's share.

She had not begun talking about the past yet but years later I'd think about that moment when she spoke about her decision. She would mention feeling small and hard, like a stone, and that's how I felt standing in front of the grocery store watching the traffic push through the spring muck, like a small river stone found at the edge of the Tanana. They were always more beautiful in the water. You'd go through the trouble of picking one up only to find it lost some of its luster in your hand.

"This is good," she said through her chewing. "It'll be good to be working again." But her face looked funny to me. She seemed to be talking to herself. She took my hand again and we walked to the car.

That night my mother said, "If the phone rings don't answer it. He's been calling and I don't want him to ambush you."

Food appeared from his sisters and his mother and his brothers' wives, desserts made from blueberries and animal fat, a soup made from the head of a moose, dried salmon I carried around with me like a lollipop. It felt like someone had died—it was that final and ceremonious. "I'm not afraid of a little charity," my mother said.

I hear this word again—charity—at the club years later, but the meaning is very different. It's the name of one of the girls who whips her hair around her head. It's three in the morning on a Saturday night and the club has closed and I can hear everything: the sound of glass being swept up in the parking lot, the cars running, her tight breathing as she holds her ice water with pink manicured fingers. She tells me she's saving up money for a boob job and that if I lost a little weight I would probably make better tips. "You have a cute face," she says. She even touches my cheek.

How did she pick this name? She's touched on some deep understanding of what she does. I know when I watch her—I watch her all the time, she's one of my favorites—it feels like she's lifted something heavy from my shoulders. I don't think about anything but the engine of her legs, her peroxide hair, the crazed action and motion.

They follow their scripts to the letter but when they're up there it seems like anything might happen.

"I'm not going to be here much longer," I tell her. "This summer I'm going to go work in a cannery. Head south or something."

"The smell will never come off," she says. "Trust me."

She holds out her arm, shiny as a salmon, and for a moment I think she's inviting me to run my face along it, sniff it up to the elbow. But she must be talking about old boyfriends. Off the stage she is all arms and gangly legs, sweat shining just above her breastbone. Her face glows. She reminds me of an athlete who has just lost a very difficult match. There's a resignation to her but she's smiling, taking pleasure in the big glass of water, the cooling of her skin. Or maybe all I'm thinking about is *my* pleasure.

I might never see her again. They fly them back to the Lower 48 and then new ones come up for the weekend. Of course, she could come back in a month with different colored hair. I need to tell her something very important about myself but I can't think of what.

"Do you want to go out somewhere?" she asks.

"No, no," I say instantly. "I have to get home. My mother, she's sick."

"So is mine," she says. "In the head."

She points to her own head and makes a funny face, tongue out, eyes crossed, and she is suddenly a little kid. Soon she will be flying back to wherever she comes from and she won't even remember this conversation. It's not so late. I could go. I could bring her home. My mother is in the hospital, after all. But as I think this I'm already rising, saying goodbye. "Hey," she says. "Are you afraid of me or what?"

I laugh like it's not a real question. But she seems to want an answer and then that's it, with a turn of her head she's given up on me. She must already be thinking about Anchorage or Portland or Detroit. She's practically up there already, in the sky, looking out at clouds. I can see it in her eyes. "You know," I say. "I'm not who you think I am."

She looks at me like I'm one of the guys getting too loud and lewd with her. It's a withering look and I recede back into the chairs and tables.

"Could you get rid of this stuff?" my mother asks when I visit her again. The room is spotted with modest flower arrangements and a basket of fruit. "They think they're being kind but it's just cruel. It's like they think I'm having my tonsils out."

Her arm is marked with thumbprint-sized bruises. She has small veins and putting in a new needle is hard. She always looks close though, as the needle enters the skin, the same way she watches the plumber when he's fixing something, the electrician working on the circuit breakers. She wants to make sure they're doing it right.

"I want to tell you something," I say.

But the wolves have returned. They follow further away, although they still follow. Just when everybody agrees that they're gone—when they start talking about missing them—then they reappear, and each time there seems to be more of them. The men start naming them after ex-wives, mothers, popular TV actors, pool players. They're scared to death and then something even stranger happens.

The temperature dips on the eighteenth of November until it hurts to breathe. Down ten, twenty, thirty degrees. Everything grows as still as a painting. You can feel it in the air—even the snow beneath your feet feels different. The welding equipment begins failing. So does the human brain. One of the men begins muttering to himself. Another says they are going to die and the wolves know it. They've known it all along. Everyone has reached agreement: the project is completely insane. Most of them talk about quitting. What good is all that money if you're dead?

And yet she spots birds the size and color of sparrows marching on the ice field. They're light enough that they leave no tracks.

At fifty below her fingers stop gripping. Metal becomes dangerous to touch. One of the generators dies an undignified death and slows their work to a crawl. At sixty below even the wolves become confused. Suddenly there is a feeling that they are allies, united against the weather. "I feel sorry for them and they feel sorry for us," she says.

They lose the jack of diamonds and the six of spades. And then they begin making a game of flipping the cards, one by one, into the center of the fire. She gives the rest of the cigarettes away.

On the third day of record lows one of the wolves enters the camp like a dog, head down, and it moves up to the bacon grease stewing on the fire. The men do not seem to care. It could drag one of them off and the rest would just keep staring at the flames.

The wolf digs into the pan, finds a square of fat, and licks it up. It's big as two dogs with a crest of black and shoulders wide as my mother's shoulders. That's what she says from her bed as I am pulling the flowers together in a bundle. "Just throw them out the window," she says.

Her blood feels like it's come to a standstill. She watches the wolf move past her and then out through the tents. Some of the men don't even bother watching, but for a moment she thinks of standing up, following it out there. That seems like one way, possibly the only way, to save herself.

There must be others out there waiting for this single explorer, this brave and curious one. She even takes a step in its direction. It stops and eats something else from the frozen ground. It bites at the snow, at some kind of human made stain, urine or maybe spilled food. Tomato soup? That's the spot. It feels like an important realization, a sign that her mind is still working. It paws the spot and lifts its head. Then it exits the stage of their campground and out toward the tree line. It seems to fade instead of trot.

"That's how I want to go," my mother says. "Just slip away like that."

So she does not go to Anchorage. Her mind is made up. There are no more tests and no more discussions of possibilities. No more good luck, no more bad.

I ask the nurses if anybody else wants the flowers. I bring them from room to room, a few here, a few there. I try to smile and ask how each person is doing. I feel imperial and strange, an angel of, well, charity I suppose, making the rounds.

She returns home with me and we make a bed downstairs.

A few days later she calls to me in the night.

"Water," she says, but when I bring it she doesn't drink. She doesn't even seem capable of holding the glass. Her hands are small things arranged on the sheet, limp as rags, and her eyes are round and amazed. "Did I ever tell you about Thompson Pass?" she asks.

"Of course, Mom," I say, and I reach for the brush. Her hair is a wet mess.

"That's where they finally got us," she says. "The people on the ground first. They came right into camp. The few of us up on the ridge watched it all happen. And then we watched them lick at the snow. Ketchup? It was blood. They took their time. And the three of us, the volunteers looking down, what could we do but wait? We knew they'd get us too."

"You're fine," I said. "You're with me. You're in your house in your bed."

"And they got us too. Each and every one. We had to come down eventually and they knew that. They stood there waiting."

I told her she should rest but her body was as rigid as a board. I climbed in next to her and began rubbing her back. "No," she said, and she pulled away as if I was one of them. "They got me. It took a while but they did it. Oh, they got me good."

⅀

When it was finished I finally asked my father the question I had meant to ask before. "Do you remember Mom ever talking about wolves?"

"Wolves," he said, and he laughed. "I have to get up early in the morning, you know. This city needs people like me."

"I know," I said.

"Your mother talked about a lot of things," he said. "That sounds like her. Wolves. You know what? I told her a story about wolves once. Was she telling you that one?"

"What was that?" I asked.

"Just a depressing story," he said. "One of those depressing stories from the village. A wolf killed a kid, a little girl. It didn't make any sense. She was twenty feet from her back door. There's more to it but it'll just get you down. You don't need to hear about that kind of stuff."

"Okay," I said. "That's fine."

"Why?" he asked. "What did your mother tell you?"

"I don't know," I said. "Just old stories."

"She was talking about me, wasn't she?" he said. "All these years and she couldn't forgive me, not even on her deathbed, and now she's infected you with it too."

"No, Dad," I said. "It's not that."

"Because I wouldn't come and hold her hand."

"She didn't need that," I said. "You wouldn't believe how strong she was."

"And also because *you* were holding it," he said and he laughed. "No room for me."

I could hear the thrumming of electricity in the line, the hissing distance. How could such a thing work, really? A person thousands of miles away talking to another person, through satellite or cables. It was just another thing I didn't understand. And anyway, I didn't hold my mother's hand, not ever. Something about them scared me, their size and stillness on the bed sheets, the spidery bones beneath the bluish skin. She was not the kind of person who liked to be touched. But I rubbed her feet with cream and listened to her as she moved through that other land. It took every bit of my will to let it all in without saying, wait, what, really?

I know strange things happen all the time, but even here it's hard to believe. It's been a couple of years since my mother's death and my father has followed her to that undiscovered place. His sisters appeared at my door one morning. "We don't want to trouble you," one of them said. Caribou stew, bread wrapped in dish towels. An old man sat in an idling truck waiting for them. His father had outlived him.

I am still at the house my mother bought with oil money from long ago. Sometimes in the early morning everything is quiet and my girlfriend and I let the dogs out and I can catch a glimpse of what my mother must have seen. They are running hard with a crazed abandon through the trees and it's because they've spotted something, something to chase down in the snow, and even if they don't catch it they'll return stupid with happiness, panting hard, and then one of us will make the coffee and the other will light the fire.

There are still places like the ones my mother described. I want to believe it's possible, just as I would have wanted her to believe that this thing unfolding right now is possible: these rituals, as intimate as her last days, the rubbing of her feet and combing of her hair. We coax the fire out of the tent of sticks and stir the cream into the coffee and the thermometer outside the window has fallen to another ridiculous number. The cold cures us of our ordinariness even when we have our jobs, our obligations, our mundane gripes about each other. We complain and we celebrate until they become the same thing. We pace the room like it's a cage. Because just look out there—what else can you do?

# *I'm Here*

The horse leans into the shed wall like a drunk, mottled skull lowered, ears flat, eyes rolled deep and black in pained reverie. They seem turned inward to some hidden place where Edison was denied access. He strokes its flank and tells it sweet words and when those run out, curse words spoken sweetly, because his fingers are getting cold.

He tells himself that work is a solace. He needs to tell himself this, he decides, because there is so much of it: two cords of wood to split and stack, a roof needing shoveling, water to be hauled, and the shed would need mending too—the horse's sleek weight had cracked the two-by-fours in the floor and south wall. He stares the task down from a distance, like a sailor falling in love with the sea. He's not ready to throw himself into the midst of it.

He concedes this: the pulling of the wire brush down the horse's neck to its finely muscled shoulder. It's not dying, of course, but it's in a world of hurt. Its hooves have softened and crumbled, first in a simple, almost graceful cleave, and then into a tree of puzzle shapes, spongy to the touch. When he tried touching one in October, when he first noticed, it splashed hot breath in his face, and by mid-November it wouldn't let him touch them at all. The goats come close to the shed and it warns them off with a low, bullish grunt.

He isn't sorry though. It had not even seemed like a choice so much as an instinct, some nerve twitch that had a flavor of self-preservation to it. He would not have been able to live with himself otherwise. The musher, she had stroked its muzzle and said she was going to buy it for dog food and it took Edison a moment to realize she wasn't joking. The next thing he knew he was doing the math in his head, adding up the money in his savings account, his checking account, in the cigar box on the top shelf in the pantry. The musher begged off, told him if he wanted it that way then fine, she wasn't going to stand in the way of love at first sight. "But that horse isn't worth anything living," she said, as it took the apple core from her open palm.

"You sure you want to do this?" the owner asked him. They had worked together on the roads in Sitka more than a decade before and still maintained a lazy kind of acquaintanceship. Edison had come there to buy some railroad ties—that was all—and maybe have a cup of strong coffee while they talked about the weather, and then there he was, saying sure, of course, as he shook the man's hand. The musher was still there, watching, her flat red face unreadable. Did she think he was a fool?

The horse's owner knew Edison's story, or at least the bare bones of it, but that didn't stop him from gripping his hand hard and smiling. "She's good company," he said. "You'll see."

❦

Early December now and he climbs into the loft, attention split between the small window and his computer screen, blanket draped around his shoulders. The window frames the slanted birch trees in the gulley, the haze of stars, and the ice crystals webbed at the corners of the triple pane. The computer screen displays the usual messages from men in the Lower 48—in other countries too—describing their bodies, asking him how old he is and where he lives. Alaska, he says, and they ask the usual follow-up questions. Isn't it cold there? Lonely there? He tells them the stories they want to hear and soon he *becomes* that person, and forgets about the broken shed, the broken hooves.

The red messages blink across the screen. So many people in the world who just want some kind of human connection. They want blowjobs and anal and much more, particular and peculiar things they can describe in minute detail, clinical as surgeons. *You must feel like an outsider there*, one of them types, the one who wants to duct tape him from head to toe. *I picture you in Hawaii. I can't picture you there in all that snow. It's like picturing you on the surface of the moon.*

*I like it here*, he types back, single-fingered because his hand is in his pants.

The man says he can't imagine the happy girl from the photograph enjoy-

ing life in Alaska, but Edison tells him to open his mind. It's just not burly
men with beards. *It's not what you think it is.*

But the man is right. Edison *does* feel like an outsider here, because of
the color of his skin, or because of the way winter corkscrews itself down
into his mind. It's a feeling he's grown to enjoy in an odd way, a kind of
nakedness of the spirit.

Of course, the girl in the photograph is white. They're always white, and
always blonde and young, and he shares them and says, *My nose looks too big
in this one.*

The man almost always says, *You're beautiful.*

The men are all white too, or at least that's how he imagines them, with
button-down shirts and receding hairlines and a Coke always on the table.
He's not sure who is being punished—if the young, blonde body he's making out of words is some kind of trap—and where fun comes into it, but it *is*
fun, and when he's finished he goes outside and pees in the snow.

But tonight, the man doesn't say that he's beautiful. The man, whose
screen name is simply *Shyboy*, says, *I've been to Fairbanks. I was in the military there for three years.*

Very cool, Edison says. The blonde girl says it too. She is his puppet, but
she's also simply *him*, that part of himself he never named until he started
fucking around on the internet. When he types the words, they come from
the deepest, most sincere part of himself.

Shyboy's history spills from his fingers. He plays jazz trumpet, was in the
military band for years. Lives in Arkansas now. Married twice and has a kid
who he loves deeply. Doesn't get to see him as much as he wants. He's into
rape fantasies, forced tattoos, gagging an intelligent young girl with a bright
orange ball. What to do with all of this? *I have a tattoo*, the girl writes back.
*It's on my ankle.*

The outside thermometer stops at twenty-five below.

The horse is in trouble, but it's nothing life-threatening, so he loads the
bed of his truck with trash and turns the key in the ignition for the first
time all week. He lets the engine idle as he picks up summer's trash—a broken plastic chair, stacks of beer bottles, stray wood scraps. It all goes into
the truck, and soon he's hurling the stuff, throwing it high and letting it
fall. The bottles break and the chair clatters. He makes a reckless game of it.

The ice fog begins at Chena Hot Springs Road and he cuts his speed in
half, then half again, as he slides down the long hill into the thick of it. He

can see the blurred headlights of another car coming at him in the opposite lane, and then it's past him and he's alone again. What had he told them about the fog? That it was beautiful. Which it was. But you had to do an awful lot of mental acrobatics to make it that way, to fix it in your mind as something other than car exhaust and ice crystals. *Amazing*, they say, or *incredible*, or they just want to lick his body all over.

The body he's created and then shared with them all.

It's been two weeks since he's come to town and he's a bit disappointed in himself, disappointed in the town too, as he reaches the first traffic light and slows to a stop. But what was he expecting, some kind of revelation? He lets go of the cold steering wheel and pulls off his cap. The truck is finally warm enough that he can begin shedding layers. By the time he gets to the dump he's gloveless and coatless.

He's not alone, because someone else across the parking lot is poking at debris with a ski pole, collecting small treasures. He pulls on his hat and gloves—it's the fingers that go first—and hurls trash into the nearest dumpster, calling up a terrific racket of metal and wood. The guy across the way doesn't seem to notice, or if he does notice, he doesn't care.

*The men here are ugly. They don't know how to treat you.*

When did he say that? It was at the very beginning, typed out to someone he never saw again, and the guy had replied, *I know how to treat you.*

He spins the truck in a big arc around the lot before moving to the exit.

The drunk girl at the Big I is practically dancing on her stool. She's trying to convince the people around her that they should all head out to a strip club, but nobody seems interested. The men around her watch the TV, smoke their cigarettes, and drink their drinks. Maybe they're a little defeated by the weather, maybe by her crazy energy, but mostly they just seem content. The girl has one foot on a chair, thigh spread open, and there's holes in her jeans, bruises on her knees. If her hair wasn't so long she'd be a boy, and a starving one, with wild, crazy eyes. She says something about every single person in the place being a big pussy.

Edison orders a beer and the bartender says, "What have you been doing with yourself?"

"You know what I've been doing with myself," Edison says, because last month he made the mistake of mentioning the horse. He kicks his boots against the bar to clean off the snow, glances up at the TV in the corner. The drunk girl, she's moving down the length of the bar, and as he glances at her face he realizes that he forgot to log off at home. His name, the name of the *fake* girl, is floating on the screen collecting messages. He fights the urge to slide off the stool and walk out. Instead he looks down at the burnished wood of the bar and tries to remember its story. It had been driven up from the Lower 48 on a flatbed truck, and it's classier than the place deserves, ornamented with little birds and so smooth he places his palm on it just for the sheer pleasure of the surface touching skin.

She says, "Are you in the military?" but she's talking to the redheaded kid next to him. They're the only two people in the place under thirty and now they've found each other. Except that the kid doesn't seem that interested. She ricochets off him and over to Edison. "Take off your coat and stay a while," she says, and he realizes, yes, he's still wearing his coat, his black hoodie pulled up Unabomber-style. The bartender moves away, down to the safe end of the bar.

"Black men," she says. "Black men."

He laughs like it's a joke. He wants it to be some kind of joke.

There are a few men on his computer who say they're Black, but he guesses that they are not, that they're wearing that disguise just like he's wearing his. They meet there in the Neverland between computers and exchange their lies and then they fuck him with their thick Black cocks. The clichés are a form of punishment, much more so than the tying of the wrists, the insults, the descriptions of urination. It's like the story of a little prince who wanders through the kingdom in disguise and finds his likeness in a dirty beggar boy. He looks into the face of the other and sees himself and he gives himself over to it, surrenders to it, by switching places, by letting that other one inside his life.

When it happens he sometimes types, *oh my god you're so big.*

The drunk girl touches his thigh and says, "I wander around, and I finally found the somebody who could make me be true and could make me be blue. It had to be you."

He decides it's stupid to drive the two hours into Fairbanks and not do grocery shopping, so he heads to the twenty-four-hour Safeway and walks up and down the aisles, collecting whatever catches his eye. It's three in the morning and by the time he's filled the cart he's lost in a woozy euphoria. The girl at the checkout is the opposite of the girl at the bar, the drunken girl; she's smart and sulky, with short black hair and a mumbled, "How are you tonight?" A nose ring, of course, and about eighty extra pounds. He's trying to be a nice guy, but sometimes it's hard.

The girl back home, the one he's created, is like neither of these people. In a way she's a solution to the problem posed by these people—more wholesome, but tougher too, and when she spreads her legs she never surrenders completely. There is always something held back, that part of himself he shares with the real world, with the grocery clerk, the bartender, the man who sold him the sick horse.

*Imagine me with my ass in the air.* Her skin is scrubbed clean every day, her experience unblemished by tragedy or failure or even a dull job like this one, working late at night in a grocery store in Fairbanks, Alaska.

When he gets home he finds messages from fifteen different men. Some of them he knows and others are first timers; some misspell practically every word and others are meticulous, right down to their punctuation. *Alaska girl?* Shyboy asks, *where are you?*

He types, *I'm here.*

�֍

The coronet is disintegrating into yellow pulp, but he only gets a glance before the horse pulls back, turns sideways, drives its hindquarters into the damaged wall. It's a relief to see it cave completely, because now he'll be *forced* to repair it. But the horse is the more immediate concern. Its eyes have turned to white and it's making noise like a dying engine and he has to crawl beneath it and push up, hard as he can, before it even moves an inch. He considers its weight collapsing down on him, and he considers the temperature, and then he pushes hard, from his knees, and the horse lurches sideways and there's nothing he can do, this is going to hurt.

But no, somehow the horse finds its feet. He falls to the ground, right on his ass, and the horse sidesteps a couple of feet away, looks down at him like he's some puzzling little creature. His tailbone hurts. So does his wrist. The wall is splintered outward. He wants to weep, but instead he dusts himself off and stands. His wrist is throbbing, although it's not bruised. He wants to tell them, *I'm crying right now. I don't know why. Sometimes I cry during sex.*

His friend from the farm in Livengood calls and Edison tells him, "It's fine. I think she's doing better." She drinks plenty. That's a good sign, right?

And he tells Shyboy, *I don't like to drink but I like to dance. It's hard to find men around here who are good at dancing. All the clichés about Alaska men are true. The military guys just want to fuck you and the local guys don't even want that. They just want to fall asleep on top of you. But I love it here. I really do. Today I saw a raven I swear was the size of an eagle. It moved in low over my cabin and I thought it was going to land right on my stovepipe but it kept going.*

*I want you to wear your tallest heels when you talk to me,* Shyboy says. *Okay. Okay.*

The part about the raven was true, except that it happened last winter, and for some reason it had frightened him. It was like something from a dream, beyond reason, and remembering it was like remembering a dream too: the incompleteness of it. That was when he was seeing that woman from Delta, briefly, and calling to mind her serious face made him feel like a weakling. He had told himself that he would not allow her into his head anymore, because she was not that important at all. He couldn't remember her last name.

Someone else messaged him and he tried something different. *Black cock?* he typed, but the man didn't respond, and he had to get back outside anyway and feed the chickens.

Shyboy writes, *You are the kind of person who everybody always thinks is doing fine.* Then they describe themselves in vivid language, one kneeling, the other pushing himself into her face. It's sort of boring and sort of exciting and he really should go outside. It's two o'clock and in a half hour he'll have to spread the chicken feed around in the dark. The day can slide right on past you if you're not careful.

*I love this.* He can't identify the source of his arousal. He's in her head, thinking about the raven and then thinking about the man's body, but he's also in *his* head, and the sex is a form of retribution. He feels sorry for her, he feels sorry for himself, but he also wants it to be as painful as possible. He types, *I've never, ever felt anything like this before.* It's December seventh, two weeks until the solstice and then everything will begin that slow spin backward toward the light. *I have to feed the dog,* he types.

*I didn't know you had a dog,* and then, *I think I'm falling in love with you.*

❧

The horse begins refusing water in late December. Its stool is a healthy shade of brown, sweet smelling, but it pushes its head away when Edison tugs it down to the bowl. He keeps his hand pressed to the warm skin, waiting for a message to run from its body into his brain. He feels like an idiot. He is an idiot.

This has become a performance that will measure him, and he's completely unprepared.

He tells Shyboy an hour later, *my mother is dying.*

*I'm sorry.*

Shyboy's replies are slow, which means he's probably masturbating. Edison's mother is alive and well in Atlanta, strong and happy, and she calls all the time and hassles him to come to visit, complains about the stiffness in her fingers. But the words he types on the screen seem as true as anything he's ever said, and he reads them again, hanging there in the middle of all the filthy language. The reply comes slowly, and those words seem true too, as sincere as the words about spreading his legs, taking the thick cock inside. Outside it's snowing now, and the birch trees have lost their uniqueness, the way they do every winter by this time. It's hard to tell where one ends and the next begins, and it's so beautiful he has to pause in his typing to consider it as a discovery. The window is small and blue. It hangs there like a mirror.

He says, *The winter gets inside you here.*

Shyboy says he can't imagine what it's like. He says, *I would like to come to visit someday. We don't have to do anything. We could just go out for coffee. We could just kiss.*

*My mother is the most important person in my life and she's dying.*

*Okay.*

*I thought I wanted to save her*, he types, *but it wasn't that at all.*

A long pause, and for a moment he thinks the name on the screen is going to turn from red to blue and then vanish. That happens sometimes when Shyboy reaches his climax. He doesn't like to stick around. But no, an answer finally comes back, a few words at a time. *Sometimes I think you are lying to me.* And then, *Do you really live in Alaska?*

*Yes, of course*, he types. *I'm looking at it right outside.*

And when he goes out there he is surprised to find the horse standing a good twenty feet from the shed, almost at the tree line, head bowed, side covered with hay. No miracle, because when he moves closer to it he notices the cut in its side where it pushed through the boards. It's breathing heavily, and as much as he tugs at its bridle, it won't comply and go back inside. It doesn't take much for him to just give up and let it be. He ties it off to the fence with the rope and climbs into his truck, not bothering to let it idle before he spins out of the driveway.

The drunken girl is talking about her Thanksgiving, and the turkey she and her friends fried in a barrel. They stayed up all night eating and drinking and then slept the next day and when she says this there's a light in her eyes like love. But where are those friends now? She's here alone again, drinking a rum and Coke, crunching the ice at the back of her jaw. She tells Edison, "I remember you."

"I was sure you would," he says.

"You have a beard now," she says. "It's curly."

"I had a beard before," he says. "I always have a beard."

The bartender is standing right there, listening to them talk while he rubs down the bar. He says, "He does. He always has a beard." He's smirking as he pours a shot. It's thirty-five below out and people perform a little dance when they come inside, banging their feet, shaking their mitten hands. Some of their cars are still running in the parking lot, waiting for them to have their fun. They'll run all night, or at least for a couple of hours, while they order a few drinks.

"You have an accent," she says. "Where you from?"

"Georgia, originally. But that was a long time ago. I've been here longer than you've been alive."

"I'm twenty-seven."

"Well, I'm exaggerating then. I've been here eighteen years. I came up for some work and I just sort of stuck to the place."

He feels like he's required to say something funny or out of the ordinary, anything but what he is saying, which is mundane as a glass of water. But she seems interested. She's leaning into him, practically falling against him, and he's talking about the way it used to be in this town before it got all civilized in the early nineties. "You can't imagine it," he says. "I didn't think twice about staying."

The thing is, the story doesn't make sense to him either, when he hears it aloud. He *liked* Atlanta, liked riding the buses with his teenage friends, a little gaggle of skin-and-bones boys with the same haircut, the same sneakers, the same slinky, overconfident way of walking. They'd ride in the C-bus up to the courts on Plymouth Heights, talking shit at the back, and play basketball all day, slump against the wire fence in the heat and talk more shit. He doesn't tell the girl any of this, of course. It's all he can do to talk to her about working on the pipeline. He feels like he's lying, leaving out some essential piece of information, but he doesn't know exactly what that particular piece might be.

"More money than I knew what to do with," he says. "It was obscene." He chooses this word carefully, but it doesn't register with her. She's laughing like he's told a joke, like he's boasting. That's not it at all. He wants to be understood. There's a point to his story.

They find her car around back and climb inside. The windshield is covered with fresh snow and there's something disconcerting about not being able to see ahead, but he stays put while she reaches across him to the glove compartment and pulls out a plastic bag. "I have some shrooms," she says, "but they'll hurt your stomach a little. I have some other stuff too."

It's cold enough that the police won't bother them. He knows what she's thinking, so he says, "I'm hung like a Jap," and immediately regrets it. At least she doesn't seem to be listening. She has her hands on his crotch, but not gently. She seems ready to hurt him. Her jaw is set, her face as calm and unemotional as a soldier's. "Maybe we should do the shrooms," he says.

He feels impossibly far away from everything. They might as well be a mile underground, or orbiting the earth in a satellite. He looks to one side and sees some headlights flash on, then off. He touches her hair and says, "I think you misunderstood something."

"I'm not a whore," she says, "but I do want to see the money."

"Then you definitely misunderstood." But he keeps touching her hair. His hand runs down her face, her skin so pale, and he tries to cast it in his memory, as something indelible, like a feature of the landscape he sees every day. He tells her, "You need to change your antifreeze," because the vents are still blasting cold air against his feet.

*I met someone tonight*, he tells Shyboy when he gets home.

A long pause that could mean one of a hundred things. *Interesting*, comes the reply.

*A really nice guy*, he types. *He's got a swimmer's body. Long crazy hair. He works for Fish and Game and we just sort of hit it off.*

*Did you fuck him?*

*No. I like him too much.* He's inventing her, word by word. He's saving her from some strange place. But he has to go there to do it. He types, *I'm going skiing tomorrow. The snow is perfect for it. I like to go with my dogs. Sometimes you have two dogs and sometimes you have one.*

They begin to describe their lovemaking, but this time there are no props. Shyboy simply gives him a dense description of a kiss. It's a beautiful description, actually, despite the couple of misspellings, and Edison can practically feel it. *I don't deserve that*, he types. *I've been horrible to you. You haven't. You're gorgeous. Would I be a horrible person if I wasn't gorgeous? You couldn't be horrible if you tried.*

He thinks of the woman from Delta again, looking for clues in shifting memories of their breakup, but there's really nothing there to see. Maybe just a signpost driving him further back, to the other woman in Atlanta and the stupid things he said to her, but that could just be a false trail too. He types, *I have never lied to you ever*, and it's true, it's true.

Another description of a long kiss. *Stuff the ball gag in my mouth*, he types, but Shyboy won't give him that. All he gives him is one kiss, then another, then another, each described in sentimental language. He types, *I have to go to sleep.*

The outside world is blasted white. He wades through it to the firewood stacked between two trees and begins to split. The cold makes it easy, and the logs crack and fly, one becoming two. He leaves them on the ground until he has twenty, twenty-five pieces, then does the difficult gathering work. His back hurts to stoop. The fire takes its time getting started, but soon it's blazing, and he throws in scraps of bark, a cereal box, and watches them burn. The box collapses in on itself in a kind of beautiful surrender.

Four days until the darkest day of the year. Everything is still as if it were arranged in careful precision, the seven chickens in their coop, the three goats gathered by the exhaust vent at the back of the cabin.

Its body is a kind of stove too, a hot thing that draws him in. The horse lets him put his head against its side and then he is stroking its black marbled head and it is leaning to him the way it did with the wall, but more gently. It seems to know the proper arrangement so as not to do him harm. He pushes back, like leaning into the wind, and he knows the wet eyes are unseeing as stones. There is some place deep inside it, where the heat originates, where the pain resides, that grows every hour. He pushes his face to it. Tuesday, Wednesday, Thursday, and then the solstice and the days run the other way.

It's a kind of journey, toward that strange place, then the arrival, finally the trip home.

⚜

*I want to tell you my real name,* he says to Shyboy on Wednesday.

*You don't have to do that.*

But he says that he *does* have to, sort of, but the name that comes out is Sandra.

*You are probably a lie,* Shyboy says, *but I don't care. I want to know you.*

Edison talks about what he wants to do with his life, the adventures he wants to go on to Greece and Italy, her older brother stationed in Iraq. It's fun to give him what he wants, but not exactly. It's an act of kindness and it's an act of revenge and even when Shyboy goes silent Edison keeps talking. He hasn't talked this much in years. *I'm sorry if I feel a little damaged. I know what I blame it on. It was an ex-boyfriend. He treated me really poorly. I never could trust people after that.*

*Liar, liar,* Shyboy says, and Edison thinks of the Delta woman again, the way she bit her thumbnail when she told him he was a difficult person to be around.

*You're right. It's not that. I want it to be that, but it's not.*

*I was just teasing.*

*Now you're the one who's lying.*

*I'm trying to tell the truth.*

*Me too. This feels like the truth.*

*I know.*

*I just wanted to rescue her,* he types, and he pushes himself back from the keyboard, considers his words, moves in close. *Or at least I thought I did.*

They begin to kiss, or at least their doppelgangers do, and then the ball gag goes in and the straps go on. This time it's described slowly and tenderly, as if he's making a present of her body. Then he splits her in two with descriptions of casual violence. Edison is outside it all, looking in, and inside it all, looking out, and the thought occurs to him for the first time that maybe it's he who needs to be rescued. The fantasy shifts on the axis of this particular thought, and in his head he creates a third person, a handsome man, a good man, who enters and stops the proceedings, removes him from the rack and says everything is going to be okay. He is both the body wrapped tightly and the man freeing the body, lifting it in his arms. Shyboy is the villain, the abuser. It's not difficult to think of him that way.

*Are you enjoying yourself?* the villain asks, and when Edison doesn't reply, the name on the screen disappears.

"Admit you made a mistake," the bartender tells him that night. "That's all you have to do. You can borrow my gun."

"Where's that girl tonight?" Edison asks.

"Nora?" the bartender says. "Who knows. She might be across the street. She might be at the Midnight Mine." He arranges a plate for him, silverware wrapped in a paper napkin, a bottle of ketchup. He switches out his empty glass for a fresh one with a quick shuffle.

There's something comforting about watching a good bartender do his job.

"She's a funny one," Edison says.

"Meth addicts usually are."

"She'll be okay," Edison says. "I have a feeling," and he considers her in that dark car, looking at the windshield like she can actually see something. She's talking, rambling, and he can't figure out what the point is, even now, remembering it. What is she telling him? She's telling him her life story, what has happened and what will happen. It's enough to make him believe.

"I have a Remington," Edison says, and the bartender nods.

So on Friday he takes the gun from the back of the closet and loads it and walks out to the shed with it pointed at the ground. He does not know how he will turn this into a story that makes sense, when he floats in the ether with Shyboy, where everything is just a story. But that doesn't matter so much at the moment. It's a beautiful afternoon, with the sun red and squat on the horizon, a new dusting of snow covering the landscape. The horse is waiting for him.

He's not the person raising the gun at the heavy skull. He's the person in the car, telling that sad meth addict girl that everything is going to be okay. He pulls back the bolt and sets himself and it's so easy not to see the horse as anything but a simple target. It's a form of rescue, he decides, or at least an act of kindness, but when he pulls the trigger he is not even there. It's *already* a story, even as the horse's dead weight hits the ground. His mother has died and everything is so sad and there are so many things he never had a chance to tell her.

But what comes out, hours later, is different. The words are like small accidents, but there they are, on the screen, and he can't take them back. The ball gag is back in his mouth, but he's talking, rambling almost. *You're right. I haven't been completely truthful to you.*

*I know but I still love you.*

*I'm not what you think I am.*

*It's okay.*

He pushes something forward in his head, an idea of himself he's partitioned off from the rest, and he types, *I bought a horse. A sick horse. I was trying to save it, or maybe I just wanted to be with it when it died.* He types another sentence, a description of the horse, but he taps backspace and erases it, replaces it with a better lie. *And she's doing good. I think I did it. She's getting stronger. She's drinking lots of water. I'm going to ride her once the damned winter turns the corner.*

*I've never seen a horse close up.*

*Beautiful animals.*

*I can imagine it, and you with her, riding her. That's beautiful.*

*But I'm not what I seem.*

*I know and I don't care. It's fine. I know who you are.*

*Maybe I'm some crazy meth addict.*

Edison forces himself to recall the kick of the Remington and the way the horse settled to the ground, as if getting ready for sleep, and then the girl in the car, with her staring, sick eyes. He tries to think of everything at once, holding their delicate weight as carefully as he can, and in his imagination, they are alive, pulsing deep inside him like his own stupid heart. And it's a gift he can share with this strange man, this villain, who knows him so well, better than anybody has ever known him before.

*You should see her,* he types, *close up.*

# Biographical Note

David Nikki Crouse is author of the short story collections *Copy Cats*, *The Man Back There*, and the collection of novellas *Trouble Will Save You*. David's work has received the Flannery O'Connor Award, the Mary McCarthy Prize, the Lawrence Prize, and additional short story awards, and been published in magazines such as the *Kenyon Review*, *Witness*, the *Colorado Review*, *Agni*, and the *Greensboro Review*. They live in Seattle, Washington, where they serve as the S. Wilson and Grace M. Pollock Endowed Professor in Creative Writing at the University of Washington-Seattle.